SHE'S MINE

A CAPTIVE ROMANCE

ELLIE MASTERS

JEM PUBLISHING

Click here to visit Ellie's Website (www.elliemasters.com) where you can view excerpts, teasers, and links to her other books.

ISBN-13: 978-0-9993888-5-3

❀ Created with Vellum

DEDICATION_

This book is dedicated to my one and only—my amazing and wonderful husband. Without your care and support, my writing would not have made it this far. You make me whole every day. I love you "that much." For the rest of you, that means from the beginning to the end and every point in between. Thank you, my dearest love, my heart and soul, for putting up with me, for believing in me, and for loving me.

My husband deserves a special gold star for listening to me obsess over this book and for never once complaining while I brought these characters from my mind to the page.

You pushed me when I needed to be pushed. You supported me when I felt discouraged. You believed in me when I didn't believe in myself. If it weren't for you, this book never would have come to life.

ALSO BY ELLIE MASTERS_

Sign up to Ellie's Newsletter and get a free gift.
https://elliemasters.com/FreeBook

The Angel Fire Rock Romance Series

EACH BOOK IN THIS SERIES CAN BE READ AS A STANDALONE AND IS
ABOUT A DIFFERENT COUPLE WITH AN HEA.

Ashes to New (prequel)

Heart's Insanity (book 1)

Heart's Desire (book 2)

Heart's Collide (book 3)

Hearts Divided (book 4)

Romantic Suspense

She's Mine: a Captive Romance

Twist of Fate

Ellie Masters writing as L.A. Warren

Vendel Rising: a Science Fiction Serialized Novel

(January 2019)

This book is a work of fiction. It does not exist in the real world and should not be construed as reality. As in most romantic fiction, I've taken liberties. I've compressed the romance into a sliver of time. I've allowed these characters to develop strong bonds of trust over a matter of days. This does not happen in real life where you, my amazing readers, live. Take more time in your romance and learn who you're giving a piece of your heart to. I urge you to move with caution. Always protect yourself.

When you find your partner, talk to him or her. Be open and honest about your needs, your expectations, and your limits, especially if you have any triggers. Never allow your partner to violate the tender trust you have put into their hands. Always remember, your lover can't read your mind. It is your responsibility to talk to them, no matter how frightening that might be. In return, you must listen to what your partner has to say and understand their limits, as you do your own. Share your hopes, desires, and deepest, darkest secrets. Most of all, don't be afraid to seek out who you are, become what you want, and share your journey with your partner.

CHAPTER ONE_

I BOUNCED WITH EXCITEMENT AS I NEARED THE THICK DOORS of the palatial monstrosity which had been my prison for the past twenty-one years. Z was out on a business trip. I'd be in and out, then gone, and would never again have to face the darkness in my father's eyes.

As long as Z and I kept our distance, me in boarding school and him with his business, life allowed me to deny the truth. I was the rich socialite daughter of the illustrious Zane Carson, multi-millionaire who collected properties and corporations for sport. I dated who I wanted. As long as I didn't sleep with married men or had my name splashed in the tabloids, Z and I maintained a peaceful coexistence.

But that no longer mattered, because I vowed to be free of his overbearing ways. I had plans to pub crawl from Scotland to Germany in one long summer of debauchery with my girlfriends before hitting the books and beginning my new life. All I had to do was stuff my backpack with a couple pairs of jeans, T-shirts, and one naughty black dress.

At twenty-one, I had a B.S. in Computer Science from MIT which set me free. No longer would I be a slave to Z's money or his insufferable rules.

I put my weight behind the heavy, ornate door and pushed. This would be the last time I entered this house. I stepped across the threshold and lurched to a stop.

Z stood in the middle of the sweeping foyer. His coal dark eyes bore down on me beneath thick bushy brows. Heavy shadows gathered in his stormy gaze and a scowl framed his face. Two men stood with him; two large, intimidating men.

Years of rejection and emotional manipulation left no love lost between me and Z. In my head, he wasn't father, or daddy. He was simply Z. I had long since whittled my father's name down to a single letter. I hated him, only because I craved the love he denied me with the irrational need of a child. In front of others, I maintained a civil facade, however, and called him *Papa*. I did that now.

"Papa? I didn't think you would be home." My sandals slapped against Italian marble as I pulled up short.

"Raven." His harsh, clipped tones made my heart lurch. There was no tenderness for me in his greeting. Disapproval tugged at the corners of his mouth and his displeasure radiated in the flare of his nostrils and the pinch of his eyes as he surveyed my state of dress.

His women wore their hair in tightly wound buns or French twists. I kept mine loose because it irritated him and it hung down to my waist. But his eyes skipped over my hair, made no mention of my lack of makeup, and moved to my summer tank top and cut off shorts. That's when his eyes widened, showing white around inky blackness.

"Papa..." My throat constricted and I subconsciously wrapped an arm across my chest, covering my unsupported breasts.

Z demanded perfection in his female companions. Seeing his daughter in cut-off jeans, and a spaghetti tank top without a bra garnered more reaction in three seconds than I'd gotten out of him in twenty-one years.

"You're dressed like a whore." His teeth ground out a horrible sound as his jaw clenched.

My gaze flew to the men. Surprise fluttered in my belly that he would speak so crudely in front of company.

"Papa?" The word hung between us as he came at me.

His fingers latched around my wrist, biting into the tender flesh. My free hand pulled at him, trying to loosen his grip, but my efforts were useless against the steel band of his fingers. He yanked me toward the men.

"As promised." He thrust me at the largest man. "Debt paid."

An impossibly huge man pulled me from Z's grip.

"Papa!" I turned wild eyes to Z.

I looked to the man who had given me life and saw the

truth etched in the granite lines of his features. Comfort never came through the cold-hearted man who dominated my life. He never once touched me with love. The set of his jaw confirmed the truth. I couldn't believe what was happening, but the men lent a certain degree of reality to the situation.

The man who took me from Z, wrapped an arm around my waist as I kicked out trying to get free. It was a useless gesture. My efforts to free myself were laughable, but then I wasn't thinking rationally. My mind reeled with my father's words. What did he mean by *debt paid?*

The man pressed his lips to my ear and whispered. "You belong to another now."

The other man came at me, bent to the ground and attached something bulky around my left ankle. I kicked at him, earning a grunt when my foot connected with his chin. Steely blue eyes promised retribution and my stomach clenched. Collecting my flailing arms, he pulled out a zip tie and with a *zip* my wrists were lashed together. He stepped back admiring his handiwork. I leaned back against the one holding me and screamed as I lifted my legs off the floor. The second man zip tied my ankles together while I tried to kick his face.

"Papa!" A screech escaped my lips and fell on uncaring ears.

Z backed away from the men who held me captive.

"I'm your daughter. How could you...what have you done?"

Z folded his arms across his chest. "You're no different than any of the others and now you will be one."

The man holding me tightened his grip around my belly as I squirmed trying to get free.

"What are you talking about?" I stared at my father, tears pricking at my eyes.

"Just like your mother." Z's voice dropped to a hoarse whisper. "She was so beautiful."

My mother? In all the years I'd lived with this man, he never spoke of the woman who had given birth to me. I knew nothing of her. I had never seen a picture and never heard any of the servants speak of her. All I knew was what was reflected in Z's eyes when he looked at me; hatred, contempt, and something dark and twisted.

"She's a fighter," the man holding me said with a grunt. "Chad, bring the car around."

A bruise formed on Chad's chin as he looked at me. Steel-blue eyes held a promise for retribution in my future. "Sure you can handle her on your own?" Chad grinned at me, then loped down the hall out of sight.

The one holding me grunted as I jerked my head back and smacked his jaw with the back of my head. Not my smartest move. I saw stars and I don't think I did anything to him other than make his grip on me tighten even more.

"Your daughter is a fighter, Mr. Carson," the man said.

"That was part of the agreement." Z backed farther away. "Her owner specified it."

I twisted and bucked, then stilled at my father's words. What the hell was I doing? All the years of self-defense classes and I had been reduced to this? Scrabbling and kicking and squirming in the grip of a man?

I knew better. I'd been trained to know when I was outmatched. My window of opportunity had already closed, but I never thought I'd be attacked in my own home. I hadn't been prepared to defend myself.

Frustration threatened tears, but I refused to let Z see my weakness. Another opportunity would come. I would wait, bide my time, and I wouldn't waste my chance. Complacency wouldn't lower my defenses ever again.

"Time to sleep, kitten." Chad approached and I flinched as he raised a ball of bunched cotton to my face.

"I'm not your fucking kitten." I kicked him in the groin, or tried to. He swiped my legs to the side without a thought.

"That's correct, you're not my kitten," he said. "You belong to Master Xavier now."

"I belong to no one," I screamed as he came at me, twisting my head to the side to avoid the noxious chemicals embedded in the cloth.

Z came at me and held my head. He immobilized me and allowed Chad to cover my mouth and nose with the cloth.

"You will sleep, Raven," my father murmured, "and when you wake you'll meet your fate. You'll serve your master as you were destined from birth, as your mother served me." Z kissed my forehead as astringent fumes assaulted the tender mucous membranes of my nasal passageways.

I screamed, huffing in the anesthetic ether, as my world spiraled into oblivion. My mother gave me beauty and grace, but Z gave me a more valuable gift. He bestowed upon me intelligence, tenacity, and a single mindedness to accomplish my goals. As much as I hated him, I was my father's daughter, and as blackness devoured my world, I vowed to destroy him.

Z fluttered kisses over my eyelids. "You were always destined to be a slave."

I fought against blackness, but this was a battle I would lose.

CHAPTER TWO_

I WOKE TO DRY, RECYCLED AIR, AND THE SICKENING SMELL OF Scotch and over-nuked dinners. Coarse male voices were all around me. A thrum vibrated through the cushion of my seat. My body was sore from what I assumed was sitting in one position for too long, but I didn't dare move. I didn't want my captors to know I was awake.

My lids scratched against dry eyes as I tried peeking out through tiny slits. Darkness greeted me, but sound flew around me. I was pretty certain I was inside a jet. I'd flown inside enough of them to know the distinct feel of a private plane. By the hum of the engines, and the noises around me, I discerned the size of the cabin. This was no puddle jumper.

Whose hands had I fallen into that could afford such luxury?

My breaths crested and crashed as terror gripped and

twisted at my core. If I was in a jet, flying who knew where, and for God only knew how long, then my chances of escape had narrowed down to the smallest of slivers. Fabric pressed against my mouth as my panting deepened to hysteria.

"She's awake." The voice belonged to the man who had restrained me when Z threw me away.

I heaved forward, hands locked together with zip ties, only to come up short by a seatbelt secured around my waist.

A hand pressed against my shoulder. "Easy, kitten."

I recognized that voice. It belonged to the man with the steel-blue eyes. The one I kicked in the chin, who I hoped now sported a bruise for my efforts.

I struggled to remember details. They would be important, later. His name was Chad. He'd been sent off to get a car. Somewhere along the way, they'd transported me to a jet. I struggled to work out how long I may have been unconscious. I bucked against his restraint, breaths sawing in and out of my chest.

My fingers tingled. My head swam. The skin around my lips pricked. I coughed. Wheezed. Gasped for breath. I hyperventilated in the darkness of a hood strapped over my head, terrified of what I couldn't see.

Who were these men and what horrors did they have in store for me? Would I be murdered? Raped? I would probably be raped. Wasn't that what men like this did?

I moaned, then pressed harder against Chad's hand, bucking against his restraint.

It earned me a second hand against my opposite shoulder as Chad slammed me back into the seat, straddling my legs with his.

This was it. The moment I feared, but I wouldn't let them take from me without a fight.

They may have me trapped, hooded, and restrained, but I was not powerless. If I struggled, they would hurt me more than if I offered no resistance at all.

If I didn't fight them, would my compliance be seen as a good thing, or bad? Were compliant girls sold for more or less? And which one of those outcomes did I want? Did it matter at all?

How many times would I be sold? Forced to whore myself while they hooked me on drugs to ensure my compliance? Dear God, I wasn't strong enough for this.

And the man I'd been given to, was he fat and ugly with slobbering lips? The idea of some sweaty, fat, slobbering old man doing that had me bucking in the seat. This couldn't be happening.

My imagination ran wild with scenes of rape, degradation, getting hooked on drugs, and being forced to be compliant as they used my body and destroyed my life.

I had a plan, dammit. I was finally going to be free of my father and make my way in the world without his loveless judgement. A choked cry escaped me with the loss of my dreams.

They wouldn't get me without a fight. If I was going to be

beaten and raped, then I would fight back. At least until all the fight had been whipped out of me. A low groan escaped me with the horrors I envisioned.

I kneed my captor in the groin.

This couldn't be real. It couldn't be happening.

"Holy, mother fucker!" Chad released me and I imagined him cupping his balls as he stumbled backward.

Serves you right.

Score one for Team Raven.

Satisfaction swelled in my chest, distracting me enough to control my breathing. I smoothed out my breaths as Chad's presence moved away from me. My relief was short lived. Someone grabbed me from behind, tugging back on my shoulders and pinning me in place.

All sound in the cabin quieted. I sensed bodies looming next to me, over me, behind me; large, male bodies, all around me. I'd never felt this vulnerable. Boldness sizzled as terrified breaths filled my lungs, speeding toward panic again. What would they do to me? Would they rape me?

"You will not do that again," said a man with an authoritative voice. He seemed to be in charge, so I named him Boss.

"Or what?" I belted out my defiance with the last dregs of my bravery.

Loose strands of hair drifted into my mouth and I spit them out as best I could. I tried rubbing my cheek against my shoulder, but only felt Boss's hands. I recoiled at the touch.

"We will restrain you," Boss said.

"For your own protection," another voice chimed in; one I didn't recognize. I still didn't know how many men were on board the plane, but I discerned four distinct voices.

"Bay," Boss said, "why don't you get the restraints. I have a feeling she's not going to cooperate. Master Xavier doesn't want her overly sedated during the trip."

I had another captor's name; Bay.

One or two pilots. From the feel of the plane, I assumed two. Whoever this Master Xavier was, they worked for him and would be of no help to me. It didn't help to list out who was on board. None would come to my aid, but I couldn't sit here and do nothing. Taking stock was the only thing I could do. It helped me focus, and I needed to think about anything other than the press of men surrounding me.

Bay moved in front of me.

It was amazing how much information I gleaned without the presence of sight. Sounds amplified themselves in the aircraft cabin. The creak of his leather shoes, and the swish of his pants telegraphed his movements.

Smells intensified as well. Bay's cologne, spice and citrus, wafted toward me as he approached. He was the one who held me while Chad tied me up. Boss smelled different, more pungent, manly and full of musk. Chad smelled clean and fresh, an Irish Spring kind of guy.

Bay pushed my legs to one side. "Do not try to kick me. Chad already owes you two, you do not want me owing you as well." I smelled mint on his breath as he leaned in close.

What the hell did that mean? Owing me?

Bay pressed my shoulders back against the seat. "Now lean back and behave."

"Take the hood off." I tried to make my demand forceful, but it sounded more like a whimper than anything else.

Boss's finger's pressed into my shoulders. "Hood stays on. Master Xavier's orders."

"Why?"

"One of your first lessons will be not to question your master," Boss said.

I wanted to scratch Boss's eyes out. I would have, if my wrists weren't zip tied together, if Boss wasn't standing behind me, if Bay wasn't strapping me in some contraption that seemed to immobilize me in a web against the seat back, if, if, if...

Hot tears burst from the corners of my eyes.

No! Damn it. I'm not going to cry.

I didn't want to cry. I wasn't going to become some sniveling mess. Not under this damn hood, but wetness trickled down my cheeks.

Bay secured me in his makeshift web, strapping my wrists in my lap so I couldn't lift them. Why was it my nose started to itch only after he restrained my hands?

"What if I have to use the bathroom?"

"Do you?" Bay stood. I felt the absence of his presence as he lifted away from me, the disappearance of his minty breath relayed his movements in place of sight.

I didn't, which meant we hadn't been up in the air for too long. Good, I filed that piece of information away.

"A piece of advice, kitten," Chad's clean fresh scent preceded him, "do not lie. Bay took time to secure you, so you had a chance to be comfortable. If you lie, then I will tie you back up, and you will not be so lucky."

I didn't think Chad and I were destined for friendship.

I took a moment to consider my options, then decided not to push my luck. "No, but I'm thirsty."

I was parched, to be honest. My eyes were scratchy. My lips felt cracked and my mouth was beginning to get that cottony feel from being at altitude for too long. Maybe we'd been flying longer than I thought. I was dehydrated, which might explain why I didn't need to use the restroom. "Can you please remove the hood and give me a drink?"

"You can have a drink, kitten," Chad said, "but the hood stays on." Weight settled into the seat beside me, clean and fresh. My buddy Chad.

Boss released my shoulders and walked away. Bay followed him toward the front of the cabin.

"Hey, Mel, toss me a bottle of water and a straw." Something whistled through the air. A solid *thunk* connected in a hand. I assumed it belonged to my buddy Chad, but I now had another name to add to my list.

"Can you release my hands?"

Chad laughed. "Hardly, kitten. You've gotten the best of

me twice, and I'm not giving you another chance. I'll hold the bottle for you."

He tugged at the hood around my neck, loosening strings. A cold bottle pressed against my chest and then his fingers as he guided a straw to my lips. "Go ahead and drink, kitten."

"I'm not your damn kitten."

Chad laughed. "You're whatever I want you to be. I'm the one who gets to take care of you."

Thinking about Chad taking care of me, and what that may or may not imply, had me cringing. It didn't quite fit with what Z had said though. "And what does Master Xavier have to say about that?"

"Kitten, it's precisely because of Master Xavier that you need someone to take care of you."

I sipped furiously at the water, sucking as if it could give me strength. I had no idea what awaited me, only that Z said I was to be a slave.

CHAPTER THREE_

WE TRAVELED FOR HOURS, MY MIND WHIRLING WITH possibilities for my future. The men talked and watched action movies for a time. I was learning to recognize their voices, along with their unique scents.

Chad's voice was full of laughter and sarcasm. Boss's voice was laced with command, definitely the one in charge. Bay seemed easy going, a smooth talker, friendly. Mel kept his thoughts close, seldom speaking, but when he did it was short and clipped. He wasn't a man to waste his words.

Chad sat beside me for the longest time. He fed me a protein bar and another bottle of water. When the press of my bladder became too insistent, he and Bay released my webbed restraints. They walked me to the back of the plane sandwiched between them. Like I could run at thirty-thousand feet. My wrists remained bound by the zip ties, chaffing against the hard plastic. I lifted them.

"I need these off."

Bay huffed a laugh. "No way are those coming off."

Trying to argue with the two men, as I wobbled between them, disorientated under the blackness of my hood, sapped the last of my strength. I sagged against the bulkhead. "Please. I promise to be good." I'm ashamed to admit I meant it.

"No can do, kitten," Chad said.

"How am I supposed to use the restroom?" I had no idea how I was going to pull down my shorts with my hands tied together. The thought of trying to do that hooded, and in an airplane lavatory, was ludicrous.

"That's what we're here for," Bay said.

What? No way!

I held up my hands, took a step back, and stepped on Chad's toe.

"Damn it, kitten, what is it with you?" He placed his hands on my waist and lifted me off his foot.

"Sorry." How had he gotten behind me? I thought he was beside me.

Disorientation flustered me and I reached out with my bound hands locating the walls. I found Bay's solid chest of muscle and holy hell, washboard abs. He chuckled as I felt him up.

I recoiled, moved my hands around, located a handle. It was a door. Lavatory?

"I don't need your help."

"Yes, you do, kitten," Chad said. "You grope Bay, but hit me? For the record, my body is way better than his." Chad grabbed my wrists and placed my hands on the hardness of his belly. He hadn't lied, solid, immovable muscle.

I backed away and moved toward where I thought the door might be. Good guess. I leaned against it, opening it, only to have Chad move in behind me.

"Hey, a little privacy here!" The fabric of my hood puffed as I screeched. Loose strands of hair fluttered into my mouth. I tried to spit them out, but it only made things worse. "Seriously, why can't I take the hood off?"

"Master Xavier doesn't want you to see where we're flying," Bay said from the hall.

I found the lavatory sink and grabbed it for support. "Are there any windows in here?"

"No," Chad said.

"Are there any out there that I can see from in here?"

"No," Bay said.

Frustration at my helplessness pegged to maximum. I needed some degree of control. I wasn't against begging to get it. "Then please, untie my hands and let me take off the hood. Just for a second so I can tie my hair back. It's all over my face and I keep getting hair in my mouth. I promise I won't do anything. Where exactly do you think I'm going to run?"

I couldn't see their exchange, but I imagined Bay and Chad's silent conversation. A raised eyebrow. A shake of one's head. A shrug. A nod. They didn't say anything, but finally, I felt a tugging at the cords around my neck.

"The ties around your wrists stay," Chad said.

I started to protest and his hands fell away from the bag.

"Non-negotiable, kitten," he said. "Don't make me regret this. Door to the lavatory stays open. You need to understand that privacy is a luxury you no longer have. Best to start getting used to that now. Use the restroom and wash up. I'll be right here in the hall, even think about shutting that door and I'll be all over you. Do you understand?" His fingers hovered at my neck, holding the cords.

I gave him a fractional nod. I had to pee in front of him? In front of the others? No privacy? *Come on Raven, you can do this.*

"Tell me you understand, kitten. Give me your word."

My chin lifted as I swallowed phlegm. I couldn't believe I was going to agree to this.

"I promise."

The hood lifted from my head. Brown strands of hair clung to the black fabric with static electricity, while other clumps adhered to my tear streaked face.

The first thing I did was lift my fingers to my mouth and pull out the hair. Then I smoothed hair away from my face, working one side at a time, limited as I was by my bound hands. Finally, I lifted my gaze to the mirror and sucked in a breath at the haggard vision staring back at me. Listless hazel eyes stared back with nothing but red streaks where there should have been flawless porcelain skin. My hair hung limp around my shoulders. I barely recognized myself. Puffy, red, I looked...defeated.

Damn. I wasn't that girl. I refused to be that girl.

I straightened the hunch in my shoulders, pressed my breastbone out, and lifted my chin. My bladder pinched with urgent need, reminding me of why I was here.

Beside me, Chad looked at me with his steel-blue eyes, silent, watchful, and concerned. Now, why would worry darken his features?

"What?" My biting comment had him rearing back.

"Nothing, kitten." His eyes narrowed. "You are a fierce woman, a lioness I think."

"You know nothing about me."

His expression softened as he stepped toward me. "I know more than you think."

I lifted my hands in defense and he paused.

"You promised to behave," he said. "Do not make me regret being kind to you. Now hold still, don't fight me, and don't you dare hit me again."

He put his hands on the button of my shorts. When I gasped, he gazed into my eyes. His body filled the lavatory, towering over me, shoulders brushing the sides of the small space. The man was built like a tank. And, yes, he had a purple bruise at the tip of his chin. His gaze softened as he cupped my chin.

An involuntary exhale pushed past my lips.

"Know this, kitten," he said with tenderness, "you belong to Master Xavier. It is my job to care for you, but you do not belong to me in that way. None of us will touch you like that."

But this Master Xavier would. I didn't find comfort in Chad's words.

He pushed my shorts and panties down over my hips and then backed away through the doorway and took a half a step to the side. He never looked down at my nakedness. I know because my eyes were latched to his the entire time.

I heard him with Bay, talking about sports, while I stood speechless with my pants halfway down my legs.

My bladder pinched, spasming with need. What world had I descended into where one man controlled others so completely? If this Master Xavier held such sway over men such as Chad, Bay, Boss, and Mel, then what hope did I have?

I didn't know, but now was not the time to push more boundaries. I discovered one thing. I had power. The hood was off. It was only for a moment, and I checked; there were no windows I could look out, but I won a small victory with my captors.

I pushed my shorts down and quickly did my business, mindful for the courtesy Chad afforded me. I washed up and did my best to dress. Chad had to help me pull my shorts over my hips. I bit my lip the entire time, trying not to let my mortification show.

Bay motioned for Chad to move out of the lavatory and then proceeded to brush out my long hair. He pulled a rubber band from his pocket and secured my hair in a ponytail. I reveled in the absence of the hood. Looking into the mirror, I almost looked like my old self and I caught Bay admiring my reflection as well.

I didn't see what my friends saw, what they told me men couldn't resist when looking at me. I saw only me, a plain and curious girl. Men saw something else, some captivating quality I never understood. I used to hold up magazines next to my face, trying to see what features I shared with those models. My eyes were not crystalline blue or emerald green. They weren't some fathomless dark chocolate to beguile men. Instead, they were an unremarkable hazel flecked with green. The only remarkable quality was in the way my eyes shifted colors with my mood. Their shape was unique perhaps, a bit too large and open for the size of my face. People said it gave me an inquisitive expression.

I thought it made me look younger than I was, more fragile than I felt. To me, it was a hindrance as I could never sneak into clubs, although I never lacked for dates, or boyfriends, or older men who wanted to buy me expensive gifts. I was guilty for taking advantage where I could. No one ever said I was a saint. I was, after all, the product of boarding school and broken curfews.

My mother gave me the gift of flawless skin with a natural ivory complexion, not too white. I didn't look like a ghost and I wasn't pasty-white. I had rosy cheeks and I tanned well. There was a luminosity to my skin my friend, Elsbeth, told me one night with only a twinge of jealousy. I never understood what luminosity meant in a skin tone. I wasn't a whore, despite Z's words. I wasn't super-model beautiful. There was nothing worth justifying purchasing me as a slave.

I lacked refinement. Z's fault. He didn't send me to finishing school, but I never lacked men's interest. While my girlfriends were learning how to blend in with high society, I learned to fight, took personal self-defense, learned to shoot a hand gun, and went hunting and fishing. I learned to dance, too. I wasn't a complete savage.

Like all my friends at boarding school, equestrian sports, swimming, tennis, the usual suspects, made up my physical education. But I also ran, did yoga, rock climbed, crawled through caves, surfed, and scuba dove. Hell, I jumped out of planes and kayaked too, and did every un-ladylike activity I could think of that would irritate my father. Whoever Master Xavier was, he was in for a big disappointment, because he wasn't getting a socialite's daughter.

Bay pressed his lips together when he saw me watching him. "Master Xavier has been waiting for you for some time. It won't be much longer now."

My eyes widened, and I wanted to ask what he meant, but

he lifted the black hood and swept it back down over my head silencing my questions.

"No, please." I cried out and gripped the edge of the hood as it lowered to my chin.

Chad spoke from the doorway. "Kitten, don't fight. You will not win. Let Bay secure the hood."

I gripped the edge, defiant and needing the tiny bit of freedom offered. Chad's clean scent pressed close and I felt small and trapped between the two men. I dropped my hands to my waist in resignation, losing that battle.

"Good, girl," Chad said. He reached around and tied the cords of the hood around my neck.

He and Bay guided me back to my seat. Bay buckled my seatbelt across my lap and then bent forward to begin strapping the webbing over my chest.

"No, Bay, please. Don't. I won't be a problem."

"Ben's orders," Bay said.

Ben? Who was Ben? Chad, Bay, Mel, and Ben. Ben must be the boss. I now had all four of my captor's names.

"Don't want you pulling off the hood and taking a peek out the window." Bay secured my hands beneath the webbing.

"Why does that matter?"

Bay didn't answer as he quietly and efficiently restrained me in my seat. I was a fly caught in a web. A pungent smell wafted toward me, full of musk and cigarettes. This was the boss, Ben.

"Hey," Bay said. "She's restrained."

"Good. I'll take over," Ben said. "Why don't you get some shut eye."

"Sure thing," Bay said.

"You doing okay, kid?" Ben settled into the seat beside me.

I turned my hooded face toward him, wishing he could see the expression on my face. Then I made a face, thankful he couldn't see what I thought of his idiotic question. I wanted to cross my arms and turn away from him in a huff, but I couldn't. The webbing made that impossible.

Mechanical whirring noises sounded moments before my seat began tilting back. I gave a start as the leg rest extended and my chair turned into a bed. Ben leaned into me. A needle pricked my neck and a cold sensation flowed under my skin, followed by a burn.

"What..."

"Time to sleep," Bossman Ben said.

"No..." I didn't want to sleep. I didn't want to lose control. I fought the sluggishness pouring through my veins and lost yet another battle. More frustrating blackness swallowed me whole.

CHAPTER FOUR_

THE NEXT TIME CONSCIOUSNESS WRAPPED ITS WARM HANDS around me, tires bounced on a runway. My ears popped. In a foggy haze, I shifted in my seat, stretching shoulders left and right. Wait, my shoulders moved? I leaned forward, the webbing had been removed. Cotton filled my mouth and my scratchy eyes burned with irritation. My mind moved at half speed as I shrugged off the vestiges of whatever Ben the Boss had given me. I had no measure of how much time had passed. Hours? Days? Did it matter anymore?

My bladder spasmed painfully, letting me know I had been out for quite some time. I leaned forward and groaned. Spice and citrus floated beside me, mixed with minty goodness. Bay sat beside me. His easy-going voice soothed the frayed edges of my mind.

"Once we come to a stop, we'll let you use the restroom."

"Where are we?" I lifted my hands to my face, surprised I had that much freedom, and rubbed at tired eyes behind the fabric of the hood.

The plane taxied and rumbled across uneven pavement. The floorboard creaked in the aisle beside me and the scent of tobacco filled the air.

"Welcome to your new home, little one," Ben said.

I cringed at his words, but didn't have the strength to contradict him. I didn't care what these men thought, or what their orders were, this wasn't my home.

Tires bumped along the runway as the plane taxied to a stop. That's when I first realized the seat I occupied was different from the plush recliner I had been in before. It was narrower too. Bay's arm brushed against mine. I explored my surroundings with my feet, marking out the size of my seat. I spread my elbows and confirmed my fears. We had changed planes during my last bout of unconsciousness, this time to a smaller craft.

I mentally prepared for the worst. Surely, this was the end of my journey. My head ached from being drugged, that and some degree of altitude dehydration. I needed to ready myself for what came next. This next stage of my life promised untold horror and I needed to protect myself. Be ready to run. Observe and gather information. I didn't want to dwell on what waited for me outside the plane.

"Up you go." Bay reached across my lap and sprung my seat

belt. He guided me by my elbow into the aisle and steered me to the back of the plane. Behind me, the unmistakable sound of the door hatch opening brought the whine of the engines powering down as well as a blast of hot, humid air. The moisture saturated my clothes and brought beads of perspiration to my brow. Now more than ever, the infernal hood suffocated me.

We repeated the embarrassing process in the lavatory, this time with Bay assisting me with my clothes. Chad was nowhere to be smelled or heard. I couldn't see a damned thing and Bay refused to remove the hood, despite my begging. He guided me back down the narrow aisle, my hips bumped against the seats and then he pulled me up beside the door. A hot breeze blew against my bare legs.

The plane engines had quieted. I heard men hefting luggage and calling out directions, and beyond that, birds squawked overhead. The wind brought beautiful floral scents to my heightened sense of smell. Exoticness screamed at my limited senses. I took in a sharp inhale, smelling a hint of brine, confirming my suspicions.

We had landed near a beach, on an island perhaps, or along a coast. Images of jungles, palm trees, ferns, exotic birds, lizards, and monkeys filled my mind. Without sight, my imagination ran wild. My body thrummed with nervous energy, terrified at what our arrival implied. I didn't care how long I'd been traveling, I wanted to see my journey's end. I wanted to explore this prison I had been thrust into by my wretched father and I needed to start making plans for escape.

Bay pressed a hand to the small of my back. "I'm going to help you down a set of stairs. Put your hands out, Chad will guide you down."

A massive hand folded itself around my bound hands and I flinched at the unexpected touch.

"Relax, kitten," Chad soothed, "and promise not to hit me." Sarcasm laced his words and a ghost of a smile tugged at the corner of my lips before I realized how easily he had endeared himself to me. His hands covered mine and he tugged me gently forward. "First step is right here." He pressed a hand to my foot, showing me the way.

With Chad and Bay's help, I navigated my way down the stairs. Hot tarmac reflected back the sun, intensifying the heat, causing sweat to bead upon my skin. The heat under the hood became unbearable and I swayed.

Bay grasped my shoulders. "Just a bit farther."

Tires churned on the asphalt and a car pulled close.

"Get her out of the heat," Chad said, "and we need to pull the hood."

"No," Ben said. "He wants to do that himself."

I didn't know where Ben had come from, but my head was spinning, floating with disorientation. I wasn't doing a very good job of paying attention to my surroundings, but I knew exactly who the *he* was that Ben referred to. My stomach twisted, threatening to empty the remnants of the protein bar I'd been fed some time ago.

A door clicked open and I was assisted into a blissfully cool, leather infused car interior. Bay moved me to the center seat, locked a seatbelt around me, and sat beside me. The door opposite opened and the smell of Irish Spring settled on the other side. My buddies, Bay and Chad, had me cocooned between them.

More doors opened and shut. The car rocked as people climbed in. I rested my head against the seat as the air conditioner whirred away. The car moved, bringing me one step closer to the man who had taken me as his slave.

Debt paid.

Z's words swirled in my head. What kind of debt demanded he give over his only daughter?

The men around me talked and laughed, while I sat in darkness. I wanted to scream at them, but kept silent as tears streaked down my face. My lack of any resistance frustrated me as much as it terrified me. All I had done so far was offer compliance, but then I'd never experienced this kind of fear before.

They had me at a disadvantage. How was I to run if I was blind? How was I to escape with shackled arms? I couldn't outrun anyone, and they knew it. And it hadn't escaped my notice that at least one of them was always within arm's reach of me. I'd be grabbed the moment I made a break for it.

I had failed before I'd even had a chance to try. My fingers curled. *Do not give up. Never stop looking for a way out. Stay strong and fight.*

The vehicle swayed and bumped as it navigated rutted roads. Dirt and gravel crunched beneath the tires. I bounced in the seat, grateful for the two overly large men bracketing me for a change, because they supported me as the car tried to shake every bone in my body loose. After a few minutes, the car slowed and came to a stop.

My gut clenched. One step closer.

Doors popped open all around me as men spilled out of the car. Bay and Chad exited. Chad guided me out of the car and led me forward with a gentle grip on my arm. Moments later, Bay joined us, taking hold of my other arm. I was once again sandwiched between my buddies. I don't know what happened to Ben or Mel, and I didn't really care.

Bay and Chad guided me up a set of stairs. The heat and humidity beat down on the hood. Sharp inhales tugged into my lungs while the fabric of the hood grew wet with my breath. My head swam with light headedness and exhaustion.

This was it. My ending.

A door opened and a gust of air-conditioned wonderment brushed over me. Chad guided me over a threshold into the welcoming coolness of recirculated and conditioned air, while Bay shut out the heat with the finality of a lock clicking into place behind me.

Chad nudged me forward, guided me into what I assumed was another room. Then he sat me in a chair.

The presence of my captors surrounded me. Their breaths pulled at my sensitive hearing as they leaned over me. Chad tugged my leg to the side. The sound of Velcro unzipping alerted me moments before he secured my calf to the leg of the chair. I jumped at the restraint, kicking out with my free leg.

A chuckle sounded as I connected with open air.

"Missed me, kitten." Chad's strong hand pressed against my shin, inexorably lowering my leg to the opposite chair leg. Another rip of Velcro and the fabric wrapped around my leg. Immobilization had become my universe.

Bay's sweet fragrance, tinged with citrus and mint, crossed in front of my body. He lifted my wrists and slid something hard and cold between the plastic of the zip tie. With a quick upward jerk, my hands were freed.

I rubbed at my wrists where the hard plastic had bit into soft flesh, but the men separated my hands, and pulled them to the side. More ripping sounds, and more Velcro bound me to the chair. Tears of frustration spilled from the corners of my eyes.

A new scent filled the room, a rich aroma full of spice and musk, layered with another deeper fragrance. A deep woodsy aroma penetrated the fabric of the hood, a decidedly masculine scent. The tread of a measured step and the rustle of fabric announced the newcomer.

Terror gripped me. That had to be *him.* I squeezed out tears and prayed for strength. Our first meeting would determine the entire tone of whatever warped relationship we would have. I needed to meet him with strength.

"That will be all, gentlemen."

The deep, cultured voice did strange things to my insides. Terror gripped me, but something more alarming occurred as well. I was eager to meet this man called Master Xavier.

"Thank you," he said. "You have earned your reward."

"Thank you, Master Xavier." Chad leaned down and whispered in my ear. "Behave, kitten." Then his footfalls fell away.

I was in the presence of Master Xavier, and if I guessed correctly, we were alone. As my captors' footfalls receded, I couldn't help the pang in my heart at their disappearance. Some twisted part of me needed Chad and Bay by my side. It made no sense, but I felt more protected with them around. With them gone, I felt naked and exposed.

My heart thundered in my chest. My breaths turned ragged and shallow. I wanted to leap out of that chair and run out of the room, but the hood stole my sight and the chair had become a prison as well.

He approached with sure-footed steps. A single tug at my neck freed the cords of the hood. A quick jerk and bright light filled my universe.

I blinked scratchy eyes against the brightness as my dilated pupils struggled to accommodate to the change in illumination. Movement in front of me revealed the blurred image of a man walking away, carrying an empty black hood. He tossed the offensive thing on a table and turned to face me.

He regarded me as I blinked away sleep and dried tears from my eyes. Slowly, my vision cleared and the details of my surroundings revealed themselves. I wasn't ready to face this person, so I focused on the room instead.

I was in a three-story, wood-paneled library supported by pillars and decorated with intricate moldings. Books filled floor-to-ceiling shelves, and ladders on rails encircled the room. Overhead a dome soared, painted with the most amazing mural of cherubs frolicking in clouds suspended in a gold and blue sky.

A massive mahogany desk filled one corner. Piles of books perched precariously on its edges. In another corner, a set of reading chairs faced each other, matching folded tartans tucked neatly on their cushions. The only other furniture in the room was a matched pair of chairs, one on which I sat. The other faced me, a few feet away.

My vision solidified, cleared, and locked onto the dominant presence in the room. I searched for evil in the man standing before me, some sense of vileness I expected from a man who traded in slaves. What I saw instead was compassion.

"Good afternoon." He bowed his head. "It is with great pleasure that I welcome you, my slave, to your new home."

My gaze soared up to the cherub filled painting. He named me slave. Evil lurked within him no matter what I'd seen in his eyes. Dear God, what captivating eyes they were, too. They flashed in the light and seared me to the bone. Twin lasers of the purest blue fixed me in place and dissected me to the smallest sliver.

"Go fuck yourself." Probably not the best first words to say to the man who held my fate in his hands, but I'd had enough of being drugged, bound, hooded, and—well, sold.

Our eyes locked, and my entire body clenched as his jaw bunched. His gaze smoldered as his lids narrowed. Everything about him screamed power. From the way he controlled the men who brought me to him, to how he held himself with a sense of absolute assurance, and to the way the suit of the blackest black conformed to his shape. He exuded confidence, authority, and mastery of everything around him. His clipped dark hair and clean shaven appearance told me much about this man's attention to detail.

If I hadn't learned that lesson already, from all the care put into my capture so far, then I was truly an idiot. Clearly, this man had planned and orchestrated every step of my abduction. There was no doubt this was his realm, his fortress. He was the master and I but his latest acquisition.

A sensation tingled across my flesh as he stared at me, not moving a muscle. I wanted him to react to my outburst. Why did he just stand there? His lack of reaction, or rather his extreme display of self-control, told me something important. This was a man in control of not only his surroundings but his reactions as well. This made him incredibly dangerous.

His lip twitched.

I sucked in a breath.

He placed his hands on a shelf. Long, strong fingers stroked the wood. The way he stared at me became too much and I cast my eyes down, breaking the connection between us.

"That is good, slave. You've discovered your first rule. You will keep your gaze cast down in my presence. Now, say hello to your master."

CHAPTER FIVE_

"YOU'RE FUCKING HIGH IF YOU THINK I'M GOING TO DO THAT." My gaze flicked up to meet his, screw his rules.

He stalked toward me, a predator playing with its meal. I pressed back into the chair, desperate to put that fractional distance between us. My heart beat a furious tattoo, fluttering beneath my breastbone, as my fingers clawed at the arms of the chair.

There was no escape. I was at his mercy. A great weight settled over my chest as my situation became all too real. Grabbing my knees, he yanked them apart, then stepped into the empty space between them. He placed his hands over my Velcro bound wrists, leaned over me, then whispered in my ear.

"Second rule, no swearing."

He straightened and some of the weight of his presence

dissipated. We stared at each other, me glaring, him assessing, until he cocked his head and took a step back. He moved to the chair facing me and settled himself into the seat. Kicking a heel over his opposite knee, he pressed those long fingers together before placing them beneath his chin. Those laser blue eyes of his bore into me, while he regarded me with stony silence. I stared back as my heart thundered in my chest and attempted to regain control of my breathing. Intimidation aside, this man terrified me.

"You know you want to say it." A chuckle escaped him and a ghost of a smile curved at the corners of his mouth.

My eyes narrowed. I wanted to kick and scream, hiss and spit. I wanted to hurl every vile obscenity I could think of in his direction, but they were only words; impotent weapons. I clamped my mouth shut, and bit at my lower lip. If he wanted me to say something, then I would say nothing.

Our staring competition stretched the seconds and continued beyond that. His brows lifted with amusement and he dropped his hands, letting his fingers tap a rhythm on his leg. When the silence stretched to minutes, it was he who cracked.

Score one for Team Raven.

One moment he was leaning back in his chair, drumming out a beat with his fingers. In a blink of an eye, he leaned forward and pressed his hands against his knees. I wasn't prepared for the sudden movement and gasped.

"Very well, slave," he said through gritted teeth. "I will spell out the rules of your new life."

I didn't want to hear his version of my new life. His gaze terrified me, but I forced myself to look directly into his Caribbean blues, another time, another place, different circumstances, and I would be entranced by this man. Now, I found myself repulsed, mostly.

The volume of his voice increased. "Eyes. Down."

His command had me obeying without thought. My gaze dropped to his kneecaps. Tension corded in the backs of his hands, ligaments stood out in relief. His nails showed signs of work, with dirt under the nail beds. When he turned his hands, callouses lined his palms. This man didn't shy away from hard work.

Then, I realized what he had done. How I had reacted, and shame heated my face. I dragged my gaze up his body, determined to meet the steel in his eyes. I couldn't believe I caved so easily to his command. My entire body shook in the potency of his presence.

His exquisitely tailored suit allowed him freedom of movement without binding the breadth of his shoulders. A pulse lifted in his neck and disappeared into the soft tissues at the angle of his jaw. Stubble covered the expanse of his square jaw. He was older than me, young thirties, but was not an old man as I had imagined during my trip. How had such a young man amassed such great wealth? But I knew the answer to that question. I breathed in his power and felt myself caving to his control.

I lifted my gaze beyond the curve of his lips and dragged it the last few inches to meet the challenge of his eyes. The power swirling in their depths made me cringe. I couldn't fight this, but I would try. I didn't care what arrangement he and Z had made. I was slave to no one.

I stuck out my chin and glared at him. I couldn't afford to have him intimidate me. This first meeting had to be between equals. It would set the tone of everything that came after. I wouldn't allow his wealth to influence me. I had grown up around wealth. Maybe not as much as this man seemed to control, but I could hold my own. I didn't care that he was well dressed, tall, attractive, or acted like he expected everyone around him to obey his every command. I had not agreed to any of this.

He held my gaze, never broke eye contact, and we waged another battle of wills. He leaned fractionally forward. I gulped, but held my ground.

The man could move. He flowed with an indomitable force, exuding power and masculinity without effort. Hell, he moved like sex, dangerous if you weren't paying attention, and I was watching his every move. Still, his erotic power washed over me, and despite myself, a growing part of me wondered what his hands would feel like on my skin.

He had yet to touch me. The only contact we'd shared had been through the thick layers of my Velcro restraints and the whisper of his breath against my ear. For a man who bought himself a slave, why hadn't he touched me yet? Why did I care? I didn't want that, right?

My heart raced with each pull of his breath, trying to figure out what sick pleasures a man like him had that would require a slave. A man with wealth and power could surely have his choice in women. I knew this, because I had orbited in those circles, much to Z's dismay. What sick pleasures did Master Xavier indulge in that he couldn't find normal, willing women to join him?

His jaw clenched. A fractional nod followed. "The question you're not asking, but should, is what will I do to you if you don't obey?"

"I have no intention of obeying you, so it doesn't really matter what you will or will not do to me."

I countered as best I could. There were so many possibilities. I wasn't sure how strong I could be if I knew those answers. The intensity in his eyes increased, establishing a connection deep within me. A magnetic pull swirled, intensified, and amplified unwanted sensations.

My heartbeat slowed and I felt myself calm. The tremors stopped. My breathing normalized as it fell into sync with the rhythm of his breath. Somehow, he was soothing me, controlling my body as I fell into a trance in his presence.

Emotions flashed across his face. Interest dominated the parade of emotions. I presented more of a challenge than he anticipated. Did no one ever tell this man *no*? Annoyance flashed for an instant, but didn't linger. Irritation landed and flickered in his eyes, but then it morphed into an emotion even more terrifying. He blinked, and his eyes darkened into a smoldering flare of arousal until it erupted into an open conflagration of pure lust. My pulse jumped and broke the connection between us. I turned my attention to the rows and rows of books, moving anywhere and everywhere except to the man sitting in front of me. My pulse slammed in my throat, speeding past and through panic, because I saw his intent. He wanted me.

And I couldn't avoid him. His hand whipped out and gripped my chin, pressed my head to the back of the chair. Hot breath coursed over my face as he bore down on me, the scent of spice and musk, and a rich aroma all deliciously male captured my lips.

So many thoughts collided as his lips trapped mine beneath his. I wanted to scream and push him away. But he stole my breath, and my wrists were bound. His lips glided across mine, his tongue tracing the seams of my lips, exploring the cleft of my mouth, but he didn't force his way inside. The grip on my chin released and disappeared. He pulled at my lower lip, tugging it between his teeth. A groan escaped him.

I should fight his intrusion, but I didn't struggle. I held perfectly still while he kissed me, sucking and pulling at my lips. His tongue darted and pressed, licked along the contours of my mouth, and still I didn't react. His lips were smooth, supple, and talented. They destroyed me, because I wanted more.

He touched my cheek and traced the lines of my dried tears. He ran the pad of his thumb along my jawline as he deepened his gentle kiss. I had expected vileness. In the end, it was the tenderness of his kiss which broke me.

Shuddering sobs wracked my body as his lips brushed against mine. He could have forced my mouth open, penetrated my defenses and invaded my body, but his fingers stroked at my cheek and wiped away my tears.

The kiss stopped, leaving the incredible flavor of him behind. Why did he have to taste so good? And why did his kiss make me want to open up to him? What the hell was wrong with me?

He kissed my cheeks, no doubt tasting the saltiness of my tears, then he released me. The cushion of air and distance settled between us once more as he retook his seat.

"There are a few truths you must accept." Master Xavier reached into an inner pocket of his jacket and pulled out a velvet pouch.

My sobs continued. His kiss had ruined me.

"You are my slave. You cannot escape, although you will try. Don't think you can resist me. You'll lose. You'll not only learn my rules, but you'll embrace and obey them. Failure to do so will be met with consequence." He stood and stared down at me.

I blinked against the upwelling of my tears. I saw him, all

of him. My gaze dipped down and met the prominent bulge behind the zipper of his pants. He reached down and adjusted himself, knowing full well I watched his every move.

"These are the foundations of your new life, slave, and it's essential you understand them." He took a step forward and I flinched as he moved toward me. He pulled something shiny out of the pouch, something flat and circular, and wrapped it around my neck. The cold bite of metal stung my flesh and then disappeared as my skin warmed the chain. His deft fingers worked quickly.

I heard the unmistakable sound of a latch or lock closing. A cold weight settled around my neck, resting on my collar bone. He moved to the side and worked with quick efficiency.

"You're exhausted from your flight." He attached a flat platinum band around my wrist. It had three rings attached to it. "We'll discuss the rules after you have rested." Another *snick* and the seam of the band disappeared before my eyes. He moved to my other wrist and repeated the process. "Your handlers will be back in a moment to show you to your room. You will obey them in all things."

I couldn't let it end this way. I tasted the salt of my tears and the lingering flavor of him. "You're a monster, a sadistic, misogynistic, rapist who buys women. You're nothing."

He regarded me with lust simmering in his eyes. "I am many things, but I'm not a misogynist nor a rapist. I love everything there is about women. I will place you on a pedestal and worship you as long as you obey my rules. You were payment for debts owed. I did not kidnap you, nor did I buy you."

He left me there, strapped to a chair, to replay our first conversation in my head. The taste of him lingered on my lips. Our first kiss. There would be others. I was certain of that. Despite what he said about not being a rapist, his erection decried his interest. Lust had blazed in those eyes. In what twisted world did that not make him a rapist? I replayed his last words, what he denied, and what he admitted by omission. My inner veneer began to crack, because I was no match for this man.

CHAPTER SIX_

I SAT ALONE WITH MY THOUGHTS FOR ANOTHER TEN OR TWENTY minutes. A clock ticked out the seconds behind me, an ominous reminder of my fate. Tears spilled down my cheeks. Frustration and anger filled my being, because I had yet to do anything to better my situation. Each moment brought me further into his world and further from freedom.

I was in his home, with a collar around my neck and silver chains around my wrists. His taste lingered on my lips, dark and sultry, and filled with a promise I couldn't ignore. But that wasn't the worst of it. Heat flowed to my core with the memory of his lips against mine.

Was I sick in the head because I found my captor attractive?

I wasn't going to think about it. Before I could delve too

far into the darkness of my thoughts, the doors to the library opened.

A smiling Bay and Chad entered. Chad had his arm wrapped around Bay's shoulders and his head leaned close as he whispered into Bay's ear. It was the first time I had a chance to really look at the men. All I remembered from before was the steel-blue in Chad's eyes. The rest I had built up in my imagination from my sense of smell, sound, and what I had felt.

They were built like linebackers, solid twin walls of muscles. Chad had a smiling face that fit his sarcastic wit. His eyes softened as he glanced at me and he released Bay's shoulder. Bay looked like the stereotypical boy next door; sandy brown hair, freckles dusting his face, and dark chocolate brown eyes. An easy looking man, a match to his easy personality. If they hadn't been a part of my kidnapping, I could easily see myself being friends with both these men. Bay reached into his trousers pocket and pulled out a pack of spearmint gum. He popped a stick into his mouth, offering a stick to Chad who refused.

"How did it go, kitten?" Chad crouched down in front of me, getting eye level.

"How did you expect it to go?" My brows pinched together.

"Hey, fly's open man. Zip it." Chad's mouth twisted and he glanced at Bay's crotch.

A flush crept through Bay's freckles as he glanced at me. He turned away and zipped up.

"I was hoping it went well," Chad said. "Master Xavier told us to settle you in your room. I just assumed…"

"You assumed wrong." I wanted to bite his head off.

"Sorry, kitten." Chad undid the Velcro at my wrists. Suddenly, he stopped and regarded me with a hard stare. "I'm going to release your restraints. Bay and I are going to lead you out to your room. It's up to you whether you choose to fight us or come along quietly."

"And if I don't cooperate?"

Bay put a hand on my shoulder. "We're here to help you. Think of us as your handlers."

"You mean guards."

Chad placed his hands on my thighs and squeezed them gently. "You can think of it like that, but we're more like bodyguards. We're here to make sure you don't hurt yourself."

"How would I hurt myself?"

Bay straightened out my ponytail. "By trying to run, for one thing. We can't allow that, and we're obligated to stop you. I don't want to point out the obvious, but we're bigger than you."

It was obvious, and they'd already succeeded in restraining me, but the three of us knew I was going to run at some point.

"This is a GPS tracking device. You can try to run, but

we're going to find you." Chad tapped the device strapped to my ankle.

"Not if I take it off."

"You can try." Bay tilted my chin and regarded me with warm brown eyes. "Don't try, little one."

Chad ripped the Velcro securing my right wrist. "Promise you aren't going to hit me?" He pointed to his chin and the small bruise at the tip.

His grin was infectious and I smiled back despite my intentions to remain angry with these men. Bay released my other wrist. As Chad went to free my feet, Bay snickered.

"Did you remember to put your cup on? She has a wicked kick."

"She didn't kick me that hard." Chad stopped what he was doing. He stepped to the side and gestured to the floor.

"Then what was all that moaning about?" Bay arched a brow and crossed his arms.

Chad cupped his balls and rolled his eyes. "I managed just fine in the end, but how about you release her."

"Chicken." Bay stooped down and released the Velcro fastening my legs to the chair.

I rubbed at my wrists, amazed at the freedom of not being bound. It had become a constant in my life, but I had two new constants. Twin platinum bands encircled my wrists. I examined the seamless metal. There were no locking mechanisms. I felt around the band around my neck. Just like my wrists, sturdy rings dangled from the collar. I didn't want to think about what those rings would be used for. Xavier had a thing for restraints. What else might he have a thing for?

Bay reached out. "Come, little one." He helped me out of the chair.

Sight had been returned, as well as the freedom of my hands, but bracketed by my buddies, I never felt so caged. Chad stood on one side while Bay took the other. They led me out of the library and I saw the rest of the house for the first time.

The plantation style mansion was full of white lines, white linen, white plantation shutters, and antique leaded glass. The shutters opened to an expansive lawn full of palm trees and exotic gardens. A long driveway ended in a circular drive. Chad and Bay led me past one set of open windows and down what seemed to be a series of endless corridors. I'd been in many large estates in my life, but the size of Xavier's home put those to shame.

My guards took me to a set of twirling staircases ascending three stories in an inner atrium with a majestic landing between the second and third floors. Floral paintings and jungle motifs decorated the walls and sculpted wooden art soared in the spaces between. We ascended in silence, and I didn't try to run.

They stopped outside a plain, white door, unremarkable in every detail. I steeled myself against what I was to find inside. What sort of quarters did a slave rank? At least Xavier wasn't housing me in a dungeon, or inside a cage. Or worse, I wasn't being forced to share his room.

For whatever reason, he had given me a place of my own. I didn't know what that implied, or what message he was trying to send, only that I was thankful to have a sliver of something private. Chad told me my right to privacy was gone, but this implied something different.

I opened the door and stopped. The room was stark and bare. In the center, crisp white linen sheets spread across a four-poster bed. Attached to the posts, four heavy rings hung empty, but filled with promise. I glanced at the rings dangling from my bracelets—cuffs—and cringed at the implication. There was a wardrobe, a dresser, a small closet, and shelves bare of adornment. A doorway opened off to the far left.

Oddly, there was a twin bed in the room as well. It was tucked into the far-right corner in an unobtrusive spot. Next to it were four metal lockers, with combination locks hanging from their latches. Initials were engraved in the metal: B, C, M, and E.

I looked to Bay and Chad. They joined me in the room.

"This is your room, little one." Bay shut the door behind him, locking it by tapping a code into a key pad.

I ground my teeth together. "My name is Raven."

Chad shook his head. "Your name is slave until Master Xavier says otherwise. We have been given permission to call you what we wish, but your previous name no longer exists."

"Who is that for?" I pointed to the twin bed.

"One of us will always be with you," Chad explained. "We'll watch over you in shifts. That way if you need anything, we'll be there to serve you."

Serve me? What the hell? They acted like they were at my beck and call, when they were anything but.

"Who is E?"

Bay laughed. "That's Ben's middle initial. Couldn't have two B's. He lost the coin flip."

"Why did you lock the door?"

Chad leveled his steel-blue eyes at me as if I'd asked the dumbest question. "Kitten, when you're in your room you'll always be locked in with one of us."

"What if there's a fire?" I tried to reason with them.

Chad shook his head. "We'll get you out."

"What if you're incapacitated?"

"Kitten, stop," Chad said. "Master Xavier's orders are for you to wash up. While an amazing beauty, a day's worth of travel has done a number on you."

A queasiness settled in my gut. I could be anywhere in the world. My escape plans, non-existent as they were, became even more impossible.

"First, a long hot shower, then we'll put you to bed." Chad ushered me toward the doorway on the left.

"Isn't your Master Xavier concerned about leaving me alone with two men? He must have a lot of trust in you?"

Bay and Chad exchanged looks and grinned.

"He trusts us with your life, kitten," Chad said. "Now, you can either take a shower by yourself, or Bay and I can strip you down and wash you ourselves." He put his arms across his chest. "Which would you prefer?"

Neither.

I walked through the doorway into a spacious bathroom practically the same size of my spartan bedroom, noticing as I did the lack of a door. True to Chad's promise, it was abundantly clear my days of privacy were gone.

I felt defeated.

My encounter with Master Xavier left me doubting my ability to fight. I had crumbled after a simple kiss. I hated weakness and I didn't understand where mine stemmed from.

Never in my life had I been this meek. I was a fighter. I was the wild child. I was the kid who sought adventure, the daredevil who jumped out of planes, dove under the ocean, and explored beneath hundreds of feet of rock in the darkest recesses of the earth.

I kick-boxed. I learned judo, Ju-Jitsu, studied Kenpo and the military S.C.A.R.S. fighting system. I learned about defensive driving and how to shoot guns.

I stared at the marble shower built for two and stripped in a daze. The men moved in the room behind me, speaking quietly to themselves, giving me what privacy they could. I turned the water on, hoping my new master allowed a lowly slave the luxury of hot water. I was going to wash away my desolation and strip away this day of defeat.

Steam, lovely, wonderful, obscuring steam filled the bathroom in fog. I may not have privacy, but for a moment I had the illusion of it. The shower was equipped with everything I needed. In fact, it was stocked with my preferred hair products. I wondered how much communication Xavier had with Z prior to my purchase. My favorite shampoo, conditioner, even my razors were all stocked.

How long had they been planning this?

I lathered up and rinsed out my hair, glad to be rid of the sweat accumulated from suffering beneath that nefarious hood. Then I put on conditioner and slid to the floor where I curled into a ball and rocked myself while I cried deep soulful sobs. I was in no hurry to get out of the shower, and it seemed my guards were in no hurry to fetch me. They let me stay as long as I wanted, and I figured, why not? Where was I going to run?

But I couldn't stay there forever. Eventually I needed to get up. I stood and rinsed out my hair. Steam billowed all around me. I reached for the handle to turn off the water and paused. I pulled away and stepped out of the shower, letting the water run.

This might be the only chance I had to really look at my room, my cell. I tiptoed quietly around the room, looking for a window, an exit. There was none. Of course there wouldn't be one.

I turned off the water and toweled myself dry, taking my time. I checked the drawers and cabinets and found a hairdryer, turning it on, and began the long process of blow drying my hair.

Gradually the steam thinned, and the fog in the mirror cleared. I focused on my hair, trying not to think about anything else. When I put the hair dryer up, a glance in the mirror revealed Chad watching me.

"You doing okay?" His eyes softened and he gave me a chin bump.

"No."

"You need sleep." He jerked his head toward the room. "Bay will watch over you. I'm going to take a shower."

"How does this work? Are the two of you always going to be around?"

He shook his head. "Bay and I have the first shift. Ben and Mel are on night duty."

"I'm tired."

"It'll get easier, kitten," he said, as if he could make it a promise. "You can try to fight him, but you won't win. It's up to you how hard you make this on yourself."

"What would you do? Would you give in?"

"Those answers are complicated." He unbuttoned his shirt and tossed it on the ground. "Go to bed, kitten. Bay is waiting to lock you in."

"Lock me in?" My gaze shifted to the bed in the other

room. Bay had a long length of chain measured out. He locked an end to one of the rings.

I squeezed my eyes shut. They had me locked behind an electronic keypad with a guard, and still felt it necessary to bind me with a chain? I only wished I deserved the degree of caution they were taking.

Bay smiled as I moved toward the bed. I had a towel wrapped around me. "Do I get any clothes to sleep in?"

He pointed to the dresser. "First drawer, panties and bras. Second drawer, nightgowns. Once you're dressed..." He waved the end of the chain.

"Right, lock the slave in for the night." And tomorrow? What did my new master have planned for me in the morning?

I dressed quickly and didn't even fight as Bay locked the free end of the chain to one of the rings on the collar around my neck. He turned out the lights. Then he went into the bathroom and joined Chad in the shower. I fell asleep to the deep susurrations of male voices locked in what sounded like pleasure.

CHAPTER SEVEN_

THE NEXT MORNING, I WOKE REFRESHED. I HADN'T SLEPT THAT soundly in weeks. I rolled out of bed and headed to the bathroom, only to be jerked to a stop by the chain attached to my neck.

"Good Morning," came a clipped greeting. A groan sounded from the twin bed in the corner. A man moved under the covers and rubbed at his eyes.

I glanced at my guard, recognizing Mel's gruff tone, if not remembering his face. He was older than Bay and Chad, mid-thirties, but just as muscular.

"Come here, sweetie."

Did they all have private names for me? I walked over and he released me from my chain.

"When you're ready," he said, "Master Xavier has

requested your presence." He pulled out a phone and sent a message.

When I was ready? If it were up to me, I would stay in my room all day.

My stomach felt queasy as I entered the bathroom. I didn't have the strength for another encounter with Xavier, but there would be no way to avoid it. When I returned, Mel had put clothes on the bed for me to wear. I looked at the yellow sundress and glanced at him. While on the plane, I rarely heard Mel speak, and when he did it was with an economy of words.

"Get dressed," he said.

While he used the restroom, I tugged off my nightgown and slipped on the form-fitting sundress. Billowy fabric floated in a cloud around my legs, landing just above my knees. Mel put out a pair of matching sandals and I slipped them on.

"Lovely," he said upon exiting the bathroom.

I blushed under his scrutiny.

"Come," he said, as he grabbed my hand and guided me to the door.

He tapped in a code, not bothering to keep the numbers hidden from my view. I realized why a moment later when he pressed his palm to the biometric key pad. Another barrier. Knowing the code wasn't going to unlock my prison. I would need one of my guards' hands and didn't see how that might work. I breathed deeply, seeking strength.

The door opened and Ben the Boss greeted us on the interior balcony overlooking the atrium. I stared down three stories, looking over the tops of the trees growing inside Master Xavier's estate. No matter my thoughts about the man, he had a beautiful home. The gentle cascading of water drifted through the space. There must be a fountain, or more likely a small pond with a stream.

"Good morning," Ben said.

I didn't have a smile to spare for Ben. Truthfully, I missed Chad and Bay. I wondered what time they changed out their shifts and hoped it happened soon. I gave Ben a nod and waited for direction.

Like Chad and Bay, Ben and Mel bracketed me. We walked in silence, tracing a path through the palatial estate, traveling a new set of hallways. Only the paintings along the walls broke up the crisp white theme. Finally, they brought me to an enclosed aviary. Tropical plants filled the space, palms stretched their leafy fronds to the tall dome overhead while ferns unfurled their greenery at the base of the palms. Orchids of every variety dotted the space, providing a never-ending feast of color to the eye, and hundreds of humming-birds flitted around.

A magical space, I would have loved to stay there forever, exploring the hidden nooks and crannies, except for the presence of the man waiting for me at the glass table in the center of the room. Xavier looked up as my entourage and I entered. He wore another dark suit; this one a dark charcoal with a silk shirt the same shade as his eyes. The colors vibrated energy and power.

Once again, our gazes collided. His command to lower my gaze was one I ignored and I searched his reaction as I defied his silly rule. He guarded himself well. It put me on edge and I stiffened my spine, readying myself for battle.

He held himself with confidence, head cocked to the side, and was the first to break eye contact. His gaze slid down my figure, inspecting me like a piece of property. His slow perusal continued until Ben cleared his throat. The sound shattered the tense silence and brought Xavier's arctic gaze back to me.

"Come here," he said.

I rolled my shoulders back and jutted my chin out. I could do this. I was my father's daughter. I was strong.

Xavier dismissed my guards with a wave of his hand. Ben and Mel departed, leaving me alone with a predator. I looked left then right, instinctively searching out escape, but there was only the one entrance.

"Do not make me repeat myself, slave." His voice carried the threat of a promise I did not wish to see delivered.

Woodenly, my legs moved of their own accord. I approached the table and he moved around it, making me falter mid-step. When he stopped to pull out a chair, I found my breath and sank into the seat he offered. He moved to the opposite side of the table and took his seat. Looking at me, he pressed his palms to the table.

"You look refreshed, slave. I take it you slept well?"

"My name is Raven." I pressed my lips together.

"That name no longer exists." His brows lifted.

"You can't take my name."

"I will take more than your name." He leaned back. "It's time to establish our ground rules."

"Right," I crossed my arms and glared at him. "Your damn rules I'm supposed to follow."

He pulled out a thin rod from his breast coat pocket. "Yes, my *damn* rules. The second rule which you just violated. No swearing. And the first, which you intentionally break with every breath."

"So?" I shrugged.

He lifted the thin rod. It was about six inches long and the diameter of a pencil. "Do you know what this is?"

"No." I shook my head.

"You're going to find out."

"That didn't take long."

I couldn't resist baiting him. If he was going to beat me and rape me, I wanted to get it over with. He was being entirely too civil about the whole thing. My image of a slave trading, misogynist was not the man in front of me.

He leaned forward. "I make promises, slave, not threats. You will either choose to obey my rules or you will accept the consequence for disobeying them." He lifted the thin rod. "This, among other things," he gave a slow blink as darkness filled his expression, "will be used to punish you."

My stomach twisted as I gazed into his eyes. Stellate blue irises flashed in the morning light, and his unwavering expression told me he was serious.

"Let me present you with some truths. You cannot run from me," he said. "You will try. It will cost you. I'm going to ask that you reconsider and reconcile yourself to your fate. There's nowhere you can go that I won't find you. Therefore, when you do attempt your escape, and after I find you, I will punish you."

I swallowed against the lump in my throat. He certainly understood me. "Who says I'm going to run. You seem to have my security detail well thought out."

"I smell it on you. You're looking for holes in my security, and don't forget I know who your father is. I know what you're capable of."

"Then you know I have a chance." I wasn't sure I believed that anymore, but I had a degree from MIT which proclaimed me an expert in computer science. Technology didn't frighten me, and I hacked computers for fun. Xavier had no idea what I was capable of, not that I would share that with him.

He leaned back. "You won't succeed." His tone bordered on victory and I hadn't even begun my fight. Such assurance had my heart seizing in my chest. My voice cracked as I leaned forward, but I needed to close the distance between us. My weakness was my greatest failing and I needed to meet his strength with strength.

"If you think I'll reconcile myself to this…" I gave a vague gesture and shook my head. "I'll fight you and I'll win. You have no rights to me."

"Your father gave you to me," he countered.

"Z had no right to do that. I'm not an object to be traded. I'll do whatever it takes to survive, and when you let down your guard, which you will, I'll destroy you. I'll destroy Z. I'll make both of you pay."

"Proud words for a slave." Xavier took in a sharp inhale. "Interesting that you include your father in your plans for destruction. Have you no loyalty?"

I pressed my fingers to the glass. "To a man who gave me to a monster? I have no loyalty to Z."

Xavier kicked his ankle over his knee and stared at me for a long moment. "Destroying me will prove harder than you think, but we might talk about what to do about your father." He searched my face, his interest intensifying in his gaze.

His scrutiny made me wriggle, but I struggled not to show him how uncomfortable he made me feel. I tried to return him stare for stare, but I wasn't strong enough. My gaze slipped to his chin, then settled on his lips.

Taking a breath, he spoke. "You belong to me. This is fact. Through a string of complicated circumstances, your father owed a debt, for which you're payment in full. He was more than happy to erase his debts, especially given my reputation in…certain circles. The how and why of it is none of your concern. What matters is that you now belong to me. As a result, you must obey me in all things."

"Your logic is flawed," I countered. "You could let me go."

"I have no desire to let you go," he said. "Now that I have you, I have an even more pressing reason to keep you."

"What is that?"

A smile tugged at the corners of his eyes. "I have tasted your charms, and felt your body's reactions. I want you for purely selfish reasons."

Holy hellfire what did that mean?

His voice dropped to sultry tones and as it did an answering heat smoldered in my belly. I should hate this man, but that magnetism returned. A wild force tugged at my core, pulling me toward him and it seemed as if the very air between us crackled with energy. I traced the lines of his lips and couldn't help but imagine them pressed against my skin.

Get a grip!

I shook my head to dispel the connection.

He stood, his athletic frame moving with the fluid grace of well-toned muscles. He walked around the table, moving toward me. "You feel it too. I see it in your eyes. Don't worry, we'll soon satisfy our mutual cravings, but first..." He spun the thin rod in his hand.

Different scenarios danced through my mind, because I wanted exactly that. I could run. I should get up right now. Most likely, Ben and Mel stood guard at the door and there was no way I would be getting past them. I could deny Xavier.

Spit in his face. Or knee him in the groin like I had done to Chad. But it was too late. He knew exactly what I had been thinking.

I had no idea what that slim rod did, but I imagined it involved pain. He mentioned a whip, and I wasn't ready to visit that possibility ever. He approached, and rather than running, I remained rooted in place.

Breathe, just pretend you're anywhere but here. Find a happy place.

A frown darkened his features as he came around the table. He glanced at the slim rod, palming it. "Some people call this a misery stick. It's an effective tool, discrete, and always at hand."

I stared at the thin rod. It narrowed at the tip and flexed in his hand. I licked my lower lip and sucked in a breath, not liking where this was going.

"Rule one," he said, "is to lower your eyes in my presence. It's a sign of deference and respect for your Master. You refuse to acknowledge this rule."

My gaze flicked to his, a direct violation. At the arch in his brow, I looked away. He slapped the rod in his palm and I jumped.

"Rule two," he said. "No swearing, in particular, no disparaging remarks aimed at me."

He placed the tip of the rod under my chin. "Rule three, from this moment forward you will address me as Master."

"You're *not* my master," I said with defiance.

He crouched before me. His liquid blue eyes bore into me and I pressed myself back against the chair.

"You were given to me by your father. Payment for a debt. I own you. No one is coming for you. No one is looking for you. You have disappeared off the face of the earth. There is no escape. You will try, and you will fail. Your entire world has narrowed down to one thing. You serve me."

He waited for an answer, one I would not give. My breaths quickened with the many thoughts swirling in the chaos of my mind. He spoke the truth. Z wouldn't report my disappearance. No one would be looking for me.

Xavier's voice dropped to a whisper. "You'll serve me, obey me, and you will please me."

"Bastard," I muttered. I hated him, because all I could do was exactly as he commanded; at least, for now.

Once again, our eyes connected. Resignation filled his expression, and a burst of something dark swirled in the depths, something he suppressed. He was good at guarding his emotions, nothing gave away what he thought. If I hadn't seen a flicker, I wouldn't have a hint of the emotions behind his mask. I didn't want to know more, because what I saw was hunger and lust.

He grabbed my wrist and pulled me out of the chair. Everything happened so fast, I was barely aware of what he did. I twirled in his grip, our positions swapping between one breath and the next. He was in the chair and I draped over his lap.

He had my hand pulled up over my back, my other hand trapped between his body and mine. I kicked my feet, but he wrapped a leg over my flailing legs, pinning me in place. His breathing came hard and fast, deep inhales thundered out of his chest. I twisted and fought, but couldn't move. I had underestimated him.

"Punishment is a consequence of a failure to follow the rules. Let this be your first lesson."

I squirmed in his lap as a whistling filled the air. The sound was followed by a crack over my backside. I howled at the flare of pain lighting my skin on fire. It hurt so damn much. Before I could take another breath, he struck again, and again, and again. He rained down a flurry of blows with that deceptive looking stick.

I found myself hyperventilating. Screaming was impossible as I had no breath to make sound. The pain cracked down to the bone. I had never felt something so intense and wanted to die. Just as suddenly as it started, it stopped. He rubbed my bottom, soothing the ache. I was certain he had split the skin, but felt no sign that would indicate blood.

What I did feel was something much more concerning. Beneath me, the full force of his arousal pressed against my belly, but that wasn't what I found mortifying. Wetness soaked the silk of my panties. A flare of desire curled in my core, sending tendrils of heat to my womb.

His labored breathing signified more than exertion from the strikes he'd given me. My heart skipped a beat. I wanted to put distance between us, but he held me down and he rubbed at my tenderized flesh. The burn began to ease up, but that only allowed a new heat to stir between my legs.

I needed off his lap.

"Let me go." I pushed, earning me a strangled groan from him as I brushed against his erection.

He pressed me down onto his lap. "Do not move." He sucked in deep breaths.

I wiggled, desperate to be free of him.

He slapped my ass. "Damn it, if you move again, I won't be responsible for what happens next. Do. Not. Move."

I bit my lip. Terrified by what he was admitting. I didn't dare move.

Many seconds passed. Xavier took control of his breathing, even as his arousal continued to press against me.

Tears pricked at my eyes. My butt burned from that damn stick. Worse, he had ignited a slow burn in my core I did not understand. It fizzled away to nothing as I lay draped over his lap, but the memory of the heat left me confused.

Eventually, he lifted me off his lap and dumped me unceremoniously on the ground. As he stood, he adjusted his erection and wiped his brow. He stepped over me and took five steps before turning back around.

"You will be punished each time you fail to adhere to my rules." He pointed to the door as he adjusted himself. "You need to leave...now."

"And if I don't?" Why the hell did I say that? I didn't need to spend any longer in this man's presence. What kind of spell did he have on me?

He captured me in his gaze, holding me prisoner by nothing more than the power of his presence. His Caribbean eyes shifted, turning a deep shade of blue. Darkness lurked there, along with an inescapable hunger. There were no illusions as to what that hunger might be.

I ignored the urgent message in his gaze, the one which told me to flee, transfixed as I was by his power. His magnetism pulled at me, the danger a potent drug.

He came at me, powerful muscles shifting and bunching as he descended on me, a ruthless predator coming for his prey. Calm acceptance overcame me as his gaze dipped to my lips and his mouth parted in anticipation. He gathered me in his arms, his touch electrifying my skin. Jolts of pleasure coursed along my nerves, twisting and shooting along a path headed to the core of my being.

He leaned in, mouth open, head tilted for a kiss, but he pulled back at the last moment, aborting the kiss. His hands shook where he held me, and his husky voice washed over me.

"If you don't leave right now, I won't be able to stop. I won't be responsible for what happens."

The strain in his voice warbled in my ears, setting off alarms. I looked in his eyes, a direct violation of the first rule. Why was he letting me go?

Like a fool, I wanted to ask, but the warning in his eyes

told me he had stretched his control to his limit. Despite my body's response, I didn't want him to touch me, not like that, not without my consent. The heat he stoked in my core made it blatantly clear he was not the only one affected. As twisted as this thing was between us, I had to admit a horrible truth. His touch electrified me.

I needed to restore balance, both for myself and to remind him of my defiance. I straightened my skirt and stared him in the eyes.

"I'll consider your rules, but you need to reconsider number one..." My voice was a breathy whisper as I gave my concession. Then I sprinted out of the aviary.

I was terrified he would chase me, half hopeful he would try, and sick to my stomach that I cared at all.

CHAPTER EIGHT_

BAY AND CHAD GREETED ME OUTSIDE THE AVIARY RATHER THAN Mel and Ben. I suppose their shift had started and Bay and Chad were now in charge. I wiped tears off my cheeks as I barreled out of the glass doors, leaving the beauty of the indoor oasis behind me and the monster inside.

"Easy, kitten." Chad's easy eyes softened as he witnessed my flight. He put out a hand.

"Stop calling me that! I'm not your damn kitten!"

He held his hands up and backed away as I brushed past him. My fingers curled and clenched as I stomped away from my guards. My backside throbbed from Xavier's punishment.

Bay's phone beeped. He read a text, answered, and waited for the reply. Then he looked to Chad.

"We're to take her to the kitchen for food."

"I thought Master Xavier was having breakfast with her," Chad said.

"Plans changed." Bay gave a shrug.

I came to an intersection of hallways and pulled up short. This place was a maze to me. I had no idea where anything was in relation to my cell of a room. I failed in my escape plans because I should've been paying better attention. My confusion forced me to wait on my jailers to catch up, and I realized how dependent I was on them for everything.

Wasn't there a psychological paradox prisoners went through? Some identification and association they had with their captors? Was I falling for Xavier? I wasn't fighting Ben, Mel, Bay, or Chad. They led and I followed, and I didn't want to think about my reactions to Xavier.

My guards made it difficult because they'd been nothing but polite, almost as if they were going out of their way not to hurt me. They used words to subdue, rather than force to coerce. Other than the initial takedown, they'd been surprisingly gentle.

My reaction to Xavier opened thoughts I didn't want to face. Did I deserve what was happening to me because of some sickness in my head? Did I crave this darkness? Self-loathing and doubt filled my soul.

I wrapped my arms around myself and held back a sob. Self-doubt filled me with recrimination and I hated how my body came to life around Xavier. Pain lodged itself at the base of my skull, a headache in the making. I wanted to cry, but I'd done enough of that. What I felt was hollow and lost. I was tired of feeling powerless and victimized.

My expectations weren't fitting with reality. I expected Xavier to rape and abase me, to strip and torture me, force me to commit unspeakable acts, and violate me in every way imaginable. Instead, I'd been pampered, given my own room, and met with the man who claimed me twice without the rape I feared. I suffered his kisses, and endured the traitorous reactions of my body. He melted me from the inside out, and whatever had happened inside that aviary left me reeling. Instead of assaulting me, he had forced me from his presence, almost as if he was terrified he would cross a line. Why was he leaving me alone?

Even his guards handled me with kid gloves. There was more going on here. Discover that and maybe I wouldn't feel powerless.

Bay and Chad led me in silence, winding through corridors as I drifted inside my mind. We passed through the stark white opulence of Xavier's home, giving me a glimpse into my captor's personality. What appeared to be understated decor on first blush was really an eclectic collection of the most amazing works of art and sculptures. Sunlight streamed through the open plantation styled shutters, casting a warm glow to the expanse of white inside and made the sculptures shine.

We traveled over Egyptian marble, Travertine stone, and thick Persian wool. Each room's dominant color was a shade of white and gray, which subtly accentuated the art displayed on the walls and in specially designed niches dispersed throughout the estate.

Did he decorate the house himself? Is what I saw a reflection of his unique touch?

Soon the sounds of cutlery clinking, and plates clacking, sounded down the hall. The aromas of a kitchen coaxed me forward. My stomach rumbled. Rich coffee blended with the billowing flavors of bread baking. My mouth watered and I realized I had not eaten last night. I had been put to bed without supper. Had that been intentional? Or was Xavier not taking good care of his new pet. From what little I knew, I had no doubt it had been intentional.

Bay, Chad, and I rounded a corner, and I halted as the kitchen came into view. Here, unlike the rest of the house, the dominant color of white disappeared. This place had a weight to it, full of roughhewn wood and stone, almost as if I had been thrown back hundreds of years into an old-world castle.

An open brick oven crackled with a wood fire raging inside of it. Shelves beside the oven held loaves of bread baking, while cast iron hooks suspended pots which bubbled over the burning logs. A massive plank table dominated the center of the room. Flour covered one end and several men stood around it kneading and rolling out dough. At the far end of the table, others perched on tall stools and chopped vegetables. A rack of copper pots hung over their heads casting a golden glow over the entire room. A smaller table stood to the side. Four men gathered around it with large carving knives. They hacked at the carcass of some animal, butchering it into smaller pieces.

Stainless steel appliances and gas stovetops blended in seamlessly with the fireplace and old world brick ovens. A miniature army worked at preparing food, but what amazed me most were the deep Caribbean blue tiles decorating the floor and backsplashes behind the counters. Even here, Xavier's presence followed me.

To my right, floor to ceiling wooden shelving stood behind a wall of glass. Crates, turned on edge, held countless bottles of wine. A gauge mounted on the wall appeared to monitor the internal temperature of the wine cellar. In front of the glass wall, three bistro tables sat with matching chairs, a tiny oasis of calm in the busy kitchen. My stomach twisted at all the strangeness around me. I didn't think I'd be able to eat, but my stomach growled at the wonderful aromas swirling around me and filled my nostrils with delicious scents.

Bay pulled me over to one of the bistro tables. "What would you like, little one?" His dark brown eyes looked on me with compassion and concern.

"What do they have?"

He smiled. "Anything you want. Master Xavier keeps a well-stocked pantry."

My lips curled thinking of that man. "Does everyone call him master?" My stomach growled loudly, causing me to clutch at my belly.

"Yes." Bay's gaze flicked to my stomach and he grinned. "What do you usually eat for breakfast?"

"Coffee." I wasn't big on breakfast and Bay's response had my stomach reeling. He hadn't hesitated in answering my question.

"Coffee I can do, but we have orders to feed you, and you missed dinner last night." His eyes returned to my stomach as if cutting off my refusal of food. "How about eggs and toast," he offered.

Ugh, I hated eggs. "Toast? I'm sorry, but I'm not that hungry."

"Your stomach says otherwise." Bay said with admonishment.

Chad came over, balancing a plate of meat and cheese on top of a bowl of oatmeal.

I looked at the oatmeal and grimaced.

Chad placed his food on the table and pulled up a chair. "You need more than toast," he said, and pushed the plate of meat and cheese toward me.

Bay left and returned with two steaming mugs. "I don't know how you take your coffee." He lifted one. "This one is black." He lifted the other. "This one has sugar and cream."

I reached for the first one and he lifted a brow. "Hm, guessed wrong." Bay grabbed a stool and joined us at the table.

I picked at the meat and cheese while sipping at my coffee. Chad and Bay watched in silence. A short while later, an older man approached with a plate of toast, butter and jam. He put it down in front of me, and then placed a tray of cinnamon rolls in the center of the table. The heady aroma of cinnamon had my mouth watering and I looked at the plate.

Bay laughed as he reached over and separated a roll the size of his fist. "Thought so, little one." He lifted the gooey mess and plopped it down on my plate. "Eat."

He and Chad exchanged glances as my eyes fixed on him. I'd been outplayed and they knew it. Again, where was the evil in my captors? Were they planning to drown me in sweetness and fatten me up for slaughter?

Bay's phone beeped. He read a text and his eyes widened. He turned the phone to Chad who read it with the same surprised reaction. "If that's what he wants."

"His orders," Bay said, lifting his brows.

Chad shrugged. "Okay." He pushed back from the table. "I'll meet you in the library." He swiped a cinnamon roll and shoved half the pastry into his mouth. His eyes closed with delight as he chewed.

Bay gave a nod and reached for a roll, waving as Chad disappeared.

I couldn't refuse and took a small bite. Heavenly sweet-ness, it easily had to be the best cinnamon roll I had ever tasted in my life.

"What was that all about?" I asked.

Bay's mouth was full of dough and icing dribbled down his chin. He licked his lips and wiped his face. "Finish your breakfast, little one."

"That was him, wasn't it? That text?" I glanced at Bay's phone resting on the table and pointed at it.

Bay stopped chewing and regarded me slowly.

"He gives you orders on it?"

He nodded.

"What did he say?"

The beat of my heart increased. Anything associated with Xavier that involved me terrified me. Only now, that terror combined with something I didn't want to acknowledge. My appetite fled as queasiness replaced the growling of my stom-ach. I put the cinnamon roll down and fought against an acid burn rising in my esophagus. I had to take deep breaths, because I felt like I was going to throw up, and I didn't want to do that in front of a kitchen full of witnesses. My terror stemmed from a growing sickness inside me. I wanted to see Xavier and I shouldn't want anything to do with him.

"Finish your food, little one," Bay said.

"I'm not hungry." I pushed my plate away.

Bay arched a brow. He shoved the last bite of his cinnamon roll in his mouth, chewed, and swallowed. Then he leaned back and crossed his arms. "My orders are to make sure you eat." He pointed to my plate, to the one tiny bite I'd taken. "You're not fed. Master Xavier will not be pleased with me if I don't follow his orders, and you know what happens when he's not pleased."

"He's going to spank me again?"

"Not you."

I gave a start. Surely Bay wasn't serious. "You?"

Bay laughed, rolling his eyes. "That's not what I meant," Bay flushed, "but failure to follow orders carries consequences for us all."

"What does that mean?" I didn't understand the root of Bay's embarrassment and didn't care to travel down that path.

"Only that we're not leaving until I'm satisfied you've eaten a proper breakfast. If you refuse, then you and I are going to have a conversation, one that won't go well for you." His arms remained crossed over his chest, emphasizing the expanse of his biceps and the difference in our relative sizes.

"You can't make me eat, Bay."

He arched a brow. "I'll do what's required. As long as you obey, you and I will get along well; as we have been so far."

"And if I don't?"

"Things get complicated. None of us want that for you, little one." Sincerity filled his voice. His smooth, friendly tones remained easy going, but I didn't miss the threat implied. What surprised me was the regret in his chocolate brown eyes. Bay didn't want to hurt me. He really wanted to make things as easy as they could be, given my circumstances.

In that moment, my heart warmed to my gentle guard.

My stomach rolled, however. There was no way I would keep something as heavy and sweet as that roll down.

Then I realized what the text must mean. "He's waiting for me, isn't he?"

Bay nodded.

The bite of cinnamon roll I swallowed tried to revisit my mouth. I gulped against the nausea threatening to bring everything back up.

"Bay, can you get me something else?" I pushed the plate with the roll on it away. "Something I won't throw up?"

"Don't move, little one. I'll be right back." His eyes softened and he nodded.

Bay was a saint. Not only did he get warm broth to soothe my rebellious stomach, but he cleared the offensive tray of cinnamon rolls off the table so I wouldn't have to look at them while I ate. He brought the broth, plus a new plate of plain toast. Under his watchful eye, I swallowed every bite, wondering what punishment a guard would be forced to endure.

"Are you ready?" he asked, once I'd cleared my plate.

Ready for Round Three?

"Not at all." I gave a curt nod and shrugged.

"It'll get easier, little one. Just remember your rules and

you'll do fine. Master Xavier is not the monster you want to believe him to be."

"He's not? Then let me go."

Bay shook his head. "That will not happen."

"Then don't tell me he's not a monster."

CHAPTER NINE_

BAY MARCHED ME THROUGH THE ESTATE, TAKING A NEW ROUTE, which only served to compound my disorientation. When we passed the main entry foyer, my heart kicked into high gear, thrumming like the wings of a bumblebee. He guided me into the opulent library full of paneled wood and floor to ceiling books.

Sitting behind the massive desk piled with books, my nemesis, Xavier, waited for me. He lifted his piercing gaze as we entered and latched onto me. My tongue thickened, whatever scathing words I had prepared died in my throat as the full force of his attention focused on me.

"You may go, Bay," Xavier said.

"Yes, Master Xavier," Bay replied with the deepest respect. My guard backed out of the library, shutting the large doors and sealing me inside.

I'd never been so overwhelmed by someone's presence and I'd grown up around the rich and powerful. This man had a quality to him which left me unhinged and struggling to find my footing. His rich scent filled the room, another overwhelming sensation against which I had no defense.

"Sit." He gestured to the pair of wing backed chairs sitting off to the side.

My feet refused to move.

"Have you forgotten your lesson so soon? When I give a command, you obey. You follow my rules. Eyes. Down." His lips pressed into a thin line and his gaze darkened.

The power behind his command washed over me. The desire to obey claimed me and my gaze began to slip. I realized what was happening in time and blinked. I refused to give in to his power, even knowing the price I would have to pay.

"You choose whether to obey." He stood and pulled out the slim rod from his breast pocket. "Are you choosing to be punished? Is this your way of telling me you enjoyed what happened in the aviary as much I did?"

He gripped the edge of the desk when I didn't immediately respond. My mind reeled with his words, because I didn't have an answer.

Urgency rimmed the corners of his eyes, an odd reaction and something I couldn't quite put my finger on. It seemed as if he hoped for something, but whatever there had been, lust and desire buried the fleeting emotion. He blinked and the moment was lost to me.

"Raven," his voice came out a strained whisper, "do you *want* to be punished?"

Why did he just use my name?

Yes, whispered a voice in my head.

My head twitched. Was he mad? Was I?

"You'd like that, wouldn't you?" I jutted my chin out and rolled my shoulders back.

His eyes narrowed and he flicked the slim rod in his palm.

I curled my fingers and let my nails bite into the tender flesh of my palms. I needed pain to help me focus.

"Answer my question," he demanded.

"That's what you want, isn't it," I said with challenge. "You make stupid rules, so you can punish me for breaking them." Heat rose to my cheeks. "It justifies your abuse." I took a step toward him. My anger emboldened me, or made me incredibly stupid. I wasn't sure which, but he hadn't moved.

He gripped the edge of the desk, turning his knuckles white.

"You think you can whip me, beat me, and claim I *wanted* it because I didn't follow your stupid rules? Because I dared to look you in the eye?"

His jaw clenched.

I was on a roll. I took another step. "I'm not giving you

permission because I choose to ignore your silly rules." I stepped within arm's reach and he had yet to move a muscle. I was practically screaming. "Don't think for a minute I want any of this."

His power intoxicated me. His control excited me. His dominance was something I craved. The man who abducted and claimed me as his slave made my body tremble. I couldn't face what that meant. Was I crazy?

Staring into the smoldering darkness of his gaze, I had pressed too far, but I was tired of being compliant. I'd done nothing to fight this man, and I wasn't going to continue being a victim. I wasn't going to make this easy on him. If he wanted me, he would have to take me. If he did that—if I forced him to act—then I wouldn't be making a choice to give in to whatever this was inside of me.

His arm shot out, wrapped around my waist and yanked me against the hard length of his body. His free hand captured my chin and, faster than I could blink, he kissed me. His fingers pinched my jaw, pressing against the soft tissues under my chin. The force of his attack crashed against my carefully shored defenses, plundering inside within seconds. His tongue forced my lips open, breaching my body.

He tasted of a rich, sultry spice, so sinfully delicious, I didn't resist him. I couldn't. Instead, I opened to him, startled by the speed of his attack and my willing surrender. Why did he have to taste so good? He growled as his tongue ruthlessly sought the recesses of my mouth, mindless with his need.

I answered with a whimper, and I gripped his arm, not to push him away, but to clutch at him with my need for more. I didn't understand what was happening.

His fingers trailed from my chin down the side of my throat tracing a path of fire that sent shivers to my spine. He wrapped a hand around the back of my neck, twining fingers in my hair. I didn't try to pull away as he controlled me with his grip. I breathed out, parting my lips, unintentionally inviting him in. I needed to fight, but found myself heady with surrender. I wanted this kiss, even though I knew it was wrong.

He took me with possession and bit at my lower lip. A moan escaped me as he stole my will. He had me unglued with his passion, and drunk with the control he exorcised over me. I couldn't let him have me, but I wanted him more than I needed to hate him.

What the hell was I doing?

I freed a trapped hand and scratched at his cheek, breaking a nail in the process. When he jerked back, breathing hard, I kicked with my knee, but he anticipated my move and blocked my attack.

His lips glistened with the stolen moisture from my mouth. He glared and pressed his cheek to his shoulder, glancing at his collar to see if there was blood.

There was none. I failed to cause more than a scratch.

He tugged my hips against his groin and gripped my ass. The long length of his erection pressed between us. He lifted my skirt and dragged his fingers along my inner thigh, tracing a relentless path along my skin as I shivered beneath his touch. Heat built between my legs and I pressed my thighs as a pulse of desire flared. Fire exploded within me. He hissed with a sharp inhale and my eyes popped open. The deep blue of his eyes held mine in their grip as he took a long pull of breath.

Then he kissed me hard again. His passion drowned me, and while I knew I should fight, I could barely hold on. The more I resisted, the more intense his kiss became. The tighter he held me, the wetter I became.

"God, I can smell you." The husky need in his voice sent my head spinning. He kissed along my jaw, my neck, and sent shivers down my spine as he nibbled on my ear. "I thought..." His breaths came in pants. "In the aviary...I sensed..." His words pulsed between bites of his kisses. "I never imagined I might be right. Are you the one?" He held me tight against him, cupping my head against his shoulder, murmuring into my ear.

I closed my eyes against the embarrassment of his discovery, over the horror of what he intimated. I tried to push him away, but my words were swallowed under the assault of his kisses. His breathing deepened, turned ragged, and his kiss became less controlled, more frantic.

Had I almost let that happen? Fire moved from my core to heat my cheeks, and I closed my eyes. I couldn't face him. I couldn't bear the truth of what he discovered.

He yanked his hand away as if stung and pressed his erection against my hip. Panting he breathed into my ear, biting at my earlobe. "This is what you do to me. You drive me mad with need."

His fingers wrapped around my hair and he pulled my head back. He forced me to look at him, but I averted my eyes, cast them down and away, according to his silly rule.

His gaze flicked from my lips to my eyes and back again. "I will not take you against your will." He bent forward and pressed his lips against mine. "You will come to me."

My breath stuttered at the gentleness of his next kiss. As his lips glided over mine, all his passion and fury from before dissipated. My body relaxed in surrender, but in the absence of his fire, my passion fizzled.

He released me from the kiss, but held me in his grip. His lips brushed my cheeks and fluttered over my lids, then settled at my ear.

"This is my promise to you, my slave. You will obey, and if you don't, I won't hesitate to punish you. You do not want to force this issue. I'm barely hanging onto my control now as it is." He gripped my hair and pulled on the strands.

I yelped at the sharp tug.

"I want to be clear. You are here for one, and *only* one purpose, and you will fulfill your role. Do not challenge me. There are things I need, things that must happen..." The tone of his voice deepened, turning dark and ominous. "I'm not against seeking out more." He released my hair and placed both hands around my waist.

I pressed my hands on his chest putting space between us, but not actively pushing him away. Beneath my palms, his heart beat a slow steady rhythm, whereas my pulse raced. I stared at his chest, watching the slow, rhythmic rise and fall of his ribcage. Moments before, he had been barely restrained with passion and now he was back in full control of himself. Why couldn't I do that?

"Look at me, Raven."

I didn't want to look at him. Why did he want me to? Wasn't I supposed to avert my eyes? If he was going to make up rules, then he needed to be consistent. I obediently raised my gaze to meet the steel blue of his eyes.

"I would rather have you willingly than not. But you must understand, I won't hesitate to use you to meet my goals. I'm giving you a warning. Work with me, or I will take you."

"You said you wouldn't rape me."

He brushed the hair from my face and his eyes softened. "I don't have to rape you, Raven. You'll come to me on your own." And there it was, my shame laid out before me and the inevitability of his victory made clear. Heat suffused my entire face. I didn't care if he saw the flush in my cheeks. He knew he'd aroused me. I only hoped he didn't know how close he'd brought me to an orgasm.

His ferocity did things to me. The danger inflamed me,

and he claimed more than I could admit. I hated him for that, but I despised his gentleness more.

He ran his thumb along my lower lip. "I release you from the first rule, slave, but don't abuse my generosity." He glared at me with cold authority.

To my amazement, my nipples hardened at his command. I think he noticed, because his eyes flicked downward, although he made no mention of it. Instead, he led me to the wingback chairs. I'd suffered another defeat and breathed out my frustration in one deep sigh.

"What do you want from me?" How was I to work with him? More was at stake here than I realized.

"Isn't it obvious?" He settled me into a chair, and then made a show of adjusting his erection.

I didn't think that was funny.

He searched my face for a reaction, when I failed to give him what he wanted, he seated himself and his tone turned serious again. "I need you to be my obedient slave, broken beneath my will."

I was free falling without a parachute here. What just happened? One moment he was brutalizing me with a kiss, and now he's telling me this? Like I can make this choice? How did we get from there to here, sitting in two chairs having a discussion about breaking me? Stunned disbelief shuttled me towards mutism. I stared at him slack jawed.

He drummed a beat on the armrest of his chair as he

regarded me. Slowly, his eyes narrowed. I was undone under the scrutiny of his gaze.

"Is this not what you want?" He paused and flicked lint off the fabric of the arm rest. "To remove one of my *silly* rules?" He waited for my response, one I did not give. He examined his cuticles and then looked up at me over his lashes. "Although, I think you like my rules. You crave the control I wield, and with time, I think you'll realize the peace it brings you to yield is exactly what you need."

Selective mutism had me firmly in its grasp. I had nothing. In fact, I couldn't breathe. Holy hell, what was wrong with me?

A soft knock broke through the silence.

"Come," Xavier barked, making me jump at the authoritative tone.

Chad entered the library. He approached Xavier. "As ordered, Master Xavier, keyed to all the public areas requested." Chad handed over a slim chain with a dolphin pendant.

"Thank you." Xavier reached for the chain.

I drew up my legs and curled into a ball. Chad looked at me, worry furrowing his brow, but he didn't make a move to interfere. My attention shifted between Chad and Xavier. When I met the power of Xavier's stare, I couldn't match it and dropped my gaze to the floor. I didn't have it in me to fight him.

Chad turned on his heel and exited the library, leaving Xavier and I to our silence. I stared at the books lining the walls, unwilling to lock my gaze with his, especially now that I had his permission.

Out of the corner of my eye, I saw him put his hands in his lap. I made the mistake of looking up, caught his eyes, and then didn't know what to do. He leaned forward, pressing his hands to his knees. He captivated me.

"Two choices face you." He heaved a deep sigh.

I quirked up a single brow. My voice had yet to return.

"First is to refuse me. I commit all the horrible things you expect. I force you to scrape and bow, to kneel before me and service my every sexual whim." His voice broke and his shoulders tensed. "I get off on control, so understand that I would enjoy that choice."

I tensed. This was exactly what I thought my fate would be. What other option would he present to me?

"Second choice, and no doubt the most difficult. You obey my rules, commit yourself to learning your place. Put all thoughts of escape firmly out of your mind. As a reward, I give you limited freedom to move about the estate. You'll be free to do the things you desire when your services are not required."

"How is that any different from the first choice?" My voice seemed to have found itself.

His lips pressed together. "Option one, I break you. Option two, you make the choice. One involves all the horrible things your mind has conjured up and many other things you have yet to imagine, the other does not."

"Why would I choose to obey you?" I didn't want to ask what expectations he referred to.

"Because, I'm trying to make this as easy on you as possible. You can't deny your response to the authority I wield. You can find pleasure in obeying me." His heavy breathing saturated the room. "But I don't want a misunderstanding between us. My needs come before yours. My authority is absolute. I'm giving you a chance to choose how you embrace your fate."

"I need to be free." I curled away from him with fear. I didn't see any choice.

"You only think you do, but I know the truth. You're not what I expected and I'm delighted by this turn of events."

"What does that even mean?"

"Only that you'll train as my slave, by force or by choice. The path you take is yours. Considering what just happened, what would have happened if I hadn't stopped? I would think you'd be open to the idea." He gestured toward the desk, to the scene of the crime so to speak. "You don't find me repulsive, and you are realizing a potent truth. You want what's happening between us."

My shame bloomed anew. A knife cut straight to my heart at the betrayal of my body and the wicked desires stirring to life within me. He'd seen right through me.

He sprung from his chair. The swiftness of his movement pulled a yelp from me. I thought he was coming at me, but he stalked off to the far side of the library. He paced for several long minutes, rubbing his face, running his fingers through his close-cropped hair.

I followed his every move, entranced with his feral power. Watching him pace was like observing a caged beast prowl. It was irrational, and probably dangerous, but I wanted to poke him to see which way he would jump. Would he snap and bite? Destroy me? Or would he claim me as my traitorous body desired?

His lean, muscular frame moved with purpose. I wanted to know more about him, peel back the layers to see what made him tick. Nothing but questions swirled in my head. Who was this man who took me from my home? Who claimed me as some debt paid? What debt could my father possibly owe this man? I wanted to dig for answers, make Xavier squirm and come unglued like he had done to me. But I held no power here. Not when I fantasized about what it would be like to be draped over his knee.

I didn't want the first option. I didn't want to be brutalized, but neither did I want the second option Xavier offered. I didn't understand how that was any different from the first, except I would choose to accept my fate. Xavier didn't care which option I chose, and I believed what he said. He would enjoy breaking me. I didn't doubt what he said, because he enjoyed dispensing pain. For him, the battle for supremacy over my will, would be intoxicating. I wasn't ready to face a battle I would surely lose. I wanted freedom, if only because I needed revenge. Z would pay for my enslavement. Whatever was happening to my mind and body didn't matter. I could endure what I must. But really? Who was I kidding? I didn't trust myself around Xavier.

Taking the second choice didn't mean I lost this battle. It would be a concession made while reestablishing dominance over my own life. The destruction of Z took prominence in my mind and I couldn't do that while fighting Xavier. Z enslaved my mother and he wished that upon his daughter. For that, I would make him pay.

Xavier remained a mystery to me and I didn't understand the feelings coiling in my gut. I feared him, desired him, craved his touch, but I no longer hated him. I could work with that. I couldn't keep my thoughts straight around him, but maybe I didn't need to? As long as I carried hatred for Z in my heart, I had a purpose which drove me forward. With that goal in mind, I would find escape. To do that, I needed what limited freedom Xavier promised, even if that freedom came at a cost. To destroy Z, I was willing to pay whatever Xavier demanded.

I unfolded myself from the chair and approached Xavier with caution. He stopped pacing when he saw me. I stepped right up to him. Boldness came from some deep fountain of strength within me. He held a hand at his waist, the silver bracelet tight in his grip. I placed my hand over his and watched his body stiffen. I met his intense blue eyes and then I made a show of lowering my gaze with deference.

"Keep your rules. I could fight you, but I'm smart enough

to know I would lose, and I don't want to live in fear. I don't want option number one." I dropped to my knees.

His breath caught and his knees locked, stiffening the fabric of his trousers.

I didn't know anything about being a slave, but I had some idea of a few of the requirements. My forehead brushed against his fly.

"What happens now?"

He wrapped an arm around my head, erasing the last bit of distance between us.

Fear fled me. My rebellious body ached for him, and I wouldn't fight it. I wouldn't pursue it, but I wouldn't fight the inevitable. Something about him triggered scary things inside me, needy things. Instead of revulsion, a twisted desire filled me with something I couldn't explain. I would turn that to my advantage and I would win. At least I hoped I would prevail.

I wasn't used to this kind of problem. I was a hacker, happy with the black and white logic of 0's and 1's. Give me a string of code and I could break it down, and build a hack to attack its most basic elements. Give me an amazingly hot man with Caribbean blue eyes, a gaze of steel, and indomitable force of will, and I fell apart. I needed my brain to work on a solution and my body to shut the hell up.

I would earn Xavier's trust and wait for him to let his guard down. Then I would escape and settle my debts with Z.

"Thank you, Raven." He leaned down and pressed his lips to the top of my head. "I respect and honor your choice."

There it was again, my name. Before I could wonder at the significance of Xavier using my name, he picked me up, and set me on my feet.

"Come, I will explain."

CHAPTER TEN_

I MADE MY DECISION. A TEAR ROLLED DOWN MY CHEEK. I'D agreed to be his willing slave. My heart stopped.

Don't think about it.

He returned to the chairs. My sinful body warmed to the vision of his retreating backside, admiring the view. Every cell in my body erupted with heat, exploding with lustful thoughts.

What an amazing ass.

Images of my father slammed into my mind, and my fantasies splintered off into darkness. Desire and want disappeared, but I was left hyperaware. If Xavier touched me now, I would combust.

He turned, noticing I had not followed.

I lowered my gaze.

He stretched out, coaxing me to join him from ten feet

away, but I recoiled. This was wrong. There was no way I was going to pull this off.

He lowered himself into the chair. "Take as much time as you need, Raven, but join me. We have much to discuss."

Something squeezed at my heart. He was giving me time to come to him. There was so much about this man I did not understand. Another tear trickled down my cheek. Damn body. Mindless with lust, and now traitorous with weakness. I couldn't trust it to help me with anything. The degradation I was about to endure had nothing to do with whatever rules Xavier was soon to lay down. I swiped the tear from my cheek, and caught him staring.

"I need a moment." I huffed out the words, surprised to find myself hyperventilating. I held my head, swaying with lightheadedness.

Concern flashed in his eyes. I blinked, but when I looked again, his stony composure had returned. I had only imagined sympathy from my captor. I was one delusional and fucked up slave.

It would be easier to believe some shred of compassion lurked under his harsh exterior. I was desperate to humanize my captor, but I had no reason to. He'd done nothing but demand and push from the moment of our first meeting. Not to mention, he had accepted me as payment for Z's debt. I needed to remember the kind of man I was dealing with. Xavier traded in female flesh.

I was nothing more than a possession. Something to be

trained and played with. Presumably, when he tired of me, I would be discarded; given to another predator, or disposed of like my mother before me.

He rose from the chair and took a step toward me.

I held my arm up, palm out, beseeching. "Please. I'm fine." My head swam and I was going to pass out any second if I didn't get it together soon. *Take another step.* I willed myself to obey.

"Raven..." He came at me, but I shook my head.

"Please, I just...I need..." My fingers clutched at the air and the room spun around me. I needed him to sit down and give me space. If he came at me, supported me in this moment of weakness, it would destroy me completely, and I wouldn't be able to put the pieces back together. I placed my knuckles against my forehead and squeezed my eyes shut. "Please," I said in a whisper, "just give me a moment."

When I opened my eyes, the world around me steadied and the room stopped spinning. He stood two paces closer, hands clenching at his sides. He scanned me, head to toe, his expression tight with worry.

I pressed the fingertips of both hands to my forehead. My eyes cast down and I spoke to the floor with a much stronger voice. "What happened just hit me...what I've agreed to do." I took a deep swallow and glanced up. "I had a small panic attack, but it's passing." I forced a smile.

His eyes narrowed, weighing my words. After a long moment, his stance relaxed and he returned to his chair. He gestured to the chair opposite him. "Come. Sit. I don't have all day."

Damn, that voice of command was back. It liquefied my insides, turning them to mush. How was that possible? I didn't understand this need to obey. But if I was to be completely honest, a tiny part of me wanted to defy him because I wanted to see what he would do. Fortunately, I didn't feel that brave or foolish right now. I obediently marched over to the chair and took my seat. I folded my knees to my chest and tucked my chin.

"Look at me," he said.

I didn't have the strength for that.

His voice deepened and his command thrummed in my chest. "Look at me. I do not repeat myself. That is the only warning you will receive."

I dragged my gaze along a path from the foot of my chair, across the expanse of wood separating our staked-out territories, master on one side, slave on the other. My journey continued, eyes climbing his legs, crawling over muscular thighs, meandering across the expanse of his abdomen, and traveling the breadth of his chest. My exploration paused at his neck, delaying the inevitability of his gaze. At the low growl issued from his side of our battlefield, I snapped my focus up those last few inches and met him straight on. I held my breath waiting for his pronouncement of my fate. He drummed his fingers on the armrest, something I'd seen him do before. A nervous tic perhaps? Or irritation?

"You belong to me," he said. "I want you to say it." His eyes bore into me.

I froze.

His fingers tapped their quiet rhythm. "You belong to me," he repeated. "Say it." His insistence frightened me.

"Why do I have to say it?"

"Because you chose option number two."

I understood, not that it made it easier. I swallowed against the sudden dryness in my mouth. *They are only words.* I fisted my hands. "I belong to you."

He shook his head. "Say it again...properly. Address me with the title you will forever use."

Forever? That was far too long. I swallowed against the bile rising in my throat. "I belong to you...Master Xavier."

There, satisfied, bastard?

I may not be allowed to curse out loud, but he couldn't control what I thought in my head.

His eyes narrowed.

I don't think he believed me.

"Who do you serve?"

Another slow blink. Why was it so hard to say these stupid words?

"I serve you...Master Xavier." *You mother-fucking bastard.*

He arched a brow. "You will refer to me as simply Master. Now, who owns you?"

I wanted to ask him how many times we were going to go

round and round with this, but I held my tongue. I smiled. "You own me, Master." *Cock-sucker.*

I could do this. Every time I had to say Master, I would curse him in my head and negate the word. It would work.

"Kneel before me, slave." He pointed to a spot on the floor in front of him.

Oh, hell no. I rolled my shoulders back and opened my mouth to refuse.

He held up a single finger. "Option one or option two. The choice is yours. The expectation is that a slave will kneel at her master's feet. I am your Master. You are my slave." He pointed at the spot. "Kneel."

I unfolded my legs and slid out of the chair. My degradation had begun. God, give me the strength to endure. I knelt before him.

"Who do you belong to?"

"I belong to you, Master." *You asshole.*

"Who do you serve?"

"I serve you, Master." *You fucking asshole.*

"Who owns you?"

"You own me, Master." *You mother-fucking asshole.*

Okay, I needed more curse words. I'd pretty much exhausted my repertoire and we weren't even five minutes into this.

"Go back and take your seat." He shooed me back to my chair with an imperious wave of his hand. "You will be expected to obey my commands without hesitation, no matter how inconvenient they may be for you, or how silly they may seem. A slave does not hesitate. Is this understood?"

I wanted to glare at him. Instead I tucked my chin. "Yes, Master."

He held up a bracelet with the silver dolphin. "This bracelet contains a microchip which grants you access to certain rooms in the house."

My eyes flicked to the silver dolphin and then focused back on him.

"It is a privilege you will earn." He made a show of tucking the bracelet into his top suit pocket. "I have mentioned several rules for you to follow. Keeping your eyes down, I'll take off the table for now. No swearing or disparaging remarks is an absolute requirement and you'll address me appropriately at all times. Over the next few days, your obedience will be tested. If you satisfy me with your willingness to comply with the choice you made, only then you will earn the privilege of this bracelet."

"And if I fail?"

He shook his head. "You don't want to fail." He stood and came to stand before me. "There is more."

I stared up at him, heart thundering, breath stalling in my chest, as he held out his hand. I reached out and accepted it, terrified at the thrill I knew would follow his touch. On cue, a bolt of electricity travelled up my arm as he drew me close.

"You'll allow me to touch you, to kiss you, to hold you in my arms. You won't draw away from me." He wrapped an arm around my waist and drew me close.

I took in a stuttering breath as desire stole all thought.

"You said you wouldn't rape me."

His lips brushed mine, soft, tender, giving. "I'll give you time. You can't deny your reaction to me. Fear is in your head. You need to decide how to reconcile the two. I wish I could give you more, but this will happen between us."

I breathed out his spicy scent. "You could always set me free."

His mouth tightened into a thin line. "That's not going to happen."

"Why not?" I clutched his arm.

"Don't make me regret giving you this choice." He pushed me away. "Now go, before I change my mind."

CHAPTER ELEVEN_

BEING A SLAVE, IT TURNED OUT, WAS ONE OF THE MOST BORING jobs I ever had. I literally had nothing to do.

Xavier rattled off his slew of rules, too many for me to remember, and sent me on my way. His stern voice locked me into near catatonic paralysis with expectations for my behavior.

I was told not to worry. He would *help* me to remember. I didn't welcome what that would bring. Memories of that slim rod came to mind. The pain of it flared in my mind and even more memorable on my backside. More worrisome was the change it had engendered in the man I willingly handed over control of my life. That rod had the power to transform Xavier into a beast. I didn't believe he'd be able to keep his promise to me if he had to use that rod. I worked hard to remember his litany of rules.

He called it incentive.

I called it foul play.

Nevertheless, I didn't argue my point. Not with the silent command in his gaze. His eyes bore right into me, cutting deep, and muted all my protests. Then his cell phone rang. As he answered, darkness gathered in those penetrating eyes. Blue turned to black as his entire body stiffened at whatever the voice on the other end of that phone had to say.

"Yes, Forest, I have the girl." His gaze flicked to me as he listened to the speaker on the other end of the call. "No, we haven't discussed it." He said nothing to me, but I found myself dismissed with a wave of his hand. "I'll call you later."

Chad escorted me back to my room and I haven't left it since.

That had been two days ago. Two days locked away. Me, myself, and my constant guard.

By now, I had all their pin codes memorized. Not that it mattered. I needed both their individual codes and their palm print to unlock the door. They smiled at me as I spent hours gazing at the electronic lock, punching buttons and tapping at the screen. That's how confident they felt in their security, but I had a secret weapon. MIT computer science graduate here. I wanted to slap them in the face. You'd think they'd learn a bit more about their captive.

What I had come to find as a truth was that I could program a supercomputer, solve the general theory of relativity, clone dinosaurs. Yet the only thing the men around me would see would be my tits, ass, and my ever-unique eyes. I let Bay and Chad laugh. They thought it was funny to watch me poke at the keypad, so I poked.

Now that my brain wasn't short circuited and fried by the constant presence of one pheromone inducing distraction with electric blue eyes, the most intoxicating scent, the darkest flavors of sin and lust, and a touch of pure electricity —okay, I fantasized a lot about Xavier—but when I wasn't awash in my fantasies, I focused on escape.

First step was breaking the encryption on the keypad. Two days trapped in my room, had me climbing the walls and my mind revved into high gear. I almost had access to the root directory cracked. I spent my days staring at the keypad. Nights I dreamt about it. If I could get into the root directory, I could bypass the biometric lockout.

When I wasn't dreaming of breaking the code, I dreamt of Xavier. Images swirled in my head, never quite coalescing, with the exception of two things. Caribbean blue eyes devoured me, and a lithe, muscular body possessed me with a hunger and violence which shocked me. It never failed to leave me waking aroused, wet, and aching with need. I didn't know if Ben or Mel heard my cries, or if I gave myself away in my dreams. If I did, they never said a word.

Days piled on top of one another. Two days turned into five. Time slowed and I paced the confines of my prison. My guards provided no comfort. Under Xavier's new rules, I was not permitted to speak to them, although when two of them were locked in with me they often spoke about me.

We shared the room in silence. I wanted to rant at them, scream at them, force them to speak to me, but I knew the price for failure. Or rather, I knew my reward. The bracelet with the dolphin pendant hung over my headboard. I saw it every moment of every day and it kept me silent when I wanted to scream. I would earn what little freedom it offered. This was my test.

Loneliness settled over me, an aching hollowness that took root in my heart. I drifted for too many days, letting time pass, going stir crazy. On the seventh day of my isolation, I established a routine, letting time settle into a rhythm, unwanted, but necessary. Half an hour of high intensity exercise, followed by an hour of meditative yoga. I ate the breakfast Bay provided, made my bed, washed my face, brushed my teeth. The next two hours, I dredged up every single combat routine I remembered.

Bay's brows lifted as I spun around the room, punching and kicking my way from one corner to the next. He stayed on his small bed, watching me work up a sweat. Breathing hard, with sweat pouring down my back and my hair plastered across my brow, I worked myself until I could barely move. Then it was shower time followed by a nap as I collapsed with exhaustion onto the bed. After a nap, I dragged the one small chair I had up to the keypad and punched in Bay's pin code. The device beeped and asked for his palm signature.

Bay gave a *hrrumph* from the other side of the room, but didn't interfere. I figured if he wasn't going to stop me, then I was free to do whatever I wanted to the device. I tapped the screen to activate the directories and spent hours frustrating myself. It shouldn't be so hard. I studied stuff like this at MIT. There was a way to break it. It was just a matter of figuring it out. An hour turned to two, then to three. At a knock on the door, I was forced to stop. Dinner arrived, and with it Chad.

For the next two hours, I listened in on Bay's and Chad's conversation. They spoke about nothing of consequence, sports, poker, cars until Ben and Mel arrived for the evening shift.

This became my routine, day in, day out for the next five days. Not one word from Xavier. For a man who went to such lengths to acquire me, he certainly seemed to be in no hurry to claim me. For myself, I woke every night, drenched in sweat, breathing deep, heart hammering, aching, and wet for his touch.

Memories of his scorching eyes kept me in a perpetual state of arousal. I wondered why he kept me imprisoned up here. If he desired me, then where the hell was he? Surely, I hadn't bored him already? Or had my capitulation in the library ruined the thrill of the chase for him?

If I didn't fight, if he couldn't ruin me, did he no longer want me? Was that it? Was he even now looking for another buyer? Was I to be passed along in trade to another sadistic creep? Terror would grip me in these moments, until I remembered the hunger burning in his eyes.

Two more days passed, two weeks without him. His absence twisted my emotions, each day increasing my desperation. My life existed around my routine. I had nothing but the endless cycle of exercise and that damn puzzle of a keypad.

I stared longingly at the door. Beyond it lay a freedom of sorts, not from my enslavement, because my guards were never far away. I also had a GPS strapped to my ankle. I tapped at the keypad. Yesterday, I had finally accessed the root directory. Chad was with me today. He stood behind me, hovering, arms crossed over his chest.

The urge to tell him to mind his own business burned in my gut. I turned to give him a piece of my mind and saw the bracelet clutched in his hand. The silver dolphin swung back and forth. He shook his head, as if to remind me of one of Master Xavier's rules.

No talking unless spoken to first.

My attention focused on the dolphin, wondering why Chad had taken the bracelet down from the headboard. I glanced up into the slate gray of Chad's eyes. His gaze flicked from the chain, to the keypad, then back to me. He gave a wink, turned on his heels and headed to the bathroom.

I shook my head. *What are you up to?*

Moments later, I heard him urinating in the toilet.

I really needed to get out of this room.

My attention returned to the keypad and the last string of code I'd been fooling around with.

There's nothing sexy or glamorous about computer programming. It's slow, tedious work. A single misplaced character can spell disaster to the simplest code and this was far from simple. I liked the monotony of programming. The beauty of stringing together code to make a program come to life always amazed me. Back at MIT, I'd been known to lose many nights to long sessions writing code. All my friends did it. There, it was considered normal. I wondered what Chad thought of my tinkering.

My friend, Sadie, used to laugh about losing time as she called it. She was a bio-mechanical engineer and didn't understand us computer nerds. If it weren't for Sadie, I'd have missed out on most of college life. I vented a deep soulful sigh. Sadie and I were supposed to be crawling from one pub to another across Europe right now, with our room-mate Elsbeth. What excuse had Z given them when I failed to show up for our trip? Did they believe his lies? Other than my friends, no one would come looking for me. Z had made the perfect *fait accompli*. I disappeared from the rest of the world and no one noticed.

My shoulders pinched from hunching over the keypad. My fingers pecked at the display, tapping away at new algorithms. I breathed in through my mouth, making my lips and tongue dry out. I did that when I worked, held my mouth open and tapped my tongue to my upper teeth. Sadie said it was the one time in my life I looked like a dork.

I didn't care, because whatever it was, it worked. I finished the code. A quick check over my shoulder revealed no sign of Chad. I listened and heard the shower running in the bathroom. Before I could think it through, I hit the RUN command and entered Bay's pin code. The light on the display flashed, asked for the palm print, and rolled right on by without it. The display blinked. Electronics clicked and whirred as the locking mechanism disengaged.

With a deep breath, I straightened in my chair. Pinched nerves in my neck and shoulders protested against the movement. I glanced to the bathroom and debated my options. Chad sang some pop tune in the shower. Another deep breath and I grasped the door handle. It twisted and swung inward. Thunder hammered in my chest. The pounding sent blood surging through my body, carrying with it a burst of adrenaline.

Fight or flight. I was ready to flee.

I took a step toward freedom, but stopped when Xavier stepped in front of the doorway. I blinked at Xavier dressed in a charcoal gray suit, wearing a Caribbean blue tie the same color of his eyes. Flanking him, my other three guards waited.

Bay stepped forward. "Looks like I win. She cracked it in under two weeks."

Xavier didn't move, but then neither did I. We stood

there, locked in a battle of wills. The only move he made was a slight twitching of his fingers.

From behind me, Chad spoke up. "I was way off. I had her pegged at a month." He came to stand beside me and held up the bracelet for Xavier.

Xavier took it.

I couldn't tear my eyes from the man in front of me, but I noticed Chad's sleeve, the same one he'd been wearing all day long. He fooled me. He hadn't been in the shower.

Chad leaned toward me and whispered. "What are you supposed to do in the presence of your master, kitten?"

Eyes locked on Xavier, I followed the direction of his gaze down to the ground. The chain dangled between us. The dolphin glinted in the light as it swung in the air, and I remembered what he said. Obedience would be rewarded.

I lowered myself to the ground.

No way was I going to spend another two weeks trapped in that room.

As I knelt, I lifted my chin with strength. I fortified myself for the ensuing battle, even as my body shook with weakness. I trained my eyes on my adversary, the man who held my fate dangling by a silver chain in his hand.

"Master," I breathed out, "how may I serve you?"

CHAPTER TWELVE_

XAVIER'S STRONG JAW SCISSORED BACK AND FORTH AS HE
regarded me in that way of his, full of possession, laced with
heat, and brimming with desire. Darkness lurked within him
as well. I saw it, along with his need for me. I'd never felt that
from a man before. His need washed over me in the way his
eyes consumed my body. With a look alone, I fell further
under his control.

A new emotion swirled in the depths of his gaze, a sense
of satisfaction and victory. I didn't understand it. While not
specifically forbidden, I had broken his security. Not that
anyone had tried to stop me, but I was pretty sure it was
against one of the many rules he had established.

Beneath his stoic control, I did not see anger. That gave
me pause, enough to really look at him and admire the force
of will he leveled upon me. In his gaze, I sensed no threat of

punishment, which relieved and disappointed me at the same time. I did not desire the pain, but the promise of the sensations he could draw from my unwilling body mystified me and ignited an inquisitiveness inside me. Memories of what happened in the aviary had certainly brought passion laced dreams boiling to the surface over the past two weeks. My skin grew hot and molten with desire. Two weeks and a look from him could do this?

Mel passed something shiny to Xavier; a length of chain. Leaning toward me, Xavier grabbed at one of the rings attached to the collar and snapped one end of the chain to the ring. A leather loop dangled from the free end. He wrapped that around his wrist. Had he leashed me like a dog?

He caught my chin in his hand and stared into my eyes. A surge of electricity passed between us with the contact. His pupils dilated and he sucked in a breath. Did my face mirror the response in his? My eyes had grown wide, and I most certainly held my breath. He stood there for a moment, stooped over me, one hand on my chin, the other holding the end of the chain.

"I was hoping you would break the code, but I did not think you would be this quick."

I gasped and drew back, but his grip tightened around my chin. He held me in place, our breaths mingling with each inhale. He smelled of dark coffee and spice. God, I wanted to taste him.

I tried staring back, meeting him with strength, but our faces were too close. I turned away. The intimacy of the contact more than I could bear. I fluttered my lashes, hiding behind the long natural lengths of them.

Pride swelled in his voice. "MIT certainly trains the best, but I didn't think you had that much skill." His brows lifted. "I'm impressed." He turned to Ben. "This is good."

I blinked and forced myself to look into the depths of his blue eyes. They were vibrant, bright, yet sharp and cutting at the same time.

"This was to be your reward..." His mouth twisted as he lifted the dolphin pendant into my line of sight.

This was to be your reward... The use of the past tense had fire rising in my belly. My breaths came deep and fast as a queasiness settled upon me. My fingers curled in on themselves, useless and impotent. The world turned black.

He moved with that incredible speed of his, bending before me between one beat of my heart and the next. One moment he was standing over me, dominating with his size. The next, he hunched down, on the same level as me, hands cupping my cheeks, and wiping away tears I did not realize had been shed.

Breaths sawed in and out of my lungs and pain sliced through my chest. For two weeks they watched me work at the security pad—laughing at me? Did they think it was a joke? Not once had they told me to stop. I guess I surprised them when I actually cracked it.

But I wasn't trying to escape—not really. I was bored to tears and desperate for something to do. He hadn't left me any books, or TV, no internet of course, and I wasn't allowed to speak to the men locked inside with me. I'd stared at the walls for days.

Hot tears spilled down my cheeks. The press of his fingertips against my skin turned my stomach. I pulled away as desolation blanketed me in a cloud of despondency. He refused to let me go.

With a mournful sob, I cried out. "I obeyed every one of your damn rules."

"Do not swear at me, slave." Shadows shrouded the crystalline blue of his eyes.

"Fuck you and your damn rules. You never meant to give me that." I swiped at the bracelet, catching it, and flung it across the hall. I dissolved into a hissing, spitting, scratching she-cat. Breath pumped out of my lungs as I launched myself at him. "They never stopped me!" I huffed as I dragged my nails across his jaw. "If you didn't want me messing with the keypad, they should have said something."

I drew blood below his left eye. I yanked on the hair behind his right ear.

"Are you that desperate to get your sadistic freak on that you set me up?" I screeched at him. "You perverted bastard."

Every obscenity I knew I hurled at him. I used every weapon at my disposal. It didn't matter anymore. Option One or Option Two was nothing more than his way to fuck with my mind. Since he wasn't expecting an attack, I got in a few good hits before Chad tried to pull me off. He was unsuccessful.

Xavier grunted as I hit him in the solar plexus and kneed him in the groin. Instead of folding over, however, he surprised me. He lifted me and held me away from himself. Truthfully, it was difficult to tell who did what. My four bodyguards descended to protect their master against the she-cat caught in his grip.

I hated being played. No longer would I think of that man as Xavier. He would now be reduced to a single letter like my father before him. I took Z's name away when I was very young, when he pushed me out of his heart. I think I was seven. I did that now to X.

"God damn it," Bay huffed, "she can fight."

My foot clocked Bay in the jaw. *Damn straight I can fight.* And I'd had two straight weeks to condition myself. I kicked Ben in the ribs as he struggled to trap my leg.

"Grab her fucking arm," Ben shouted, as he helped X drag me back into the room, restraining one of my arms. I twisted out of his grip, scratched his chest, leaving three long raised welts in the skin as I ripped his shirt.

X had me, supporting me under the arms as he lifted me through the air. I bucked against him, spitting, hissing, biting. Bay gripped one of my legs. Mel had the other. Ben secured my arm; Chad took my other arm. The four of them walked in lockstep, carrying me suspended between them.

"Get the restraints," X grunted, as I clocked his jaw. He threw me on the bed.

I bounced, fire surging in my belly. "I hate you. I hate you. I hate you..."

Words dissolved into sobs as he launched on top of me, straddling me and effectively pinning me in place. I was immobilized and trapped again. X held me down by my shoulders as Ben, Mel and Bay restrained my arms and legs. Chad opened up his locker and returned with leather strips. Through blurred tears, I watched him thread the long strips through rings in the four poster supports of the bed. He tossed one to Ben, who lashed it through the ring in the platinum band around my wrist. Then he threw the ends of two others to Bay and Mel who looped them around my ankles.

Sobs wracked my body as I thrashed beneath X.

Chad secured my wrist, tying back my last extremity. I pulled against the restraints, effectively bound.

"Leave us." X said with a low, ominous growl, heavy with need.

Beneath him, I bucked against the press of his body. The men had trussed me up, spread eagle, arms out to the side, legs straight and slightly spread. There was no give to the restraints. I was at the mercy of X, and they were going to leave me alone...with him.

I knew what came next. I'd been dreading it for weeks, fantasizing about it in twisted eroticized dreams. But now, with him straddling me, restrained as I was, terror streamed through me. The last of my anger burned out as the door to my prison shut. The finality of the lock cycling sent panic surging through my veins. I didn't want X to rape me.

Strangled gut wrenching sobs escaped my lips, struggling between desperate attempts to breathe. I blinked to clear my vision and to face the monster sitting on top of me.

X braced his knees on either side of my hips and rested his weight over my pelvis and thighs. His warmth penetrated my clothing, a persistent heat that brought no answering swell of arousal from me. He held his arms crossed over his chest and stared down at me. He swiped at his left eye and wiped away the trickle of blood.

"What the hell, Raven?"

Adrenaline still pumped in my blood. Fight or flight? Well, I had fought, and now I lay beneath X in defeat. My vocal cords pinched. What did he expect me to say?

He blew out a deep breath. "This is all fucked up." He rubbed his palms against his trousers.

You don't say?

The man was a fucking genius, stating the obvious.

Roaring filled my ears, blood rushing to my brain. If only that blood helped to make smarter decisions, I would find it more useful. I had snapped. It had been a mistake, and now I was going to pay. Part of me was ready to get this over with. I was resigned. The other part of me cringed with the horror of rape.

The longer X took to go about it, the longer he left me to

think about it, only made things worse. I had to look at him, at his body, at his face, and into his eyes. He had an amazing physique, muscular and athletic, and he had a handsome face, but it wasn't X's looks that drew me. It wasn't his attractive features that had me spiraling in an unwanted direction.

There was something about the way he held himself and how he commanded the respect of the men around him. There was a quality in his expression, a sharpness of intellect, that drew me in every time. He was a potent cocktail of good looks, intelligence, masculine power, and some sort of raw primal energy. Those eyes drew me now and obliterated all thought.

"I don't have time for this," he said.

His nostrils flared and his pupils dilated. Power swirled in the air between us, cloaking him, and choking me.

"You agreed to cooperate. What has gotten into you?"

I found my voice. "How long does it take to rape a woman? Get on with it. I know you don't have a problem getting it up. Hurting women gives you a guaranteed hard on. You're probably stiff right now."

"You do not want to push me." Nostrils flaring, his eyes widened as scorn dripped from my voice.

I spit at him. Stupid because my spittle sprayed the air between us and landed back on me. I lunged at him, teeth snapping, until my restraints pulled me back.

He gripped my chin, then he was on me. His mouth crushing mine.

I bit at him, drawing blood as my teeth punctured his lip.

He howled and pressed his fingers to my jaw. Pain forced my teeth open and I released his lower lip. The pain didn't stop him; if anything, it made him more frantic. Deep panting breaths smothered me as he mouthed my neck, kissing, biting, licking his way from my ear to the tip of my shoulder. Fabric ripped as he tore at my dress. He pulled it apart, kissing the soft hollow of my throat as I shook my head from side to side. I couldn't shake him off.

With the bodice of my dress shredded, he tore at my bra. It fell apart in his hands with a tug and a snap of elastic. Then his hands were on my breasts, squeezing and pawing at me. Then his mouth was on me. I moaned and arched into his mouth. Heat flooded my core, licking between my legs as I grew wet for him. My fingers clenched and unclenched as my head shook side to side. My body, my treacherous body, betrayed me again.

He pulled up the skirt of my dress, leaving a scrap of sheer fabric as my only defense against him. To my horror, it was drenched with my need for him. He laid a line of kisses from my chest down to my navel. His tongue swirled around my belly button as his fingers clutched at the lace of my panties. A sharp yank and I was exposed to him.

I gasped and sucked in my lower lip. Powerful waves of desire pulled at my core.

"I may get hard hurting you, but you like it, Raven. You're fucking wet for me." Satisfaction filled his voice.

My mindless desire for stimulation drove me into a frenzy. I barely noticed him cupping my mound, or the fact that he had stilled. His breath swept against my belly, cooling the trail of his passionate kisses.

"You're so wet." His voice dropped to a whisper.

His violation of my body would soon be complete. My insides coiled like the wires of a spring, tightening with tension. Hot shame burned my cheeks. Tears poured out of the corners of my eyes and pooled in my ears. I hated him with every fiber of my being, and yet I wanted him as I had wanted no other man. I twisted against him.

Harsh ragged breathing filled my ears. Not my breaths, but rather his.

He fumbled with the fly of his trousers and drew the zipper down with a sharp jerk. His body twisted over mine as he kicked off his shoes and freed himself of his pants. Hot, naked skin covered me, and between us, the pulsations of his erection decried his desire. The tip of it dragged against my hip, wet with the promise of what came next.

I hated what he did to me. I despised the sickness in me. His body pressed over mine and he whispered in my ear.

"Tell me you want me," he growled.

I couldn't.

His insistent voice burned in my ear. "You're wet for me. Tell me you want me inside of you. Beg me to fuck you, and I'll give you the release your body needs."

How he kept me balanced on the knife's edge of desire, I

had no idea. Pleasure built up within me to a point where it became painful. I wanted to fall over that cliff, and let passion overcome me, but I couldn't allow this.

"No." My voice was a whimper, all strength fled.

"You can't deny it. I now know the truth. I thought I imagined it in the aviary, but now I know. Look at me." The command in his voice had my eyes snapping open. He measured out his words, control but a thread behind the desire burning in his gaze. He lifted his hips and settled between my legs. His erection pressed at the entrance to my pussy, waiting. "You can't help but submit to me. You crave it with a passion I know too well. Give in to your desires, Raven. Embrace the truth of what you are, what you want, and the things you need."

My chest heaved. Each breath brought taut nipples in contact with the silk of his shirt. The touch unhinged me. I couldn't invite him in. I wouldn't be a willing partner to my violation, no matter how hard I wanted him to plunge inside. He moved with me, never venturing past that last remaining barrier.

"I hate you."

His brusque laughter tore at me. He lifted his hips, gripped his erection in his hand and lined up to thrust into me. This was it. I cringed against his onslaught.

"You're nothing more than a cowardly rapist," I breathed out. "You're going to have to kill me after this, because if I ever get free, I'm going to destroy you."

My entire being ached to be taken, to be brutally owned by this man in the most perverse way possible. My tears weren't for him. They were for the depths of my debasement. Who could want this?

Me. I wanted this.

I wanted to drown in his strength. I wanted to struggle and rage against him as he ripped control from me. He did things to my mind, stirred up dark fantasies from nowhere and fanned them into life. His entire body stilled. He pressed his head against my breast, pulling deep lungfuls of air into his chest. The beat of his heart hammered against my belly.

"You're wrong." His voice came out as a whisper. "Until you say yes, this is where it ends." He lifted off me and began to dress.

My eyes drifted closed. I didn't understand his withdrawal.

"Open your damn eyes." The shout filled the room.

My eyes snapped open.

"You think you can absolve yourself of responsibility?" He bit out the next words. "That's not going to happen. You want this as much as I do. If you want me to fuck you, you're going to beg me for it. I'm not going to take it from you."

My eyes widened at what he said. He couldn't possibly believe that.

"I'm not going to fuck you until you beg." He sat beside me on the bed, eyes glowering.

"I don't want you to fuck me," I said, spitting the words out in denial of my true desire.

"Yes, you do." He withdrew his touch. "And you will."

"No," My cheeks burned with his assurance I would do just that. "You're wrong."

His lips twisted and his brows lifted. "I know you better than you know yourself." He leaned down and brushed my brow with a kiss. "And I know exactly what you need." He cupped my cheek. When he kissed my lips the taste of spice and copper swirled around my tongue. His lower lip swelled from where I bit it, but it no longer bled.

"You're wrong."

"Don't worry, slave..." The word slave rolled off his tongue heavy with the promise of dark desires yet to be fulfilled.

My eyes widened and I shrank away from him, but he loomed over me.

"There will be plenty of opportunities to punish you, and I'll enjoy it nearly as much as you." He pressed his palm to my belly as if cementing a promise. His hand dragged up my belly. His fingers walked between my breasts, traced a line up my throat and wandered over the angle of my chin until he brushed his thumb over my lower lip. Holding pressure, he forced his thumb between my teeth.

A knock sounded at the door.

"Yes," X said with an irritated growl.

"Master Xavier," Ben said, "the plane has landed. Your guests will be here in ten minutes."

X blinked and ground his teeth. "Thank you, Ben." He turned to me. "Business calls."

He stood, leaving me strapped to the bedposts. He ran a hand through his hair and it shook. A sign of weakness? Did I do that?

"What do you want me to do with the girl?" Ben said in his gruff voice.

X paused as he adjusted his shirt and tie. He turned to me as he adjusted his erection inside his pants and zipped up his fly. A gleam shone in his eyes.

"Bring her downstairs."

"Downstairs?" Ben looked to me, confusion scrawled across his face.

X traced the swelling of his lower lip with his fingertip. "She's to learn a lesson in obedience. Attending the sellers' meeting will allow her to understand her place."

"Sir," Ben said in a warning tone, "that is not wise. She is...unpredictable."

"And very much overdue for a demonstration of what it means to be a slave." X stepped away from the bed. "Release her and bind her wrists to her collar. Meet me in the library in five minutes with the rest of your team. And Ben..."

"Yes, sir?"

"Do not forget your place." X leveled a stare at the hulking form of my bodyguard.

Ben's shoulders curved inward and he bent at the waist into a low bow. "Forgive me, Master Xavier."

X walked back to me and put his hand over my forehead. His thumb dipped between my lips and pressed between my teeth. He stroked his thumb against the roof of my mouth, his lips parting as a hooded expression heated his gaze.

I glared up at him with all the hatred I could muster, only I had to force the emotion. I didn't hate X. An odd attraction pulled me to him. My heart thrummed in my chest wondering how he intended me to please him. The way he pulsed his thumb in and out of my mouth didn't make that difficult to guess. Anticipating his need stirred more heat in the apex of my thighs and I squirmed on the bed.

"Think about what happened here. Your punishment will be the main entertainment of the evening." The roughness of his thumb brushed against my lips. "The men coming today work for your father, and I'm sure Zane Carson is eager for news on how the training of my new slave is progressing. I hadn't intended on including you in today's event, but now I know I must."

CHAPTER THIRTEEN_

OF MY FOUR GUARDS, I LIKED BEN THE LEAST. I HADN'T bonded with him like I had Chad and Bay. Or maybe it was because he was the oldest, with a marine close-cropped shave and a gruff voice to go with it. Maybe it was because he snored and kept me awake on the nights it was his turn to watch over me. Or maybe it was because he had been the one in charge of my kidnapping.

"Don't kick me, kid," he said as he released a leg. He rubbed out the kinks in my muscles as he undid the restraint tying me to the bed.

I didn't fight him. I knew futile when I saw it.

He freed my other ankle and rubbed at the abraded skin. "I want to tell you not to judge too harshly, but I know I can't." The scratchiness of his voice slowed the beat of my heart. "You have no reason to trust any of us, no reason at all."

He released a wrist, but then shackled it to one of the rings at my neck. "Sorry, kid," he said with his low susurrations. The deep tonalities of his voice soothed me, such a contrast to the violence moments before. He released my other hand, checking the skin under the bracelet for abrasions, before locking it in place at my neck. "Sit up."

I lay in the bed, staring at the ceiling, feeling desolate and lost. X's revelation destroyed my center. Hatred for a man I desired made no sense. Not being able to hold on to that hatred filled me with shame.

Ben helped me to a sitting position and swung my feet around to hang off the edge of the bed. He crouched down before me and searched my face.

"Do you need to use the restroom?"

I shrugged and breathed out a sigh.

Behind me, someone leaned against the doorframe. "Car's arriving in five. Master Xavier wants her downstairs in position when they arrive."

"Gotcha, Mel," Ben said. "Look, there's no telling how long you're going to be tied up. Best to take care of business now." He lifted me off the bed and settled me on my feet.

"Four minutes," Mel called out.

"Tell Bay to stall them at the door. I'm not taking her down there in this condition. Master Xavier can whip my ass for it later." He nudged me toward the restroom.

I gave him a look and turned my locked wrists to him.

A flush bloomed in his cheeks. "Sorry." He released one of my hands. "Go, but you don't have much time."

I retreated to the restroom and took care of business. A quick glance into the mirror had me exiting fast. X had a scratch under his eye and a bloodied lip, but I looked like I'd been in a war zone. Red puffy eyes stared back at me. My hair scattered in all directions and I couldn't help but try to smooth it into place. Not for him. I didn't care what I looked like for him. Straightening my hair calmed me and restored order to my world. I controlled nothing in my life right now, but I could control this little bit. When I turned around, Ben leaned against the doorway watching me.

"Are you ready?"

"No."

"No, I suppose you're not." He turned to the dresser and pulled out lace panties and a bra. "You need to change."

I shrugged out of the tattered remnants of the dress and changed. I stood there in delicate pink lace, expecting another dress.

"I'm sorry, little one, but that is all you'll wear. It's expected of a slave."

I barely reacted to his words. I was to be paraded in front of my father's men as the slave I'd become. Ben clipped my wrist to a ring at my neck.

The corners of Mel's eyes softened. "He's really taking her in there?"

Ben nodded.

"What is he thinking?"

"Trust him, Mel."

Mel's mouth twitched. He looked like he was going to say one thing, but then decided on something else. "Are you going to prepare her?"

Ben gave me a long hard look and sucked at his lower lip.

I no longer cared. Despondency had wrapped me in a cloak of protection. If I didn't care, then nothing could hurt me.

"Come on," Mel said when Ben didn't respond. "You can't let her walk in on that."

I gave a shrug. I wanted to tell him it didn't matter, but X's rules blanketed me in silence. Ben and Mel were not my allies. Any infractions of the rules would be reported.

Ben took the end of the leash and stepped forward. "Time to go," he said.

Mel gave an agonized sigh of frustration. "It's a slavers' meeting," he blurted out.

"Mel," Ben said in warning.

"Ah fuck me," Mel said. "I'll gladly take the strikes." He put a hand on my shoulder as Ben led me out of the room. "The men coming today are selling a group of slaves. This is the delivery meeting."

I stumbled at the revelation. These were men who worked for my father. Not that it shouldn't surprise me to discover X and my father were doing business together. X was more than a simple buyer of women. My future suddenly became very unsteady.

He paused and I willed Mel to continue. "Each slave will be tested to make sure he or she is ready for market."

What? Not just women? Holy crap.

Ben breathed out. "You're scaring her," he said. "She's shaking like a leaf."

"You know what's going to be expected," Mel said. "He's going to have to convince them he's claimed her as his own."

Ben scrubbed the top of his head with his palm. "Mel, you're so fucked." Ben led me down the stairs into the atrium. One more hallway to go, if my memory served me, we would arrive at the grand foyer of X's home.

Ben pulled up short and turned toward me. His dark eyes rooted me in place. "Not everything is what it seems. Keep your mouth shut, follow Master Xavier's rules. Obey him in *all* things." Ben tugged me forward. He pulled me around a corner and the grand foyer yawned with malevolent promise.

In the very center stood X in his signature dark wool suit, silver shirt, and brilliant blue tie. His eyes pierced me like twin lasers searching for a target. I melted before him, my insides turning molten in the blink of an eye at the longing leveled in my direction.

Ben whispered. "Don't forget the rules. Eyes. Down. Kneel at his side. Obey all his commands. Serve his pleasure."

"Why bother?" The words fell from my lips in a whisper of despair.

Mel wrapped a silver chain around my wrist. A dolphin dangled from it. "He told me to give this to you tonight, sweetie."

X watched Mel attach the bracelet. His shoulders rotated back and his chin elevated. His imperious gaze slammed into my chest.

My voice cracked. "Why?"

"He said, obey him and it's yours," Mel said.

"But, upstairs? What I did..."

"Don't question the generosity of your master, girl," Ben cautioned. "And don't fuck up this meeting, or you'll have more than a whipping to worry about."

A car pulled up in the drive outside.

"What could possibly be worse than a whipping?" I asked.

Four men exited the vehicle and were greeted on the steps by Bay.

Mel inclined his chin toward the car outside. "He could send you home with one of them."

X heard Mel's pronouncement. His jaw clenched. "What the fuck have you been telling my slave, Mel?"

Mel took position to X's left. "Only what she needed to know."

Ben handed the end of my leash to X and stood to his

right in a position of parade rest. He was definitely ex-military. "He told her to obey you in all things, Master Xavier." Ben looked to me and pointed to the floor. "Such as kneeling at your feet." Ben took half a step to the side and pressed down on my shoulder. I went to my knees as the front door opened.

X hissed. "Eyes. Down. Hands on your knees. Whatever the fuck you do, do not say a word."

I gritted my teeth. "As you command."

He gave a sharp tug on my leash, and I straightened my spine. I kept my head bowed.

Men entered. Their shiny black shoes clacked against the expensive tiles.

"Welcome to my home." The tone of X's voice lowered. "Well, what is this? I wasn't expecting you, Zane."

"It's so nice to see you Xavier." A man walked forward, stepping up to shake hands with X.

My heart stuttered upon hearing my father's voice. As I lifted my head, X palmed my scalp pressing down hard.

"And you too," X said. "I hope the flight wasn't too rough? I would have come out and met you in person had I known you were coming."

"A bit of turbulence as we landed, but nothing too bad." The false cheer in my father's voice evaporated and turned cruel. "How are you enjoying your newest slave?"

X laughed. "The bitch tried to scratch my eye out and bit my lip, so you could say I'm having the time of my life. I have something special lined up for tonight's entertainment for her punishment."

"Really?" Z rubbed his palms together. I hated that gesture. Made me cringe every time he did it.

"Unless you have a problem watching, considering she's your daughter. You know my reputation with a whip."

Z paused and I thought I heard him swallow. What an offensive man. "I'm always a fan of the whip, boy," he said with a sneer. "But, there are so many other...effective forms of punishment."

"You knew who you were giving your daughter to when you made the deal, Zane. You know what I like."

My father stepped back. "It doesn't matter what you do with her. She's yours now. As long as you and I are square. Tonight, we have new business to discuss and pleasure to enjoy. This crop of slaves is superb."

"Well, that sounds promising." Dangerous undertones laced X's words. "My men tell me your cargo has been unloaded. I'm sure you'll want to check on it."

"My associates will see to that," Z said. "Let me introduce Braxton Bastion, Derk Paulson, and Mark Bennett." He introduced the three men accompanying him.

X shook each of their hands.

I tuned out the introductions. My head spun in the presence of my father. I'd long suspected our wealth didn't come solely from my father's legitimate business dealings, but this dark secret was news to me, though not unexpected since my kidnapping.

I'd long suspected something wasn't the same about the women in Z's life. Sometime in my early preteens, and probably subconsciously much younger than that, I noticed a difference. They acted differently towards Z than my friends' mothers did to their fathers, always deferential and fearful. None stayed in the house for very long. I think the longest lasted eleven months.

At twelve, a late-night escapade found my father's private chambers. I never knew we had a dungeon, but I found it and had nightmares for years thereafter. At thirteen, suspicions about my mother's death grew. By fifteen, I put the pieces together. Z was a collector. I took some solace in the knowledge my mother had been his favorite. Unfortunately, she gave him a daughter and not the heir he demanded.

What I never expected were Z's plans for me. I thought I had a life to lead, never knowing I was merely an object to be traded and sold. The fire burning in my belly ate at my insides. This was what hatred felt like. It was nothing like what I felt for X.

X turned to Ben. "You remember my associate, Ben Chambers, and his business partner, Mel Abrams."

My back stiffened and my head jerked up, only to be pressed down by the firm pressure of X's palm.

"Mr. Chambers is looking at a sizable purchase." X continued. "I invited him for a private viewing."

"Mr. Carson," Ben said, as he shook Z's hand. "It's an honor to see you again. I've heard about the quality of your merchandise, and I've seen the tenacity of your daughter first hand. Xavier assures me your training methods ensure the most excellent, and compliant, slaves."

Z's voice peaked with interest. "They have been suitably broken. How many girls are you looking to buy?"

Where did my father get these women? And how could I save them? I needed to find a way to make my father pay. For now, I was smart enough to know I needed to learn. That began by observing and learning as much as possible.

"I want the whole lot," Ben said.

The whole lot? My insides twisted with a spark of hope. If Ben was taking the entire lot, maybe those girls wouldn't wind up in a real slaver's auction. Was this how it worked? I glanced at X, dying to know the inner workings of his operation.

"Excuse me?" Z's leather shoes squeaked on the marble floors.

Ben laughed. "I'm opening a resort." He rocked back on his heels, presenting a cocky air. "My clientele expects compliant subjects. If your product meets with my specifications, we may be able to do business."

"How do you intend to control so many slaves?" Z asked.

"I train my employees well and use technology to the fullest," Ben said. "Xavier is trialing some of my tech now. On your daughter in fact."

My guts twisted with that. I didn't like my father's eyes on me. I hated that he sat above me with that smug expression on his face. He did this to me and would make him pay.

"Is that so? You have interesting friends, Xavier," Z said.

"Don't we all," X replied. "Come. My slave, Bay, will show you to your rooms. I know the flight can be exhausting. Once you have time to refresh yourself, we'll enjoy cocktails. In the meantime, your associates can check on your cargo and examine the demonstration area for tonight."

CHAPTER FOURTEEN_

THE VILENESS THAT WAS Z RADIATED OFF MY FATHER AND flowed over my body, drenching me in a sourness that made me want to retch. Kneeling in nothing but a bra and panties before that horrible man intensified the queasiness ransacking my belly. I held back the strongest urge to vomit. I wanted to leap up and gouge his eyes out, tear his heart out with my bare hands, only that man had no heart. I would only find a dried-out husk beneath his breastbone.

With X's hand pressing down on my head, keeping me firmly in place, I certainly wouldn't make it to Z. That weighed on me with a sourness turning the bile in my throat into an unpalatable treat.

Two men to hate. I quivered with inaction. For one of them, my emotions remained conflicted.

X motioned to Bay.

"Gentlemen," Bay said, "if you will follow me."

I wasn't allowed to lift my head, so I couldn't see Z looking at me, but I felt every sweep of his gaze. The pressure of X's hand kept my eyes rooted to the floor, but I felt the vileness of Z. His toes pointed toward me, hesitated a fraction of a second too long before turning to follow Bay.

Z and his entourage departed amid the scuffing of leather over priceless marble. The swishing of expensive Armani suits faded as the muscles between my shoulder blades pinched. Hot tears pricked behind my lids, but I kept my tears in check.

For X, tears flowed because I had yet to develop a defense against the tide of emotions he drew forth. For Z, I had a lifetime to shore up my defenses. I blinked against the heat behind my eyes, shoved my tears back where they belonged and swallowed my hatred into the pit of my stomach where it could ferment into the strength I would need to kill.

X jerked at my chain. "Come," he said, tension rolled off him as he strode toward the library.

I obediently followed.

Ben fell into step behind X. Tapping on a cell phone sounded behind me as X dragged me into the library. Ben shut the door. X spun and his voice heated with displeasure.

"Why was I not told he was on the plane?"

"Master Xavier—" Ben began, but X cut him off with an upraised fist.

"Don't you dare break character, one misstep and this all

comes crashing down." He poked a finger at Ben. "Text Chad and tell him to bring her some damned clothes." His face turned red and he dropped my leash. "Forgive me, Raven, I would never have subjected you to that if I had known he would be here."

The door to the library burst open as Chad entered. "Master Xavier—"

X cut him off. "Get her some clothes."

Chad pulled up short, his mouth hung open, a look of indecision scrawled on his face. "Um, what kind of clothes?"

X ran fingers through his hair. I watched this strange exchange with a rising tide of unease. What was I missing?

Ben stepped forward. "If I may, sir, clothes may not be the best choice."

"I will have her covered." A distraught expression flashed across X's face, followed by anger.

"This may not be the best time to have this conversation." Ben's gaze flicked my direction and he caught me staring.

I averted my eyes before X caught me.

"Fuck that." X spun to me and lifted my chin. "Raven," he said in a voice that practically barked it was so abrupt.

I jumped at the harshness of his tone. "Yes, Master."

He lifted a finger and pointed at Ben. "We might be able to salvage something of this." X turned to me. "Do you know any of your father's access codes?"

Was he kidding? Breaking Z's security codes had been my favorite pastime for years. Once I learned how to program a computer, I'd hacked every account he had. Although, except for mandatory summer vacations, I hadn't spent much time around Z in the past eight years. Anything recent, or anything business related, I wouldn't be much help with.

I shrugged.

X pounced on me, lunging in close and gripping my collar. His face, inches from mine, practically growled out his demand. "I asked a question, slave."

Holy crap. Rather than recoiling in fear like a normal person, his show of power turned me on. Heat bloomed between my legs, confirming I was twisted in the head. My breaths came out in shallow pants and I couldn't help but lick my lips, preparing for an assault on my mouth.

He leaned in close. His eyes followed my tongue and I thought he might kiss me, but he focused back on my eyes. "Answer me," he said through gritted teeth.

I gave a sharp inhale. Oh, he was just as hot and bothered as I was, only he had more self-control than me.

I breathed out and took in a breath. "I used to know some of his codes at home, but I don't know any of his business codes." That was the truth, but it wasn't the whole truth. I didn't need to know Z's business codes to access Z's accounts.

X released me and stood. He paced the length of the library.

Ben spoke with Chad, and after a moment, Chad rushed out of the library. Ben took a seat in one of the armchairs. His gruff voice sounded throughout the tall chamber. "So...

Xavier," a slight pause hitched at the use of his name, "how do you want to proceed? Are you bringing the girl in or not?"

X glanced at me and looked to Ben. "What do you think?"

Ben shrugged. "It's too damn late, and she's too damn smart. And so is he. He's going to know if it's not real. You don't have a choice but to continue."

"Know what?" Screw the damn rules. I wanted to know what they were talking about.

"Don't forget your place, slave," X said.

I stood and walked toward him. Confidence bloomed in my heart. "I'm thinking my place is becoming more negotiable." In what way, I wasn't entirely certain, but something was about to change.

Ben chuckled. "Oh, sweetie, you truly do not know your master." He stood and came at me. Ben approached from the other side. A stern expression plastered on his face.

I glanced between the two men, alarm bells sounding loudly in my head.

In front of me, X shook his head. "Then let's make this real." He took off his jacket and draped it over the back of the chair behind the desk piled high with books. He rolled his shoulders and cracked his knuckles. "Time to make you a slave."

Like I wasn't already? I didn't try to flee as Ben grabbed my arms.

X opened a drawer of the desk and pulled out a long strap of leather. A swallow got stuck in my throat as he ran his hand down the length of the strap. Ben turned me around.

X's voice dropped to a low whisper, "I own your ass."

I cried out as he traced a finger down my spine. The soft touch was not what I expected.

"Count to five," he said.

Without warning the air whistled with the crack of the leather strap. Pain striped over my left ass cheek, lifting me up onto the balls of my feet. I cried out as a shrill piercing wail of agony pushed past my lips.

Ben murmured beside me. "Count slave or the number is reset at zero."

Oh my God, he couldn't be serious. I glanced at Ben, and by the look in his eye, I received my answer. I huffed out the count.

"One."

Another whistle of air. *Crack*. And pain over the right side of my ass became my universe. Another scream tore past my lips as I rocked forward. I gasped for breath and Ben reminded me to count.

Crack. Pain over my thigh. *Crack*. Fire over the other thigh. *Crack*. My lower back lit up. I screamed at the top of my lungs and fell against Ben.

"Five." I huffed against the pain. One strike to each of my buttocks, both my thighs and one against the small of my back. Shallow breaths did nothing to ease the fire burning against my backside.

"Turn her around," X commanded.

Ben pushed me to my knees. Tears flooded out of my eyes blurring my vision. My damn eyes had sprung another leak.

"You were given a choice," X said. "An easy or a more difficult path. You made your choice, and now your father has arrived, making today's transaction...complicated."

"Expectations of a slave are clear and hesitation by you will spell disaster to my plans."

My nose ran with the flood of tears spilling down my cheeks. I blinked against the blurriness in my vision, but saw only the blackness of X's trousers pressing near my face.

The anger of his beating had not aroused me as before. The power I had felt flowing off him, feeding the desire within me, had faded, evaporated with the knowledge of what tonight implied. The reality of enslavement, sandwiched against my fantasy of slavery, exposed the sick underbelly of this dark world. It took the arrival of Z to make it real. I could no longer walk around in a dreamlike haze, allowing a mindless attraction for X to override the very real terror behind my situation.

It didn't change my desire for X. Didn't dampen the magnetic allure of the man standing before me. What it did was sharpen and focus my place. The men standing to either side of me were my jailers, no matter how gentle they had treated me these past two weeks. X said he wouldn't rape me. I needed to know if I could trust his word.

"You don't want me to do anything against my will." I

believed that. I hoped I was right. I licked my lips and took a chance I had figured things out. "Tell me what my father is doing here."

"I don't take orders from slaves," X said with an indrawn hiss of breath.

I glanced down at the floor. "You don't know Z." Images of long suppressed memories flooded through my mind, things a daughter should never have witnessed. I dragged my attention back to X, but I couldn't hold his gaze as I spoke. Horrible images flashed past my eyes.

"I know him better than you think," X said. "Remember who I got you from?"

I cringed at the loathing in his voice, but he was wrong. I stiffened my spine and lifted my gaze. "Z won't be satisfied with watching you punish me. He's going to want more. And the..." my voice hitched on the next word, "...the *merchandise* he brought with him..."

Ben's hands clenched.

I extended the fingers of both bound hands under my chin. "He won't permanently harm them, bad for business. If you're selling his product, you know this. But, if he gave me to you, he knows you're a sadist. He'll have certain expectations."

X took two steps back. He turned away, but not before I saw a look of disgust march across his features. I had no idea why the idea affected him so strongly, especially considering he had no such difficulties with abduction, enslavement, restraint, or using physical force against me. A sadist who couldn't stomach rape. What a contradiction.

"Sir," Ben said.

X gripped the edge of the desk. A stack of books tumbled to the floor, crashing into the silence that hung around all of us. He hung his head. "I didn't know he would be here." He lifted his head. "Ben, why wasn't I informed?"

Ben's cheeks flushed. "None of us knew, sir. He wasn't listed on the manifest, but it does give an unprecedented opportunity." Ben took my elbow. "Sir," he said in a strangled voice. He pushed me forward and took two steps back.

Had I just been presented as a sacrificial lamb?

X gave Ben a long hard look. Finally, with a sharp wave of his hand he barked out a command. "Leave me."

Ben bowed and backed out of the library, but not before Chad returned with a shimmering length of fabric. Ben snatched it and laid it on a rail of one of the book cases and quickly ushered a very confused Chad outside.

X lifted my chin. "There are worse monsters in the world than me, Raven. Men such as your father. With your help, I'll bring him down, but I can't allow your defiance to jeopardize my plans. You're right, your father has certain expectations, and I'll do what I can to protect you, as much as I'm able, but you must trust me to know what that is. You must obey me."

"But..." I shook my head; certain I hadn't heard him correctly.

"I don't have time to explain every detail, except trust me

when I tell you I'm not the monster you believe me to be, but I will do whatever is required to bring one down." His jaw clenched.

Questions would wait. Power flowed in the strength of his gaze. He left me in the library with instructions not to leave until my guards returned. No lock on the door held me. The front door lay just a few feet away. I could run, but X had left me with the dolphin bracelet wrapped around my wrist—a reward for my obedience. Although, I didn't know what that bracelet allowed me to do.

The only thing holding me in place was the force of his will and an insatiable curiosity about his plans for Z. My eyes darted to the door of the library. Outside was the foyer. Beyond the foyer, doors led outside. Outside lay freedom. Yet, I stayed on my knees and waited for my guards.

CHAPTER FIFTEEN_

I WASN'T KEPT WAITING LONG, WHICH WAS A GOOD THING. Thinking about the short distance from where I knelt to outside that door did things to my head. The temptation to flee overwhelmed me, but the anchor wrapped around my ankle, that damned GPS tracking device, held me in place. Not to mention, X had not freed my wrists. They remained manacled to my collar. Running with my arms flapping, wrists bound to my neck, pretty much ensured I would trip and fall.

That damned bracelet was no gift of freedom. X knew what he was doing in giving it to me. It was a chain like any other, though it taunted me with the illusion of freedom. He was so much better at this game than I was.

Ben opened the door to the library, drawing me out of my

contemplation. He snagged the discarded fabric Chad had brought in earlier and brought it to me.

"Go ahead and stand," he ordered.

With my hands bound, it was harder than it should have been to get to my feet, but I managed.

He shook out the pearlescent gauze, more of a filigree of interlocking spider-web than fabric. Tiny gems glittered in the light as he held it out for me.

My brows lifted as I examined it. "I'm supposed to wear that?"

He nodded.

"Why bother?"

The garment reminded me of a harem slave outfit, billowy leg coverings, with long flowing fabric that offered no coverage apart from a very minimal and questionable thicker weave around the groin. As he thrust it at me, I arched a brow and turned my palms up.

"Either you dress me, or release my hands so I can dress myself." I shook my head as I took another look at the outfit. "Does it come with a top?"

"Come here," he said.

I took a step toward him and he released my wrists.

"Get dressed." He thrust the delicate fabric into my hands.

I plucked the harem pants from him and stepped into them. The GPS anklet tangled in the hem. The pants hung low over my hips, exposing the expanse of my back. I turned to him feeling more exposed in the fabric than I had without clothes.

He handed over a mass of silver strands.

Oh, my God, he expected me to wear this?

My eyes met Ben's.

"Here, let me help you," he said.

Ben fastened the contraption of silver around my chest and breasts, encircling them in a birdcage bra of...well, I'm really not sure what I was wearing. I was dressed, but I had never felt so on display in my life.

I looked down at myself. Sterling silver ropes draped over my breasts. My abdomen was bare. The sheer filigree did little to conceal the pink lace of my panties, but the thicker weave over my groin hinted at some degree of modesty.

Ben fingered the bracelet lying next to the silver cuffs. "We will go over this later. I'm happy to see he let you keep it. You must have pleased him."

I frowned at Ben's praise, knowing how true his words were. X's pleasure had stirred a reaction in me that I had to face. I needed to understand why I responded to X the way I did.

"What does it do?"

Ben flicked the dolphin with his finger. "The dolphin holds a sensor that allows access to different areas of the house. You're being granted some degree of freedom, but not tonight. Don't wander off alone. It hasn't been activated yet."

"Why?"

"Because, you've been ordered not to. Don't lose this privilege so soon after earning it."

"I have so many questions, Ben."

He curled his upper lip inward and I watched him shut down to my questions. He gestured with his fingers. "Give me your hand."

Heat bloomed in my face, frustration at the lack of answers, irritation at my helplessness. I gave him my hand and my stomach sank as he reattached my cuffs to the ring at the collar.

"Other one," he said.

My compliance frustrated me, but I didn't know what else to do.

"Now tell me," he said in a casual voice, "how confident are you that you can hack your father's systems?"

"I don't know his codes."

"That's not what I asked. Can you or can you not hack into your father's systems? Xavier wants to know if you can crack his network the same way you cracked our security."

I diverted with a question of my own. "Why did you call him Master Xavier before but only Xavier now?"

"Excuse me?" Ben's brows lifted and his chin tucked in as he stepped back in surprise.

"Answer my question and I'll answer yours."

He huffed a low laugh. "Silly slave, that's not how this works." His finger flicked the dolphin dangling at my wrist.

"It can be taken away before you even have a chance to see what you've earned."

"Why won't you answer me?"

"Because you haven't earned it."

"You know, that's the first time you called me slave. I know why X does it, but..."

"What did you call him?" Ben turned on me, his face turning red.

"X." I took a step back as Ben advanced on me.

"Do not disrespect Xavier like that. Ever. He's a man to be admired."

"Admired?" I huffed a laugh. "I'm sorry, but I disagree."

"There are many things you don't understand about Xavier."

"Then tell me."

"That is not my place, but I will give you this one warning. Do not cross Xavier. You won't appreciate what happens. I'll tell him of our conversation. You need to understand my loyalty to Xavier is beyond reproach."

"I wasn't questioning your loyalty. I was simply asking a question."

"You disparaged his name. Xavier is your master. I suggest you don't forget that."

"And what is he to you?"

"My life is his."

How did X instill such loyalty? I needed to understand

the power he held over my guards. I ground my teeth together as Ben clammed up on me.

"Now, follow me." He grabbed the end of the leash and led me out of the library.

"Where are you taking me?"

"You're ordered not to speak," Ben commanded.

"I take orders only from X." I squared off my shoulders and jutted out my chin. No way was I going to let Ben boss me around, not if he wasn't going to answer the simplest of questions.

I stumbled as Ben came to a sudden stop. His face turned a dark crimson as he turned dangerous eyes on me. "Perhaps I wasn't clear about insulting your master."

My jaw dropped as I realized my slip of tongue. "Ben, I'm sorry. It's just something I say in my head." Was he going to tell X? What was the punishment for disparaging X?

Ben yanked my collar and pulled me up on my toes. Heavy breaths surged out of his lungs, bathing me in fury. "I'm allowed to punish you, but for this weekend I'm playing the role of a buyer, so I cannot." His breath pulsed onto my cheek. "Xavier is your master. Do not denigrate his name as you do your father. You have no idea what sort of man your master is."

While my body shook with fear, I found my backbone and straightened it. My eyes narrowed. "I have a fair idea what sort of man Master Xavier is Ben."

Ben released me. "You will call me Mr. Chambers from

here on out, and you will refer to Mel as Mr. Abrams. You will never refer to your master by a letter again. Is that understood?"

I cocked my head, my voice taking on venomous tones of its own to match his. "And Chad and Bay? What roles are they playing this weekend?"

Ben took a step back. His body visibly shook and I could see the effort he took to control himself. Deep breaths moved in and out of his broad chest, and the muscles of his jaw clenched. "They are as they always were. Now answer my question. Do. You. Understand?" He grabbed my upper arm and pinched the tender flesh.

"Yes." I yelped as his grip tightened. "Yes. Ben." His fingers dug into my skin. I danced away from him, but he had me in his grip. I was certain I would bruise. "You're hurting me."

"Answer me," he said through gritted teeth, "appropriately this time."

"For the love of God!" I pulled away, but he yanked me against his chest.

His breath blew against my hair. "What is my name, slave?"

"Mr. Chambers!"

He released me and I stared at the red and purple handprint forming into a bruise. With a jerk on my chain, he took off down the stark white hallways that dominated X's estate. No wonder I was constantly lost and disorientated.

"Now, we have a few hours before the evening demonstration," Ben stated as he rushed me through the halls. "You can spend that time in your room, or doing something more interesting. Perhaps even answer some of your questions."

The thought of returning to my room filled me with mind numbing boredom. All I would do would be to stew about my punishment, my father, and X. I had no idea what Ben had in mind, but it had to be better than sitting all alone with my thoughts.

"Like what?"

"Well, let's start with your father."

"I have no interest in my father."

"Really?" Ben gave me a look which said he didn't believe a word I said, but the truth was I didn't care about my father. I wanted him out of my life.

"What if I told you what we have in mind will cause your father great harm?"

"Excuse me?"

"Aren't you interested in how you came to belong to Xavier? Or why your father is here?"

I had all kinds of questions, but no one answered any of them. I'd given up looking for reasons why. I'd pretty much given up on everything and I didn't like what that said about me. I hadn't been raised to be submissive. What had happened to me?

I shouldn't be eager to help whatever X and Ben had in mind, however, if it had anything to do with hurting my father I was all on board. I needed something to activate my brain and shut off the needy pieces of me.

"What do you have in mind?"

"Now, that's my girl."

Ben pulled out his phone and tapped out a text. With another series of twists and turns down a maze of hallways I had not yet travelled, Ben succeeded in getting me thoroughly lost in X's home yet again. He led me into a nondescript room full of linens, bath towels and other toiletry items. A door led out from the other side of the maid's closet. I could only wonder why he brought me to such a room, but he silenced my question with a finger raised to his lips.

"Wait here," he said in a hushed whisper. He pulled out his phone and stared at the screen. After an agonizing wait, the screen glowed blue. Then, he led me to the door, opened it, and ushered me inside.

I gasped at the opulence on the other side of the utilitarian linen closet. A massive king size bed dominated the room. Red velvet drapes framed the ever-present plantation shutters. The drapes had been pulled back and the shutters opened. I gasped at the view of a patio garden full of lush green plants and blooming flowers. The delicate aroma filled the room with a heavenly fragrance. I couldn't help but inhale. There was a fountain out there. The tapping of falling water soothed my nerves. This was a room for a king, and I briefly wondered if Ben had brought me to X's quarters. That sent my insides tumbling about.

Wealth dripped from the crown moldings down the walls, settled in the intricate details of the carved wooden furniture, and spilled across the floor. But this wasn't X's room.

At the foot of the bed, sat Z's signature luggage. I stopped in my tracks. Ben placed a hand on the small of my back and urged me toward the massive partners desk in the corner. Z's briefcase rested on the stamped leather tabletop. Beside it, his black laptop had been plugged into a charging cored along with his other electronic accessories.

"We don't have much time," Ben said in a low whisper.

My eyes widened. "Much time for what? What exactly do you expect me to do?"

A chin bump in the direction of the laptop gave me a fair idea what the answer to that question might be, but there were a lot of things someone could do with a computer. Ben fished out a USB stick and handed it to me.

"If you can log on, all we need is to insert this."

"What's on the stick?" No way was that going to work.

"You don't need to know."

"Like hell."

I lived and breathed computers, as did Z. Since I didn't know the degree of sophistication X and his crew possessed, I didn't trust what was on that USB drive or what security protocols it would trip once attached. The fact they relied on me to hack into Z's computer told me plenty about their competence.

"Z will detect that when he logs back onto his computer," I said.

"It's not staying."

"Doesn't matter. I helped Z upgrade his security. He'll receive a notification of a new device. It'll ping his cellphone and leave a trail. What is it you're trying to do?"

With your help, I'll bring him down. X's words whispered in my head. What was going on here?

I wasn't against doing something to hurt Z, but I needed more information. Specifically, what did X need off Z's personal computer? But, I would help because while I had no idea what X's agenda might be, I had one of my own. This presented an opportunity I couldn't ignore. I could get a message out to my friends.

Ben and I traded stares. It was important I put up some degree of fight before giving in. My fingertips itched to begin, I was that eager to get at Z's system. Two hours wasn't much time, but I only needed to write a few lines of code. And I didn't need Z's password to gain access to his laptop's operating system. Ben didn't need to know this. I wasn't giving up all my tricks. At least not until Ben answered a few of my questions.

I didn't think Z had remembered to shut me out after handing me into X's eager hands. My father was a businessman, not a hacker, and he could be sloppy at times.

"I can't give you details," Ben said.

"Then I can't help you." My blood roared as it rushed

past my ears. I was playing a dangerous game of chicken with Ben, one I needed to win. "Look, you don't have to give specifics, but I need to know what you're trying to access, or download. It matters in how I proceed, and Ben?"

"Yes?" His lips twisted in a frown.

"If you want my help, a little give and take. Master Xavier said I could help bring my father down. What did he mean? Why am I'm here?"

"In this room? That's obvious. You have skills Xavier requires."

"That's not what I mean. Why am I here?" I made a more expansive gesture. "Why did he buy me?"

"I'm surprised you haven't figured it out, and Xavier didn't buy you. You were traded to settle a debt owed."

"Figure what out?" I had been focused on the first part of what Ben said that it took a moment before the second half slammed into me. "My father planned what?"

"Xavier is many things, but unlike your father, he's not a monster."

"I have every reason to believe Xavier is just as bad as Z, if not worse."

"No, you don't."

I gave him a look. Our conversation was going in circles.

"He kidnapped me and forced me to—"

"Forced is a relative term. He's done nothing that you didn't want."

You need me to force you, Raven. You and I both know this. X's words became more intrusive and insistent, repeating over and over in my head. *I'll do what I can to protect you.*

Was that true? Protect me from whom? Z? Could any of what Ben said be true? I shook my head, trying to clear it and focus back on my argument.

"How can you say that? I didn't choose this! I didn't choose to be raped."

I may get hard hurting you, but you like it, Raven. You're fucking wet for me.

"Xavier has never, and would never, force you against your will," Ben said.

"What about what happened in the library? He's not a nice man. I don't know what world you're living in, but he beat me, forced me to...to..."

"He's forced you to face a truth within you, something buried until he came along. And honestly, you helped him find truth in himself. You're right about one thing. Master Xavier is not a nice man. He'll do whatever it takes to get what he wants, but think about what he has done, and consider what he's asking of you now."

I fisted my hands on my hips. "He put bruises on my ass and welts on my skin. He forced me to my knees. I think that speaks enough to his character."

"And the rest? Have you forgotten what happened in your room."

"Where he practically raped me!"

"Where he specifically *did not* rape you. Little one, you

171

can't see the forest for the trees. Let go of your anger and open your mind. More is going on here than you know. Now, why do you think you're here?"

I couldn't admit the truth. I'd been here for weeks and yet X had barely touched me. The few times he had...I turned my back to Ben. I didn't believe him. I couldn't. Swiping tears from my face, I gestured to the laptop.

"I'm here to hack that." Was this the truth? I was nothing other than a tool. Evidently, I was a tool positioned with expert care. How much planning had gone into this moment?

"You're here because Xavier couldn't bear what your father intended for his only daughter. Xavier saved you from a fate worse than death. That your presence here has turned into... something else, is merely an unintended, but welcomed, benefit. Now, you present an unprecedented opportunity, one Xavier won't pass up on. I'm asking on his behalf, will you help us?"

My thoughts tumbled about, spiraling with the implications of everything Ben said, and those things he didn't mention. It was too much to take in, and I needed to take a step back, regroup, and reorder my thoughts. Nothing made sense. My father, I understood. X? I had no idea what game he was playing at. For now, I would focus on what I could and take down the devil I knew.

As for X? I'd figure that out later.

"What do you need me to do?"

My face paled and my guts twisted. I was going to do this. USBs were good for only a few things: downloading programs or uploading files. I needed to know what X wanted before I could proceed. Ben guided me over to the desk and sat me down. I trembled as I stared at the computer. When he reached over my shoulder to open the laptop, I knocked his hand out of the way.

"Stop!"

"What?" He jerked back.

"You don't know Z like I do. He has security on top of security and not all of it is high tech."

I checked for his paranoid first layer of security, and arguably the most robust. It could be anything, but would appear innocuous to the untrained eye. For me, it didn't take long to find the tiny down feather primed to fall the moment someone opened the lid. I took note of its position, every rotation of the feathers, and very carefully caught it as I opened the lid.

Z taught me that trick himself. *Thank you, papa, you wretched man.*

"Now, what is it that X is looking for? Files? A program? Access to Z's accounts?"

Ben gave me a long hard stare. "Yes... to everything." He handed me the USB. "This has a program that will grant remote access."

"And trigger every security layer in place." I brushed away the USB. "Give me a moment..."

I could ask more questions, but it was clear X didn't trust me to be anything other than his tech monkey. He counted on my hatred for my father to help him. In this, X was right on track. What he didn't know was what I planned next. I swiped the track pad and got to work.

CHAPTER SIXTEEN_

NEARLY TWO HOURS LATER, BEN DRAGGED ME THROUGH THE white halls of X's estate again. My back ached from hunching over the keys while writing lines of code into the operating system of Z's laptop. I would have to show X what to do next, but all of Z's business files would be open. I'd given X exclusive backdoor access to everything, and I inserted something for myself.

I gave up trying to keep track of the twists and turns. We passed through several open-air atriums. It seemed X liked to build around a series of courtyards surrounding inner gardens. I counted three such structures before Ben brought me to a large set of carved double doors. Despite all my misgivings, I couldn't deny an anticipation growing inside of me.

X brought all the emotions boiling to the surface; anger,

fear, disgust, confusion, interest, excitement, guilt, anxiety, and more simmered together and left me feeling wrung out. I was anticipatory, eager to see him again after the revelations of this afternoon. I was scared of the steel in his eyes and the predator within, but excited as well. His dominance had uncovered something within me, something I was only now beginning to accept. I approached the evening with cautious excitement, but steeled myself for the reality Z's presence would bring. I didn't know what I would find when Ben delivered me to X.

I gasped as Ben tugged me past erotic sculptures, getting only a glimpse of the men and women engaged in every imaginable sexual act. It would have been beautiful if not for the circumstances of my situation. I stumbled, neck craned as I looked at the doors, but Ben dragged me into a large chamber. After the stark white and gray walls, I wasn't prepared for the crimson and black, or what awaited me inside that room.

"Come slave." Ben was back in character, calling me slave and referring to X as Xavier rather than Master Xavier. Ben dragged me toward the center of the room taking very little care to be gentle with me.

The multitude of chains hanging down from the ceiling made my mouth go dry. My entire world slowed to a stand-still, even the beating of my heart seemed to pause. A large cross dominated the center of the room. This was my initiation into X's twisted world. Everything that came before had only been a prelude, but this, that cross, those chains, this was his domain. The hood and restraints on the plane had been child's play compared to this.

I scanned the crimson walls. Implements of torture hung on hooks screwed into the walls. Whips of every variety were placed with the precision of an obsessive mind. Floggers and crops, paddles and canes had been laid out according to type and size. Chains and cuffs and shiny metal devices I could not identify occupied shelves and hung from pegs along the walls.

My gaze fluttered around, terrified of the next revelation, but I couldn't stop looking. If I could take everything in, then I could destroy the power of the unknown. Blindfolds, hoods, gags, feathers, dildos were all represented. Chains, thin, thick, short, and long, hung from the ceiling or were attached to the walls. Cages lined the far wall and some even swung from the ceiling. Surrounding everything were red leather couches, chairs, and other oddly shaped furniture forming wedges and rolls. All of them had rings attached to them.

I teetered with the undeniable need to flee, but that route had been firmly denied. There was nowhere to go and I wondered if I would ever see the light of day again. What horrors did X have in store for me? What must I endure? My throat constricted against the thread of panic welling up inside me. I struggled to swallow, but my tongue felt thick.

"Come slave." Ben pulled me to the center of the room.

My voice cracked. "B...Ben?" Turning to him for support made no sense, but reason had left me many heartbeats ago.

He hissed. "Silence, slave!" To my horror, but not much to my surprise, he brought me to the center of the room. His voice dropped to a whisper. "Do not forget what name to call me by, and don't speak unless asked a direct question. This begins now."

I nodded as he unclipped my wrist and attached it to the cross. He spun me to face the cross and attached my other wrist to the last support. The wood pressed against my belly and upper part of my hips.

"You wait for your master, slave."

Do I have any other choice? As if confirming everything Ben said earlier, a heat of arousal flooded through me with the thought of seeing X again.

I listened to Ben's footsteps as he left and then the deafening silence of the room folded around the beating of my heart. This was it. My end would come in this room. Seconds stretched to minutes. My breathing deepened then turned frantic as I tested my restraints. Ben had left my feet free, but it didn't matter. My arms spread above my head, shackled to the cross, I was helpless. My fingers clenched and unclenched with each of my breaths, fast at first and then slowing as I gained control over my breathing.

I wouldn't let panic rule me. There was nothing I could do about my situation. The only thing I could control was myself, so I would control what I could.

A door opened, not the set of double doors behind me, but a door to the side. I didn't have to look to know who approached. It was X. I knew his step intimately. He came to stand behind me and stroked my throat. I jumped at the warmth of his skin. His fingers clamped down, wrapping around my neck. I winced as I attempted to swallow beneath the constriction. The heat of his breath whispered against my ear.

"I won't apologize for hurting you. I can't deny it's what I need. I thought I would be able to hold off, that I would be strong enough, but you ignite a darkness I can't control." His hand tightened against my throat.

I gasped as he squeezed the soft tissues of my neck. My body reacted to his touch, burning, melting, igniting beneath his undeniable power. He pivoted around the cross until he stood before me. The heat in X's eyes acted as an accelerant to the fire smoldering in my belly, turning the embers there into a blaze. Within seconds he incinerated me with his gaze.

"Good," he said as he cupped my cheek, "you feel it too."

Such a tender move, but with him it was a move engendered to establish dominance. His hand tightened and then released around my throat. Gulping air, I gave a strangled groan. I lost even more ground in our battle as he collected my hair, twisted it together and brought it forward over one shoulder with a tug. I couldn't help but shiver, even though the room was more than warm enough. I stared into the eyes of a man blinded with lust. My attention skittered to the wall of whips and crops.

"We'll get there." He turned to follow the path of my gaze. His finger pressed against my lips. "Ben told me what you did. Thank you, it will be rewarded, but first you need correction for your disrespect. And of course, you have your punishment later tonight to endure."

Damn, Ben. I closed my eyes as hot pinpricks threatened tears. This was the thanks I received? X stroked my throat with his thumb.

"Pain doesn't always need to come with discipline, Raven. With time, I'll show you how pain becomes pleasure."

Had X finally snapped beyond reason? I wasn't permitted to speak. If I broke one of his rules, would he hear me? Or would it push him to punish me faster? I struggled not knowing the rules of this world. There was so much to learn. I didn't know how brave, or how strong I could be. Looking at the wall of torture devices, I prayed my pain threshold was higher than I imagined.

His hand dropped to my breast. "You're beautiful, and perfect for me; the other half to make me whole." He brought both hands to cup my breasts, hefting their weight.

I fisted my hands as my nipples peaked at the stimulus. My back arched, pressing my breasts into his hands. A smile tugged at the corners of his impeccable eyes.

"God, you're so responsive. We have just a few moments before our company joins us..."

I breathed shallowly as my body betrayed me.

What was I afraid of?

He kissed a tear on my cheek. "Don't worry, Raven, I will not force you. There's a promise hanging between us, one you can't escape." He traced the line of my jaw and lifted my chin as tears poured out of my eyes. He vented a deep sigh. "For what I must do to you, you'll hate me. I have a role to fulfill, it's everything you believe of me, but not who I am. Believe me when I say I would rather die than do this to you. I ask you to forgive me." His words cooled me off. "Don't hate me for what happens next."

I pulled away, my heart pinching with pain. He made no sense. Closing my eyes, I berated myself for my weakness. Whoever X was, he had mastered the female body and he had certainly mastered mine. I was a fool, because I wanted to believe him and a piece of me already forgave him.

I despised the power he held over me. This man was my captor, not my lover, and I'd forgotten that along the way. It was time to take back control of my mind, if not my body. I had lost so much, so fast. I couldn't believe I had caved under his dominion and shuddered at how far I had fallen. I sagged in my restraints with defeat.

"I don't hate you. I hate myself." I said it in the faintest of whispers, never meaning for him to hear. Although it was against the rules to speak, saying it aloud made it real. And I certainly needed to hear the truth.

"What?" The hiss of indrawn breath alerted me I hadn't said it quietly enough.

"Nothing."

"You hate yourself? Why would you say that?"

I turned my cheek, avoiding his demands.

"Answer me." His voice lowered, a dominant tone, the one full of command that turned my insides to jelly.

"No." I shook my head and ignored his command.

He could do whatever he wanted. I'd already given in, what more could he take? He'd stolen my dignity, and would make me beg for him to take me fully. I would, too, as sick as that was. It was simply a matter of time. I was ruined, but I would not give him my mind. He already had everything else. We both knew what would happen later tonight. I had lost this war. I would beg and he would take everything.

"Raven, don't deny me."

I glanced back at him. "Or what? You'll whip me? Find some other way to punish me? Have sex with me in front of my father? Or maybe you'll sell me to some other sadistic freak?" I shrugged. "It doesn't matter. You win. I'm not going to fight you. I'm yours."

He pressed his forehead to mine and breathed out a sigh. He shook his head, rocking his forehead against mine. "Life is not so simple, slave."

"Why do you do that?"

"Do what?" He lifted his head and our eyes collided in an intimate embrace of wills.

I breathed out, releasing some of the tension in my body. "Sometimes you call me slave. Sometimes you use my name."

His eyes hardened, and he drew back. "Don't." The muscles in his jaw clenched as if I'd hit upon a nerve. He turned away and walked to the far wall. "It means nothing."

He ran his hand along the line of whips hanging from the hooks, pausing to caress the long bullwhip and cat-o-nine tails. My stomach clenched, then relaxed as he moved down the wall, fingers trailing over implements of torture I wanted nothing to do with, but which he seemed intimately familiar. He stopped at a length of hard flat leather, nearly the length of his forearm, something between a crop and a paddle. He lifted it off the wall and hefted its weight in his hand.

"This should do." How easily his voice carried in the room, although I was sure he projected the callous tone for my benefit. He made a show of walking back to me, carrying his chosen weapon before him. "Ben mentioned you failed to call me Master."

I drew in breath, certain what came next. No way was I going to break another rule.

"You call your father Z. Is this not so?"

"Yes, Master."

"When did this begin?"

"I was young. Maybe six or seven."

"But to his face you call him Papa?" He slapped the

leather thing in his palm. A solid *thwack* sounded in the room.

I jumped at the sound. "In front of others, I do. When it's just him and me, I don't call him papa."

"So, Z? The letter? It's derisive?" The arch of his brow told me X already knew the answer to his question. I was so screwed.

My attention latched on to the device X held. I couldn't make myself answer because I knew what would come next. Fear kept my mouth closed. My lower lip trembled. X stepped up to me and lifted the flat leather rod in front of my face.

"It's called a tawse." He pressed it to my lips. "Kiss it, and when I'm done, thank me."

Prickly heat, the precursor of tears, burned behind my lids. My lips trembled as I kissed the leather. I despised the surge of heat blooming between my legs. This thing within me that wanted X to hit me with that thing confused me as much as it aroused me. I couldn't understand how I wanted it —him—so badly.

X stepped behind the cross and rubbed the leather tawse up and down my back. "There's something you need to learn about sadists, Raven," he said. "Pain excites me. I like the power in forcing your body to turn pain into pleasure."

Thwack! Thwack! Thwack!

I screamed.

His breathing came hard and fast. His words turned frantic, guttural, primal. Deep breaths panted in my ear. "For me, nothing gets me harder than dispensing pain. Every time you disobey..." He pressed the hard length of his erection against my hip. Then stepped away from me.

Thwack! Thwack! Thwack!

Deep sobs burst from my lungs as intense sensations flared to life.

Thwack! Thwack! Thwack!

My bottom pulsed with pain, hot lines throbbed with each beat of my heart, radiating out with white hot fire. I sobbed and cried for him to stop. I begged him to end it. He unchained me, flipped me around, pressed down on my shoulders and forced me to my knees.

"Nine strikes with a tawse, Raven, and my dick is ready to explode. This is what you do to me. When I punish you, my cock swells with need. So, when you disobey, you'll feel the bite of my whip, then see to my release when I'm done."

I glanced up. Big mistake. Fury and lust swirled in his eyes. The double doors to the Hall of Horrors opened wide and Z's clipped voice called out.

"Starting without us, boy?"

CHAPTER SEVENTEEN_

MY FATHER PUFFED OUT HIS CHEST. MY DEGRADATION WAS complete.

"Glad to see you're making use of your new slave," my father said.

"I'll be with you in a moment." X glanced down at me, a look of regret filling his face. "String her up in the corner, out of the way."

"I thought she was to be our entertainment for the evening," Z said from one of the leather chairs lining the center circle. He sounded disappointed and pouty.

If my father were closer, I would spit in his face. As it was, I had to endure his derisive comments and do nothing.

His associates lounged in identical chairs around the room, forming a semicircle with the cross at the center. Ben and Mel had joined them, leaving two leather couches unoccupied. A quick glance around the room revealed Chad standing guard at the set of double doors. Bay marched toward me.

I couldn't help but flinch. I'd been lulled into thinking I was safe, untouchable even, in X's home, but everything about this reminded me what my true status was. I was a prisoner and a slave.

"Come, slave." Bay said as he collected me at the cross. He looped the leash around his wrist and headed for a far corner.

X headed to one of the empty couches. "So eager to see your daughter whipped?"

"I've been itching to see the bitch strapped since the day she was born."

My step faltered, not because of the cruelty in my father's voice, but rather at his eagerness.

"Then why didn't you do it yourself?" X fell into the couch with a sigh. "Damn that felt good."

Z didn't answer. If a look passed between them, I certainly didn't see it.

Bay took me to a far wall and locked me into one of the many chains hanging on the wall. He leaned in and whispered into my ear. "Whatever happens, keep silent."

I opened my mouth to ask a question. Whenever someone said *be silent* a hundred questions pop to mind.

I had thousands of questions. Right now, most of them had to do with X, and I had a fair idea he knew it too. His laser eyes pierced through the dimness of the room and cut right to me where he stopped my heart for a beat. Then he glanced away and responded to a question one of his guests asked. The taste of him filled my mouth.

Bay pressed a finger to my lips. "I'm serious. Already, you're to be whipped. Don't force Master Xavier into punishing you on top of that. Not in front of guests, and not in front of your father."

"I don't understand." Nothing about this made sense.

He pressed against my lips. His eyes shifted left as his shoulders tensed. "Not another word. Trust your master."

"Bay?" The hoarse whisper in my voice pleaded with him to offer some sort of answer, but all I received was firmer pressure on my lips.

He shook his head.

"Bay," X barked from the comfort of his couch. "Go fetch the slaves."

Bay rolled his shoulders. "Yes, Master Xavier." He gave me a significant look, turned, and gave X a slight bow.

Z waved to the man sitting next to him, a man with curly black hair and a dark pointed beard. "Derk, go with him."

"Sure thing," Derk said.

Bay walked to the small side entrance X had used when he entered the room. He gestured to Derk. "Mr. Paulson, the slaves are this way."

As they left, X leaned back in his couch. "Can I interest you in something to drink?"

Z laughed. "Would love some Scotch...neat. What about you Braxton?"

The man sitting to Z's left rubbed his hand over his bald head. He looked to be in his late forties or early fifties. "Nah, if I start drinking now I won't be able to get it up after the first time. I plan to fuck all night long. I'll stick with water. How about you Mark?"

The remaining man, younger than Z, sandy brown hair, with a body that had once been fit but now sagged with a pot belly, turned to X. "I'd love a beer."

"I've tried to turn Mark into a Scotch man, but he won't give up his beer," Z said with a sneer.

Ben and Mel gave their drink orders. The shift in the dynamic between X and my guards confused me. What was going on?

X flicked his wrist, giving some signal. Nothing happened for some time, then men appeared carrying trays with the requested drinks. I recognized a few of them from my one foray into the kitchen.

Z turned to Ben. "Now, Mr. Chambers, tell me about this resort of yours. I have to tell you I'm entranced."

Ben snorted a laugh. "It's been a dream of mine for years." He took a sip of Scotch, lifting the glass in salute to Z. "Having a personal slave is a privilege few can enjoy," he said with a wistful expression. "And having a well-behaved slave is a rare pleasure. I had heard of your slave acquisition program. That, combined with Xavier's conditioning program and I figure I'll get the finest and most well-behaved slaves my money can buy."

Z toasted Ben. "Sounds like you've done your research."

Ben took a sip. "Difficult research."

Mel snorted. "Expensive."

Z turned his attention to Mel. "You two are in business together." It was a statement. Not a question.

"I'm the tech support," Mel said. "I handle all issues of security, client screening, and overall resort security. Our clients want to ensure their safety and anonymity."

Braxton nodded. "Don't we all?"

"My clients are more interested in the fantasy aspect of slave ownership. They want to live on the dark side for a weekend, then go home to their wives and children."

Mr. Bennett drank his beer and gave Ben a sneer. "Why not hire prostitutes?"

Ben sat up straight. "For the prices I charge, my clients want to know they're purchasing the real thing. I'm not some fantasy sex shop making a quick buck."

X held up a hand. "I'm sure Mr. Bennett didn't mean to insult you."

Ben glared at Mr. Bennett. "If they happen to bond with a slave, I offer a sales service. This works well for me, and if this weekend works out, we may find a mutually beneficial ongoing business arrangement."

Dollar signs spiked in Z's eyes. "How many slaves do you think you might sell?"

Ben held up a hand. "Gentlemen, I'm only now looking to open up my club. A few have expressed interest in purchasing private slaves. Part of my services and fees include the boarding of their future property. I don't yet have an answer to your question."

"I'd like to visit your club," Z said, "before making a commitment."

Ben hesitated, but not Mel.

"Out of the question." Mel pointed to X. "We haven't even allowed Xavier to tour the premises yet." He leaned forward with intent. "Have I mentioned yet the exclusivity of our clientele?"

Z's mouth firmed into a thin line. "Considering we're the source of said slaves, I think that can be waived."

Mel examined his cuticles and leaned back in his seat. "I'll consider it." He paused for a long moment. "But, you'll have to fill out the forms."

Silence filled the room.

I glanced between all the men, watching their body language. Knowing Z and how he dealt with rejection, or worse, straight out confrontation in not getting what he wanted, this deal was going south fast.

It was X who broke the tension. He threw his head back and laughed. "Holy fucking shit, Ben. Can you call off your dog?" He turned to Z. "I filled out Mel's mountain of paper-work two weeks ago. He still hasn't cleared me for the resort." He turned to Mel. "What do you say? Send Mr. Carson the forms. Except for selling you his first born—who he's already given to me—he'll tell you whatever you need to know." He laughed again. "Maybe we can combine our visits when Zane delivers the slaves?" X twisted in his seat, craning his neck around. "Now where did Bay go? Who's ready to fuck?"

Braxton threw his hand in the air. "Took my Viagra. Little prick is ready for some action."

Ben thrust his finger at Mel. "Send the forms to Mr. Carson."

Mel grumbled. "There had better be some pretty blondes in this group."

Z's coarse laugh grated on my ears. "Oh, blonde, brunette, red head, Asian, Hispanic, black, and white. All the flavors of the rainbow are well represented."

"Are they well behaved?" Mel finished off his drink.

"They know what a whip is." Z lifted a remote control. "And for tonight, they've been fitted with extra motivation."

Mel nodded. "I see you know the utilities of a shock collar."

"You're familiar?"

"My favorite motivator," Mel agreed.

My stomach squeezed with the men's talk. I couldn't believe Mel's coarse tones as he discussed such cruelty, but I also knew there was more going on here than I understood.

Then the side door opened and Bay led a string of women into the room chained together by their collars. All hung their heads in submission. Their hands had been manacled in front of their waists. They were naked too and had cuffs around their ankles. I knew exactly what those would be used for as I scanned the many rings scattered around the room. A tingle ran up my spine as I stared at the darkness flashing in the maniacal eyes of my father.

My attention went from the women to X. He caught me in his gaze, and with the slightest shake of his head urged me to remain silent and stay in my darkened corner. I had no problem complying with either of those requests.

Then the other man entered, Derk. He led a smaller procession of three slaves urging them forward with what looked like a cattle prod. I gasped at the shackled men as they stumbled and jerked with each touch of the black rod. Unlike the despondent expressions of the women, angry stares and murderous expressions filled their faces.

Z lifted a hand, gesturing to the new group of slaves. "Mr. Chambers didn't you mention you were in the market for male slaves as well? These have yet to be broken, but with a little work..."

Ben's brows lifted. "Oh my." He licked his lip and he turned his attention to X. "Now this is a surprise."

X lifted a hand. "I have first pick of the male slaves, Ben."

Z huffed a laugh. "What is it with you and male slaves, boy?" He made a gesture toward Bay and Chad. "I know for a fact you don't swing that way, but you always gobble up the male merchandise."

"You have your secrets and I have mine." X turned narrowed eyes on Z.

Z turned to Bay. "Slave, tell me why do you serve your master? I don't see any chains keeping you in place."

Bay's fingers tightened around the chain holding the string of female slaves. His lips tightened into a thin line and his eyes flicked to X who gave him permission to speak with a nod. I leaned forward desperate to hear the answer, because I'd been wondering about the relationship between X and all my guards. How did X control these men? What did he offer them that make them follow him with such devotion?

Bay gave Z a half bow. "Master Xavier's rules are simple and his discipline unwavering. He gave me a choice to submit or challenge his authority."

Z threw his head back. His coarse laughter reverberated through the room. "Somehow I don't see a man like you submitting to someone like X. What are you, ex-military? Marines? Army?"

"Navy Seals, Sir." Bay straightened with pride.

Z pointed. "And Xavier mastered you?"

X cleared his throat. "Bay took some convincing." He gestured to Bay. "Bring the girls to the middle of the room."

Bay led the string of female slaves forward. Chad took up the end of the slave chain. When Bay had them in position, he and Chad attached individual girls to chains hanging down from the ceiling. This blocked my view of the couches and the men sitting in them.

"I'm intrigued," Z continued. "What about you?" Z pointed to Chad.

Chad looked to X for permission before speaking.

X granted it with a nod.

"Master Xavier gave me the same choice. I listened to his terms and agreed to submit. I've never once regretted my decision. I am his, fully."

Z whistled. "What loyalty, boy. Truly impressive."

The muscles in X's jaw clenched each time Z called him *boy*. It was equally obvious to me that Z knew how much it annoyed X. My father had always been a bastard with his normal business partners. It was the way he established dominance. I knew all his tricks though, and he certainly was getting on X's nerves. It was precisely where he wanted to be, better to unnerve X and force his opponent into a position of weakness.

From where I stood, I had the perfect vantage point to observe their exchange. Really, it was no different from any of the hundreds of business meetings I'd suffered through as a child. Z searched for weakness and exploited it, only I had a suspicion he was reading X wrong.

I'm not sure why I thought that, except Chad and Bay's answers to Z's questions were not what I would have expected. Why would Chad submit to X, whereas Bay had to be convinced? Knowing X as I did, the subtext was not lost to me, or what that implied. What had X done to Bay? And that didn't begin to explain why Ben and Mel were playing the part of slavers in this twisted business meeting.

Ben walked over to the three male slaves. He put a hand on the chest of one of them. The well-built man flinched at the touch and he covered his genitals with his bound hands.

"Damn," Ben said with respect. "This one is too much for what I'm prepared to handle." He pointed to the two smaller men standing behind the muscular slave. "But these two might be of interest to some of my clients interested in exploring their alternate sexuality."

X unfolded himself from the couch, expressing a bored disaffection as he walked over to the three male slaves. He walked around the three men examining them with a critical eye. "Chad, string the men up next to my slave."

The two smaller men cringed as his attention settled on them, while the taller man held his chin level and gazed X squarely in the face. X stared down the man. Although matched in height, X was physically smaller than the slave. This proved insignificant in the battle of wills waged between them, because the man couldn't stand up against the full onslaught of X's indomitable will. I watched, entranced as X dominated the man with nothing other than silence and a look. The man's gaze shifted left and then dropped down to the ground in defeat. Is that what happened with me? I knew the power behind X's presence.

"We'll deal with them later." X put a hand on Ben's shoulder. "Come, it's time to test the merchandise. Let's see if any of these slaves are worthy of your time."

Interesting how X didn't mention price, but rather the investment of time. Did Z note X's choice of words? My attention wandered to my father, but his attention was not focused on X, or Ben. Rather, Z had the fly of his pants undone, and fisted his cock. His eyes were locked onto the string of women standing before him. I jerked my focus away from the disgusting sight.

To my right, Chad secured the men to the wall. He looked at me and his lips pressed together as his gaze traveled back to where I had been looking. He gave a sharp jerk of his head, as he locked the muscular man to a ring in the wall.

"Things are not what you think, kitten," Chad said.

"Please don't call me that." I closed my eyes and stifled a groan.

"When I get free, I'm going to rip your balls off and make you eat them." The man Chad chained to the wall said with a growl.

Chad clipped the man's other wrist to the wall and then secured a chain to the collar around his neck. He leaned in close. "If you're really lucky," he said in a hoarse whisper, "Master Xavier is going to give you a choice to serve him."

"I'm not gay, you mother-fucking queer." He jerked against his restraints.

"Right, but girls don't do it for you." Chad smirked. "Your cock is half hard right now thinking about getting fucked by me. It's up to you. Master Xavier is a fair man. You choose to serve him, and that will be the first and last time you'll ever be forced against your will. Your other choice is much less appealing." Chad moved to the next man in line.

The man stilled and glared at Chad. "What the fuck does that mean?"

"Only that some choices are worse than others." Chad pointed to Z. "Instead of saving you, Master Xavier can leave you with him."

The man coughed. "What about these two."

Chad thumped the two smaller men on their chests. "These guys aren't gay. Master Xavier has no interest in them. Mr. Chambers will buy them."

The middle man struggled in his bonds. He gave a strangled gasp. "What are they going to do to us?"

Chad shook his head. "You're being sold as a sex slave. Figure it out." He turned around and went to the middle of the room where Bay pulled a woman off the chain and led her toward one of the men seated on the couch.

"Who the fuck are these men?" The muscular man turned toward me.

"How the hell do I know?" I looked at him and shrugged. Really? What did I know? It had been weeks since my kidnapping and I still had little idea about who X was, or the four men who were my constant guards. Except I did know something. X may be involved in the active sale of slaves, but there was more. I needed to understand what was going on.

Bay and Chad led woman by woman off the chain and placed them in front of each of the men sitting on the couches. I had a fair idea what was in store. I squeezed my eyes shut, not wanting to watch the abuse of others. My heart went out to those poor girls. I'd been sold, abducted, and transported against my will. I was an unwilling prisoner, but the longer I stayed, the more willing I became. I knew what they were going through and felt like the worst hypocrite. I had become a willing participant in my enslavement. They had not, although they didn't have X. By the way, where was he? I didn't see him among the men.

CHAPTER EIGHTEEN_

BAY CAME TO COLLECT ME. I TUNED OUT THE SOUNDS COMING from the couches. I would never get the image of my father and what he did to that poor girl out of my head. As Bay attached my wrists to my collar, Z called out.

"Where are you taking her?"

"She's to be returned to her room, Mr. Carson." Bay said. "Master Xavier's orders."

"And where is Xavier?"

"My apologies, Mr. Carson, but he only gave instructions regarding his slave."

"Will he be returning?"

"I would assume so. Once I lock his slave inside her room, I will find out."

"No hurry, as long as the food, drink and slaves keep coming, it's all good."

"Of course, Mr. Carson. I will return presently."

Bay cut me a sharp look, perhaps reminding me to keep my silence. I couldn't get out of that room fast enough with its noxious flesh slapping on flesh and slurping sounds. The door closed behind us and took the offensive noise with it.

"Come," Bay said, "we don't have much time. Master Xavier is waiting in the library."

"But you told Z…"

"I don't serve that scum. Now, we must hurry."

The maze of endless white walls had my head spinning, but Bay new exactly where he was going. I wished I had the freedom to explore this place and gain my bearings. A part of me even wanted to stop and admire the many priceless works of art, or sit in any one of the many interior courtyards and whittle away the hours of the day absorbed in a good book. When had my desire for freedom left me? Was the blanket of complacency settling over me? Because I couldn't *want* to stay here. Could I?

We turned a corner and I found myself in the main entry foyer. To my right, X waited for me in his study. Bay gestured for me to go ahead, but I paused in front of the massive doors.

"What does he want?"

"You," Bay said. "Go, little one. Don't keep Master Xavier waiting."

"Why do you serve him?" Unlike me, Bay, and the others, didn't wear collars around their necks or slave bracelets around their wrists. There was no sign of a GPS tracker attached to their ankles either.

"I owe him a great debt and I give my service freely. Master Xavier is a noble man."

"Who owns slaves."

"Who owns slaves," Bay said with a nod, "but not as you think."

"Bay!" X's cutting voice snapped Bay's head up.

"Master Xavier," Bay said, bowing his head and bending at the waist. "Forgive me."

"You were not instructed to engage in conversation with my slave."

"Yes, Master Xavier."

"You will record the infraction and we will deal with it later."

"Yes, Master Xavier."

"Now go. Return to the lounge. Ben and Mel need your support."

Without another word, Bay turned on his heels and rushed out of the foyer.

X held the door to the library and ushered me inside. "Come Raven. It's time we had a talk."

I found myself speechless but I hurried inside, jumping at his command. X held an unquestionable power over me. His dominating presence crawled inside me and took root deep inside. I couldn't ignore the power he held over me, or how I was growing to crave it. Power was an essential part of him, one which left many questions swirling in my head. Once inside the library, I came to a stop, uncertain where to stand or whether to sit in one of the wing backed chairs.

X closed the door behind me and turned the lock. "I don't want us interrupted and we don't have much time. My absence will be tolerated for only so long." He gestured to a chair. "Sit."

Without thinking too much about the command, I took a seat and curled my legs beneath me.

"Ben gave me an update. He said you did not use the thumb drive."

"Z would have known someone tried to tamper with his computer."

"You didn't have to help me."

"Did I have a choice?"

"You always have a choice, but for what it's worth, thank you."

Where did that come from? A thank you? X wasn't a man to show gratitude, but it felt sincere. I felt as if we were actually working toward the same goal. When did we start working as a team. I couldn't wrap my head around this.

Instead, I bowed my head and mumbled. "You're welcome."

"You must have questions."

"I have tons."

He held up a hand, forestalling the rest of what I had to say.

"First, know that nothing changes between us."

"But…"

"Nothing. Despite what I'm about to tell you, our arrangement continues."

"Our arrangement? You talk about kidnapping me and keeping me against my will as if it's some social arrangement. It's anything but that."

He cocked his head. "I speak of a truth between us; mutual needs met in our truest selves. You know this. You feel it, as I do."

"Truth?" I spat. "In what fucked up world is this thing between us the truth?"

He rushed me, moving too fast for me to follow. In the blink of an eye, I found myself draped over his knee and the thin fabric shredded with a single yank. His hand slammed down on my ass, the deafening *Smack!* echoed in the spacious library. I screamed and kicked while he held me down.

"Count, slave," he commanded between strikes. "Or don't." *Smack!* "It's up to you, but the count doesn't begin until you do." *Smack!*

Pain seared my flesh, then burned a second later. I cried out, begged him to stop, and tried to get free. He held me in an iron grip and struck me three more times before my brain caught up.

I never threaten. His words came back to me.

This was going to end only one way. I had to do as he said.

Smack!

"One," I cried out.

Smack!

"Two!" I howled against the pain. He hit both cheeks in rapid succession. "Three. Four." I could barely breathe.

"What rule did you break?"

The sternness of his tone lit a fuse in me, one which spiraled me into a mindless state. I couldn't breathe. I couldn't think. Pain filled my world. My skin felt like it was on fire. It burned and I could feel it beginning to swell. I felt something else as well, a growing ache inside of me.

Smack!

He paused, waiting for something, then struck me again.

"Six!" I screamed.

"No slave, we begin again at one. I was very clear you were to count each strike."

No. No. No!

But I knew there would be no arguing with X. He set his expectations and held to them with rigid control. He hit me again and I dutifully counted. I counted to ten, thinking he would stop there, and then sobbed as the number passed twenty.

My ass would be bruised. Tears streaked down my face and my nose ran. I was a blubbering idiot, but I counted. It wasn't until we rounded on twenty-five that I finally gave in. I stopped fighting and collapsed over his knee. My body absorbed the strikes and soaked up the pain. There was no escaping this.

Smack!

"Twenty-five."

I barely got the words out through my sobs. I was a complete mess, drowning in pain, but that ache stirred in my belly. Something I didn't want to admit. X lifted me off his lap and deposited me on the floor. I collapsed and curled in on myself.

"Never doubt my willingness to assert my authority. That is a binding truth between us and my promise to you."

I looked up at him, then shut my eyes when his lustful gaze fell on me. His erection tented his trousers, but instead of coming at me, he adjusted himself and sat down. Leaning forward, he propped his elbows on his knees and bowed his head into his hands.

"Why do you do this to me?" I couldn't help but choke back my sobs, and I didn't know if my question would be allowed. I wasn't prepared for the answer.

"Because this is what we both need."

"You're wrong."

"Raven," he said with a sniff, "I can smell you from here. Tell me, are you wet for me? Are you aching for more?"

I could lie, but he spoke the truth. My entire body burned for more of his touch and I didn't understand any of it.

"I asked a question."

"You already know the answer." I looked up but I couldn't hold his gaze.

"I do."

"You're cruel."

"I can make that ache go away. All you have to do is ask."

"No!"

I wouldn't ask. I wouldn't cave to his demands, but neither could I deny the throbbing ache between my legs. Arousal coiled in my belly, not because of the pain, but rather because of something much more potent. His authority drew me like a moth to the flame and I drank in his darkness, filling up an emptiness inside of me. I wasn't going to ask, but it horrified me to know that someday soon, I would beg.

"Yin and Yang, Raven. Light and Dark. Pleasure and Pain. Dominance and Submission. You feed my darkest desires as I nourish yours. We're opposite sides of the coin. You can refuse to admit what is plain to see, but you're hanging on by a thread. You want what's brewing between us, what's been growing from our very first encounter. You need my dominance as surely as I desire your surrender."

"You're wrong."

He stared at the juncture between my legs. "Do you want me to spread you wide and show you exactly how right I am?"

"No." I wanted to curl in on myself and disappear.

He tilted his head back and ran his fingers through his hair. "You're lucky, you know that?"

"How is any of this lucky?"

His glare caught me off guard. "Because, if I didn't have to return to conduct business with your father, I would take what I wanted rather than wait for you to ask."

"What's keeping you?" I tried to screech my indignation, but my words came out a weak whimper.

"Because, I'm not that kind of man."

"Aren't you?"

"I get off on dominating you, taking control, exercising my authority, and yes, in giving pain, but I don't rape the innocent."

I met the hardness of his gaze and saw a softening there. His shoulders slumped and he wiped his hands on his knees.

"Unfortunately, this exchange, while necessary, has taken too much time. I need to know what you did to your father's laptop and how I can access it."

I pushed on the floor and curled my knees beneath me. It didn't escape my notice that I was kneeling before him, or how right that seemed in my head. Blinking away my tears, I took a long hard look at X and took a leap of faith.

"I wrote what's called a back door. It's untraceable. Once Z logs in and goes on line, you'll be able to track everything he does."

"I'll have full access?"

"Limited, but you'll have the most important parts."

"What is that? I need access to his business files."

"You'll have access to his keystrokes."

"How does that help me?"

"Because you'll get all his account information and pass-words. My father backs everything up to a secure central server. I've given you the keys to that."

"You truly despise your father."

"Yes. Now isn't that worth my freedom?"

X's eyes pinched together. "Your freedom is not on the table, Raven. Get that out of your head. I have no intention of ever letting you go."

"But..."

How could he deny me when I'd handed everything over to him? I didn't tell X everything. Once he accessed Z's infor-mation, another door would open. One which granted me access into everything X controlled. I wasn't done fighting. I never would be.

"No buts. I have spoken and this is the last we'll speak on this matter. Now, you have yet to answer my first question."

I didn't remember his question and stared blankly at him.

X bent down and placed a finger beneath my chin. "You were punished for swearing, for violating my rules. This is the foundation which defines everything. You choose, Raven. You choose your path. Punishments are a part of your world now, but only you choose how much they intrude on your life. In time, I'll show you another side of pain, the kind of pain that turns into the most exquisite pleasure."

"You're crazy."

"Am I? You can't deny it, and when you accept this part of yourself, you'll finally understand."

"Never."

He gave a short laugh. "Never say never, Raven."

And with that, he left me in the library. It took ten minutes before I realized I'd been left alone. The door to the library stood open. The front door, and freedom, was only steps away.

CHAPTER NINETEEN_

It took everything within me not to rush that front door. It called to me, as if I could sneak out of the library, slip out the front door, and race to freedom.

If only it were that easy.

The anklet defined my captivity as much, or more, than the collar around my neck and the steel encircling my wrists.

That didn't mean I didn't make good use of my time, or the opportunity facing me. It was a test. X and I knew this. In the weeks since coming here, I'd never been left alone. I understood something was happening with my father, a transaction involving slaves, but there was more at stake. Ben and Mel played the roles of wealthy businessmen setting up a Master's paradise full of obedient slaves, men and women who were ruthlessly broken. But I knew Ben and Mel, or thought I did. With the exception of my kidnapping, they'd been nothing but kind to me.

I didn't know how much time I had, not that it mattered. I would pass this test, but I would also work toward freedom. The backdoor I implanted on Z's computer wouldn't activate until he connected to the internet. X would need a key to access the vulnerability I created, and I had a point to prove. X spoke of choices and having control over what happened to me. He needed to know I could be dangerous and that he didn't hold all the cards.

A quick search of the desk and I located a laptop. I didn't know if it was his, personal or business, but it didn't matter. Like my father, X was paranoid and had layers of security protecting his assets. It took less than ten minutes to crack his system and set up the key he would need. I considered inserting the same code into his operating system as I had on my father's but understood the depths of the test X subjected me too. I was under no illusions I wasn't being watched.

Once I was satisfied X had what he needed to take Z down, I closed out the laptop and took a stroll around the library. I loved books. It was hard to find a real book anymore. With the advent of e-readers, few people collected books. X had all manner of books, from true antiques to modern bestsellers. He preferred mystery thrillers and I gave an approving nod to his reading choices. I wanted to spend more time here, exploring, reading, and escaping into other worlds, but I had more to do.

I wasn't sure how much time had passed. It seemed well over an hour, but there was still no signs of my guards and no movement outside the library. A glance at my ankle and I decided to test X while we were at this game. Leaving the library felt like I was breaking some unspoken rule, but X had left no instructions as to what I could and couldn't do. I stepped lightly and peeked into the foyer. It sat empty. I didn't think twice when I went for the door.

The strap around my ankle didn't have anything that looked like it would give a shock, but I had no illusions it could track me around the globe. I still pressed forward with my plan. X was testing me, but I tested him as well. How far would he let me get? How far could I go and prove to him that I wasn't a flight risk?

The door leading outside opened. No lock held me back, but I didn't need locks to keep me imprisoned. It had been weeks since I'd been outside. Most of my time had been spent in my room, my guards watching my every move while taking bets on how long it would take for me to crack the cypher lock on my door. I wondered what bets they had on me now? I stepped outside.

Late afternoon, the sun dipped toward the horizon, and I took note of my surroundings, building a mental map. One day, I would need it to escape. A long driveway headed away from the estate, arrowing due west. Tropical foliage lined the drive, a mixture of palm trees, hibiscus, and bougainvillea. The floral perfumes permeated the air, and I couldn't help but take a deep breath. I spread my arms wide, splayed my fingers, and luxuriated in the gentleness of the breeze tickling my skin.

X built his home in paradise and I never wanted to leave. I grew up in a palatial monstrosity surrounded by pine forests and hemmed in by the jagged peaks of the neighboring mountains. It had always felt cold and unyielding. X's estate felt rich, vibrant, and welcoming. The faintest scent of the ocean tickled my senses. I closed my eyes and tried to soak it all in.

My skin warmed with the fading rays of the sun as I stepped across the large porch and took a seat at the top of the steps leading down to the pebble drive. I pulled my knees against my chest and wrapped my arms around tight.

"It's beautiful out here, isn't it?" X's deep, cultured voice spoke from behind me.

His presence didn't surprise me. I'd been expecting someone. It had been a toss up between Chad and Bay, or him. I should be surprised he took time out of his business dealings to attend to me. I twisted around, craning my neck, and caught the magnificence of the man who called himself my Master. A tiny flutter tickled my stomach; there was simply something captivating about this man. It was time to see who passed the test.

"It's beyond beautiful," I said. "It's gorgeous."

He glanced down the long drive, took a look at the

tracking device around my ankle, and then came to sit beside me.

"You didn't run."

"I didn't think it was an option."

"It's not."

"It seemed silly to try, not when I know you would find me and what will happen afterwards."

"True." He stretched his long legs on the steps and leaned back on his elbows, placing himself beneath me. I had to look down on him, and his chisel features nearly stole my breath. I struggled to remain calm and unaffected. In this I failed miserably.

"Would it be possible to allow me outside from time to time?"

"Privilege must be earned," he said with a tightening around his eyes. "You have yet to prove yourself to me."

"I would have thought I earned quite a bit of trust and privilege."

"It's a start, but you are out here without permission."

"You left me alone and I don't remember any orders that I stay put."

"And if I had given that command?"

"I would still be in the library."

He gave a soft laugh. "Do you really expect me to believe that? When you're sitting on the steps contemplating escape?"

"I'm sitting. I'm not running."

"But you are thinking about escape."

"I was, but I was also admiring your home. It's very different from where I grew up."

"How so?"

"It's warm, inviting..."

"Do you see yourself living here, my sweet Raven?"

I turned away from him. The smoldering desire in his eyes drew me too far, made me want things I shouldn't, and promised a world I could escape into.

"I don't know."

"It will come, with time."

I didn't think so, but I didn't want to discuss it further.

"By the way," I said, changing topics, "I set up your laptop."

"Is that all you did? Did you insert any code I should be worried about?"

I gave a deep sigh. This felt good, a civil conversation between us. I enjoyed talking to X rather than constantly walking on eggshells around him.

"The thought crossed my mind."

"That's not really an answer, or are you not answering one of my questions on purpose. Is the fire burning inside of you to feel my punishment again that strong?"

My insides clenched, not with fear, but rather with something much more damaging. It spoke to a truth I wasn't ready to accept. I pressed my thighs together, trying to soothe the needy ache brought on by his words. He brushed a lock of hair over my shoulder and trailed his fingers down my back.

"I decided against it," I said, making sure to answer his question.

"Tell me what you're feeling," he said with a growl.

The low sound rolled through me, stirring up the embers inside of me and fanning them to life. No way in hell was I telling him that.

"I don't want to be punished."

"Perhaps, but there is something you do want instead? Someday soon, you'll embrace this thing between us. And spankings can be used for fun. You don't have to break my rules to get what you need."

"We don't have a thing and I want nothing to do with punishments or spankings. Didn't anyone ever tell you that you shouldn't hit women?"

"First off, I don't hit women for sport. I do it for mutual pleasure."

"But that's not true." I shifted away from him, stunned by his comment. "I haven't asked for any of this."

"That is where you're wrong. Your body asks with every breath. Your eyes beg each time you look at me. Your lips whisper the truth with every kiss I give you. You need exactly what I give, and more. I've never experienced the depth of connection we share. You're not a victim, and soon you'll be a willing participant, begging for more."

My head whipped around at that comment and I caught

the smugness of his expression. A small gap of space separated us, and yet I felt him all around me, breathed him in, and sank beneath the overwhelming presence of him.

"It's true, and we will share more truths between us. This is one more I think you should know. I haven't had a slave in years."

"What about Chad and Bay and..."

"Let me rephrase. I haven't had a female slave in years."

"Just men?"

He gave a smirk. "Yes, just men, but not how you're thinking. There is no sexual relationship between me and my male slaves."

"I don't understand the power you have over them, or why they allow it."

"They allow it because they've embraced the truth within them. My slaves desire guidance. They thrive in the control they give surrendering to me. And the authority I wield over their lives meets their deepest needs."

"So, you didn't force any of them like you did me?"

"Oh, some were forced. Those who needed a demonstration of my ability to master them, required that display, but most were not."

"That's not what I want. I simply want to go home."

He bristled beside me, then leaned back and closed his eyes against the sun. He took several deep breaths before responding. When he did, the tone of his voice changed. We were no longer having a simple conversation. Master Xavier had returned.

"You're never leaving, Raven. I'm your beginning and your end. I'm your Master and you'll respect my position and the authority I hold over you. You don't believe the truth of your new status in life, but you will."

"That's never going to happen," I said in a whimper.

"Never say never. You haven't tasted my whip."

I gave a shudder at the promise laced in his words. He touched the bracelet with the dolphin. It sparkled in the fading light. I glanced at the freedom it promised and groaned. I shouldn't want it as much as I did because it meant I would be less of a prisoner. I didn't want to accept this place, but taking that bracelet felt like giving tacit approval to my kidnapping.

"I intended to give this to you, a reward for your assistance today." From his tone, this would no longer be happening. What had I done wrong?

"But you're not going to," I said with more disappointment than I expected. "Why doesn't that surprise me?"

"Rewards are earned, but they can be taken away. You earned this today, but lost it when you denigrated my name. You were told to never refer to me as you do your father."

"I didn't..."

"You called me X, whittling my name down to a single letter as you've done to him. I know why you do it, but it stops now. From here on out you'll call me Master each time you speak, until it's ingrained in your head and becomes second nature."

"I'm sorry. I didn't mean to..."

"I have no doubt it slipped out, but all that tells me is that is how you think of me in your head. A few days of having to say Master each time you speak will take care of that. You'll eat, breathe, sleep, and dream of me. And each time you fail to give the appropriate address, you'll earn five strikes of my hand. And you know what happens when I punish you."

He gets hard, and I get wet. I swallowed against the thickness in my throat.

"I'm sorry, I didn't mean it." I needed to be more careful.

He gave me a long, hard stare and I wrapped my arms tight around my legs bringing my knees to my chin.

"I didn't mean it...*Master*." I made sure to emphasize his title. A tiny jolt of pleasure sparked deep within me, and I hated that less than I should.

"Much better." He stood and offered me a hand. "Come, it's nearly time for dinner. You have several punishments waiting for you tonight. We have just enough time to dispense one before dinner."

I'd lost track of what punishments I'd earned. It seemed the simple act of breathing brought on one of X's punishments. I held back my anger. It didn't matter what I called him out loud, he couldn't take away how I referred to him inside my head. Z hadn't and X wouldn't either. What I couldn't ignore was the heat in his eyes or the response that stirred in me.

CHAPTER TWENTY_

X LED ME BACK TO THE LIBRARY AND I FOLLOWED WITH trepidation and a shaky anticipation. My body did strange things around him. It hummed and vibrated, heated and glowed; it betrayed me with malicious intent because it wanted everything X promised with an insatiable hunger.

I thought my punishment would be delivered immediately and steeled myself against what would surely follow. Instead, X lifted a white sundress off the back of a chair and thrust it at me.

"Get dressed."

"You're giving me real clothes?"

I didn't immediately take it and regretted this when he yanked the dress away. The scowl on his face deepened and his gaze heated with lust.

"I've demonstrated what needed to be seen. There's no

reason for you not to be clothed. Think what you will of me, Raven, but I have no desire for other men to see you naked. Some things needed to play out, proof given of your compliance and my control."

"You used me." How easily I played into his hands.

His eyes hardened. "As is my right. You serve me in all things." He crooked a finger at me as he sat down on the chair. "Come."

I clasped my hands in front of me, not trusting the smoldering anger swirling in his expression, but I didn't dare disobey. I stepped in front of him. He shook his head.

"Closer."

I gulped and took a step closer. He might be fully dressed, but I had no protection against this man. I glanced at the dress, but he caught the direction of my gaze and set the dress down behind him.

"Closer." The tone of his voice lowered, turned sultry and intoxicating, but hardness lurked there as well.

I took a step closer until our knees nearly touched. He reached out and took my wrist with firm possession, but he didn't tug or pull. Instead, he looked up at me with fire in his eyes.

"You have a choice. Accept your punishment with grace, or resist and add five strikes to the ten you've earned."

"What?" I took a step back, but his grip on my wrist tightened, holding me in place.

"Are you that eager for punishment my dear Raven? That makes fifteen."

I reeled with his pronouncement. Fifteen? How had I racked up fifteen strikes? And then it hit me. My eyes widened.

"I see you've remembered. Understand the truth of your new life and understand me. I don't threaten. I don't issue empty promises. Your rules are clear. The punishment for failing to meet them will always be stated clearly and swiftly delivered. These are the ties that bind us. The expectations are as clear as our roles. Now, you have fifteen strikes. You can choose to bend over my knee, or I can force you into place. The choice is entirely yours, as is the price."

Another five strikes!

I berated myself for forgetting his stupid rule. It shouldn't be that hard to say Master, but to say it was to acknowledge a truth I couldn't face. I'd foolishly thought it wouldn't matter, but having to call him Master each time I spoke turned something inside me. I didn't like his choices, but the thought of another five strikes wasn't something I could stomach. He wouldn't be easy on me. He never had been. That had been demonstrated time and time again, and I knew exactly what delivering fifteen strikes would do to him. I squeezed my eyes shut as I closed the distance between us and stepped to the side of his legs. That was where I stopped.

The times before, he'd surprised me, lifting and spinning me until I landed in his lap, but how did I do that now? I glanced at him and he patted his lap. A glance revealed his growing arousal. I was not getting out of this unscathed.

Without any of the grace I might possess, I awkwardly positioned myself over his lap. X placed a hand over my shoulder blades, and I knew exactly why he did that. Once the blows started, there would be no way I could hold still.

"Do I need to secure your hands? Or will you keep them out of the way? A word of warning, you'll find it even more painful if I strike your hands."

Everything about this was going to be excessively painful. I remembered the other times he'd spanked me, the way I squirmed and fought to get free of the agonizing burn. Both times, he had kept control of my wrists, binding them at my lower back while using his elbow to form a brace against the bucking of my body. I licked my lips and swallowed nervously because I didn't want to ask for my hands to be bound. I folded my arms beneath my breasts and gripped my elbows. Only my shoulders and head hung free. No matter how bad it got, I wouldn't ask for his help.

"No...Master." I ground out the title he forced me to use. There was no way I would earn more strikes, and I made a mental note to remember to use the title from here on out. No matter how hard that might be.

He gave no warning. It was like he purposefully caught me off guard. The first strike fell hard and fast, cracking against my skin and stealing my breath. I remembered to count.

"One!"

He ran his hand over my aching skin, soothing the burn.

"Are you forgetting something?"

Amusement tinged his words and I realized my mistake too late. It shouldn't be this hard.

"One, Master!"

"Oh no, my sweet Raven. We begin again, and will continue to return to the beginning if you fail to address me properly. This is the price of disrespect. You'll call me Master until you dream it in your sleep, until you feel it in the deepest parts of your soul, until it's inseparable from your thoughts. Do you understand?"

Tears leaked from my eyes and I sniffed. Such a simple yet effective punishment, he had me exactly where he wanted me.

"Yes, Master."

"Good. Now, let's begin again."

Twenty strikes later, I sobbed at X's feet. My entire backside burned. X spared no mercy and added five strikes for my failure to call him Master. The word came easily to me now. Twenty times, I said Master, counting through and past fifteen. He didn't give me a pass for forgetting to use the word on that first count. X would never give leniency. I stared up at him, trembling before him as I sat on my knees. He handed me the white dress.

"Put this on."

I glanced at the tenting of his trousers and he looked to his lap.

"Tell me what's going through your mind," he commanded.

I yanked my attention from his lap and met the tenacity of his gaze. What to say to him? I began with the truth.

"You're not an easy man, Master." The word spilled easily from my lips.

"No, but that is what you need."

"Me? I don't want this. You keep saying I do, but..." I squirmed at his feet, trying and failing to find a comfortable position. "I don't want to be forced and punished and devalued and..."

"Devalued? Is that what you think?"

"I'm your slave, Master. There is nothing more degrading than this."

"Degrading and devalued are two completely different things. You're priceless, and my most treasured possession."

"But, I'm not a thing, Master. I'm a person."

"You're right."

"But you can set me free, Master. You don't have to do this."

"I'll never set you free."

"Why?" I couldn't help the sob from escaping me.

"Because I don't want to. There's a war being fought within you, Raven, and it's a battle only you can wage. You must fight before you can surrender to the inevitable."

"I don't understand." I swiped at my cheeks, and then quickly remembered to add the name I must. "Master."

He leaned down and scooped me up. I found myself cradled in his arms. I couldn't help but curl against him, tucking my head beneath his chin. My backside throbbed with the spanking, ferocious and intense, but it barely hid another, more needy, pulsation.

X wiped away my tears and then tilted my chin up. Lust burned in his eyes, barely held back in check by his restraint. He ran the pad of his finger across my lips. I parted for him. That small action unleashed the wildness trapped within him. X bent down, capturing my lips with his. He forced my lips wider and invaded my mouth with his tongue. Sweeping inside, the dark, overwhelming taste of him sent my body flying. I clutched at his neck and twined my fingers in his hair.

Everything shifted and I found myself carried across the library. With one sweep of his arm, he cleared the desk and gently laid me down. With his pupils blown out by his lust, a ferocious energy bunched in his body. He was like a beast on the prowl, waiting for the moment to pounce. He released me and I scooted back, oblivious to my pain. My entire focus centered on X as he undid his belt and unzipped his fly. He freed his cock and held it in his fist.

My entire body ached for him, and I no longer cared to fight the inevitable. Not with the very air crackling between us. He said nothing, but his gaze drilled into me. The skin over his knuckles turned white where he gripped his shaft, a stark contrast to the red and engorged velvety skin of his cock.

I leaned back on my elbows, knees drawn up as a serenity overcame me. Then ever so slowly, with our gazes locked in the fiercest of battles, I gave him everything he craved. His eyes widened as I let my knees fall to the side, giving him an unrestricted access to my most private parts.

"Raven..." His voice came out a harsh whisper. "I won't be able to stop. Don't do this..."

I lifted off my elbows and lay back with my hands by my side, a sacrificial offering of flesh and surrendering of my will. He stepped forward and yanked my hips to the edge of the table, lifted my legs and wrapped them around his hips.

"If you don't say no, now... Fuck, Raven, tell me this is what you want."

I shook my head, letting tears fall. He'd been right about everything, a battle raged in my head. Heart, mind, body and soul, I was at war, but I couldn't ask. I wouldn't. I forced myself to look at X, truly look at this man who enraptured and enraged me at the same time.

"Don't make me ask for it. Just take what you need." That was all I could give him.

Whatever was happening between us was an inevitability I couldn't escape, and I no longer possessed the strength to fight. X released my legs and stepped back, surprising me. He shook his head and tossed the white dress over my belly.

"I don't take what isn't freely offered. I won't become the monster you think I am, but I will be the Master you need, even if that means stepping away from this. This is not over, Raven. It's barely even begun."

He tucked his erection back into his pants, turned, and left me trembling. The fall of his steps was all I heard as he left the library. This time, he shut the door behind him, an unspoken command that I wasn't allowed to leave. I curled in on myself, sobbed, and examined the ruin of my thoughts. I'd lost the battle, only it wasn't the one I thought I'd been fighting, and I couldn't deny an inescapable truth.

I wanted Xavier.

CHAPTER TWENTY-ONE_

X LEFT ME IN THE LIBRARY FOR HOURS. MY STOMACH RUMBLED, telling me the dinner hour had come and gone. A glance at the closed door kept me in place. Not once did I venture out of the library. I didn't want the temptation it would bring. If I did leave, there would be no stopping me from attempting escape. That long driveway teased me with the promise of freedom, but I understood one thing about X. He didn't leave anything to chance. I might have a GPS strapped around my ankle, but I was certain it wasn't my greatest barrier to fleeing this place. That didn't stop me from examining the anklet, though. I was obsessed with it.

I'd had plenty of time to look at it. I hadn't been idle during the time spent in my room. I never examined it in front of Bay, Chad, Ben, or Mel, but every shower brought another opportunity to figure out how to defeat it. Unlike the keypad at the door, this was one puzzle I wouldn't be solving anytime soon. If I cut the strap, an alarm would sound. No doubt, a signal would be sent to whomever monitored the device. X and my guards would be on me in an instant. I also couldn't run with it still attached. I had no illusions of a perimeter which monitored my whereabouts. Break the perimeter and the anklet would not only alarm but send my location, not to mention the punishment from X which would follow.

I couldn't cut it.

I couldn't run.

I had been neutralized.

Which left me looking for alternate escape. After combing the library, and the plentiful offering of books, I turned my attention to his laptop. I curled up in one of the chairs and cradled it in my lap.

The first thing I did was check the program to track my father's activities. His computer wouldn't ping until he connected to the internet, so I expected nothing. To my surprise, the code had been activated.

The backdoor I installed gave me access to everything on Z's computer and more. I was a virtual ghost in his machine. I hadn't mentioned that to X, keeping that gem to myself. One question burned at the forefront of my mind and I used my time to find answers. Over an hour later, all I had left were more questions.

Beneath the layers of shell companies and holdings, I

uncovered a shadow organization which turned my stomach. The business of trading human flesh brought millions into my father's accounts. He had his fingers involved in every aspect of illicit human trafficking. My stomach roiled with the depths of his depravation. From stealing orphans from foster homes in the United States, to sweeps of the homeless in Central America, my father filled the orders of those wealthy enough to purchase humans for any number of different reasons. One name kept reappearing and I wondered who John Snowden might be. He and my father seemed to have extensive business dealings.

Not all of the hapless victims became sex slaves and it was this which sent chills down my spine. An entire segment of his operation dealt in the trafficking of young boys meant specifically to live or die in illegal death matches organized across the globe. Thoughts of what those poor boys endured nearly had me emptying the contents of my stomach.

Each slave came with a bio stating where they'd been taken from, a list of their characteristics, and the potential roles they might fill. Prettier boys were slated for the sex trade. Those who were scrawny, and those who were filling out, went to the fight rings. They pitted the weak against the strong in an ugly contest of survival.

Never in my life would I have believed such brutality existed, although I didn't know why I shouldn't be surprised. Like cock fights and dog fighting, there were too many people who took sport in the misery of others. Why not boys fighting for their lives?

I slammed the lid down on the laptop and swiped at my cheeks. It seemed all I ever did since coming here was cry. The door to the library opened and I looked up. X entered, his discerning gaze looked to the laptop and then to my tear-streaked cheeks.

"Raven? Are you okay?"

I shoved the laptop away from me as X closed the door behind him. He approached me cautiously as anger surged inside of me. I'd almost given myself to this man. Hell, there was no *almost* about it. I'd willingly spread my legs for a monster.

X's rules put me in an untenable position. His questions had to be answered, and if I spoke to him, I now had to call him Master or accept punishment. If I didn't answer, my fate would be the same. With no good choice, I chose the direct approach.

"How long have you been trading slaves, Master?" I crossed my arms over my chest, trying for defiance, but coming far short of my goal. My entire body shivered and goosebumps prickled on my skin.

He glanced at the laptop and pulled a chair to the opposite side of the desk. I appreciated having something between us, but understood there was nothing which could keep X away from me if he decided he would have me.

"I'll answer your questions, but first I have some of my own. Do you mind?"

"Do I have a choice?" I gritted my teeth and closed my eyes, then added the formal address. "Master."

"You always have a choice, but in this, I need a few questions answered first."

"Of course, Master. We always do things your way. Why should this be any different?"

"You're angry." Astute in all things, it didn't take a rocket scientist to read my mood.

"I'm disgusted...Master, and angry." I was angry at myself, not him.

He reached across the desk and pulled the laptop to him. "Why are you disgusted?"

I pointed to the laptop. "Never leave me alone with a computer when I'm bored. I tend to dig stuff up."

"I take it your anger has something to do with this?" He tapped the laptop case and continued, not waiting for me to answer. "I don't think it's too much of a leap to assume you did some digging."

"I did...Master." I injected venom into the word now, not caring about the consequences. Did it really matter? He could claim disrespect whenever he chose and punish me for it as he pleased.

His long fingers tapped the laptop and silence descended between us. I shifted in my seat and bit my lower lip.

"Raven," he finally said, "let's dispense with titles for a moment."

"Fine by me." I hated having to call him Master.

"Maintain a respectful tone. You won't be warned again."

"Does it matter?"

"You know the answer to that."

Yes, I did. Nothing had changed between us. He was still the Master, and I the lowly slave. I ripped my attention from him and tried looking anywhere else, but I failed. His magnetism pulled me back and some of my anger crumbled with the overwhelming power pouring off him.

"Now," he continued, "what did you find?"

"As if you don't know."

"I actually don't. Despite what you think, I can't read minds."

"You said you're not a monster and yet that's exactly what you are."

"You don't know what I do."

I pointed to the laptop. "You're in business with my father, and my father is in business..." My voice cracked, but I refused to break down in tears. From somewhere deep inside of me, I found the strength to continue.

"What about your father?"

"He's at the center of it all: sex slave trafficking and worse. Innocent boys are dying..."

X clenched his fist and sucked in a breath. "I know."

"Of course you know." I wanted to leap across the desk

and strangle him. I wanted to stab him in the heart and watch his life bleed out on the floor. I wanted to scream and rage, and...I just wanted to curl into a ball and pretend none of this existed.

"You haven't asked me the most important question."

I really hadn't asked any questions. At least, not the ones I wanted.

"I'm disappointed." His eyes pinched and he leaned back, returning my anger with exquisite patience. "I thought you were a better judge of character. You haven't asked why I had you access your father's laptop."

"To spy on him." My face heated with indignation. "I presume it's a power grab. You're trying to take over his slave empire."

"Be very careful of assumptions, Raven. They're never what you think."

I wanted to hate X. I needed to hate him because I'd fallen too far under his spell.

"How about we talk about what you saw." He flipped open the laptop and turned it toward me.

I'd already closed out of everything. Nothing but a black screen faced me.

"I don't want to talk about it."

"Yes, you do." He pushed the laptop toward me. "Tell me, did you find his business associate?"

"You mean John Snowden?" That man gave me full body shudders. For that matter, my father did the same. The depth of their depravity wasn't something my mind could process.

"You found Snowden?" X leaned forward, his entire body wound tight with tension. "Did you find anything that says where he might be?"

"What, so you can meet with him and conduct your *business?*" I sprung to my feet and pointed an accusing finger at X. "I'm not going to be a part of that." I grabbed for the computer, intent on shutting down my little backdoor into my father's illicit dealings, but X was faster than me. He was always faster, stronger, and more cunning than me.

"Give that back to me," I screeched.

"Sit down, Raven, before I lose my patience and turn you over my knee."

I laughed in his face. "Go ahead. Without the right protocols, you'll trip the self-destruct code I placed."

His expression darkened. "What did you do?"

"You didn't think you could lead me to my father's chambers, force me to write code on his laptop and not leave an insurance policy behind?"

X might be stronger and faster than me, but I had outsmarted him in this. He surprised me by not reacting. Instead, he pulled out a cellphone and dialed a number.

X paused, waiting for whomever was on the other end.

"Forest?"

Was *forest* some sort of code word? X didn't try to hide his conversation and I couldn't help but listen to every word he said. I strained to hear the other voice, but my efforts were in vain. I couldn't make out anything.

"We have access, but Raven wrote in a self-destruct code." Anger set X's eyes ablaze, retribution would soon follow. In that, I had faith. I wouldn't come out of this unscathed.

"Yes. I have it. Do you want me to—" X paused, listening. "Okay. I'll leave it."

I leaned forward, intent on hearing the other half of the conversation, but failed.

"No," X said. "Don't come. Her father is here. You need to be invisible in this, but Forest..." X glanced at me, a look of admiration in his expression. "She found Snowden. Just like we thought, Carson is working with him. What do you want me to do?"

A long pause followed. I strained to overhear, but all I heard was a deep bass rumble through the speaker. X listened. Every word brought tension coiling in his body. He glanced at me and gripped the phone.

"No. Raven isn't leaving the island."

Well, that answered one of my most pressing questions. If X's estate was on an island, there really was no place for me to run. I'd have to find a boat to take me away. Certainly, there was no way I would be escaping in a plane.

"You know the answer to that. Whatever happens, Raven is mine." X glanced at me again. "I can send it via courier."

More time passed as the other man spoke.

"A day or two at most," X answered. "My business with

Carson should be concluded tonight and the slave transfer completed tomorrow. I expect he'll leave no later than noon."

More words I couldn't hear.

"That's cutting it close. If he sees you...If Snowden finds out we're on to him..."

X placed the laptop on the desk. When I shifted my attention to it, X gave a sharp nod. "Don't even think about it." He motioned for me to sit in the wingback chair. I was beginning to hate that chair.

My fear for what X could do kept me from moving and I sat. He cupped the phone to his ear, talking to the stranger the whole time while he stepped behind me. For a brief millisecond, I contemplated rushing the desk, opening the laptop, and activating the RUN command which would unravel everything I'd done. But in the time it took me to think through that, X clicked something to my neck. I reached up and traced out the links of a chain. I'd been locked in.

I didn't even fight when X attached a chain to my right wrist and then snapped a third to my left. With me immobilized, he returned to the desk, took his seat facing me, and opened the laptop. He swiped at the screen of his phone, pulled out a stand from a desk drawer, and placed his phone in the cradle. A few seconds later, he put earbuds in his ears, removing me from the conversation entirely. I had a fair idea what was going on, but there was no way X, or that stranger, would break my encryption.

They were royally fucked.

Their conversation continued for minutes. X listened, tapped at the keys, and cursed. I watched his expression turned from consternation to defeat. I didn't know what he was up to, but felt confident he hadn't broken through my security. I'd given him access to exactly what he'd asked, Z's business accounts, but that hadn't been what I had uncovered. I'd gone layers deeper. My intimate familiarity with how Z's mind worked told me there would be much more buried beneath the surface. X could scan all of my father's bank accounts, but none of what I'd seen would be visible to him. He looked up at me and darkness swirled in the depths of his eyes. I swallowed reflexively and guarded against what would come.

"Yes, that'll be all. I'll see you soon."

With those words, X ended the call. He stood over me and bent down, placing his hands on the armrests of the chair.

"You have been a very bad girl."

CHAPTER TWENTY-TWO_

X LEANED IN AND I PRESSED MY SHOULDER BLADES AGAINST THE chair. With no place to run, I was trapped and at his mercy. I should hate him for this. I did. I really did, or at least I told myself this was true. I wasn't a very good liar, at least to myself. The truth was much darker and harder to face. It was inescapable and I was only just realizing how helpless I was around X. I craved the indescribable power he held over me. He made me tremble in fear and I ate it up. He delivered pain and I craved more. More of his touch. His mastery. More of his control. I fought him because the act of resisting turned me on. Nothing about him made sense.

This man did things to me that I didn't understand. His intensity flicked on switches inside me and turned me into a submissive, yielding, wanton thing. I hungered for him. I challenged him if only because I needed to know if he would push back. My pulse fired. My breaths accelerated. The blood in my body burned as it raced merrily along and ignited sensations I didn't want to face. But I couldn't ignore the thrill of meeting X's strength with my own. I needed to clash with him before I could yield. Our struggle for supremacy defined our roles and I never doubted how our war would end.

That didn't make me weak. I was stronger than X. The battle of wills raging between us would end only one way, but not until I accepted the truth of what I was, what I needed, and the same for him. Xavier would win in the end, because I let him. Because he would make me.

"You have earned a punishment my dear Raven."

"You're a monster."

I searched his face, needing to see the evil I claimed lived within him. What I saw instead made my insides clench and my nerves light up in anticipation of what would come; not the punishment. I knew how difficult that would be to endure. The punishment didn't excite me, but rather what came afterward and what I would finally give.

"Know this, my slave, nothing is as it seems. There are things which must be done, horrible things, but sometimes it takes evil to fight evil. I would explain, but you continue to resist me. Until we're on the same page, you'll be denied certain things. Know this, I crave the darkness and I'll do terrible things to you. Your days of resistance are behind you."

The air between us sizzled with sexual tension. It vibrated in the space between us, melding our breaths, and forging our future. The inevitability of it pulsed with every breath, echoed with every beat of my heart, and filled every word he spoke.

X continued to lean over me, invading my space, dominating me with his presence, and I soaked it all in, craving the delicious torment he promised and hating myself for needing it. Then, suddenly, something within me released. All the tension inside of me disappeared. I searched his face and made my peace.

"Then take me."

X took in a sharp breath, then he was on me, kissing me, licking me, biting my neck, my shoulders, and pawing at the dress I had just put on. It shredded in his hands as he ripped it from my body. I'd been chained in place, but not truly restrained. If I wanted, I could have fought; pushed him away and squirmed out of his touch. I did none of these things. He devoured me with a ravenous hunger and I sacrificed myself to his need.

Eventually, the chains fell away. Naked, he clutched me tight to his chest. I burrowed into him, tucking my head beneath his chin and clutching his neck. He carried me out of the library, down one of the endless white hallways, and brought me to the doors that led into the room with the chains. I wrapped my arms around his neck, terrified, and yet accepting of my fate.

The cross had been removed from the middle of the room. The couches had been pushed back against the wall. X said nothing as he deposited me in the middle of the room. A storm brewed in his eyes as he steadied me and attached the first chain to one of the three rings around my neck. He clipped the second and then the third. Without resistance, I met the steel of his expression, compliant and, if not willing, at least finally in acceptance of my fate.

He left me standing there, forced to watch as he went to the wall where all manner of torture devices waited for unwilling flesh. Instead of grabbing something from the wall, he went to a set of drawers and pulled out something which made a clinking sound. Returning to me, he held out a sturdy leather cuff with silver rings attached to it. Much different from the delicate bands I wore around my wrists, the cuffs looked to have been designed with industrial strength. My stomach clenched and I swallowed, wondering for a moment if I truly had lost my mind. X thrust out the cuff and the deep timbre of his voice settled my nerves and burrowed deep into my chest to lodge in my heart. I chose this fate.

"Give me your wrist."

This would be my last chance to refuse what came next. My attention turned from the cuff to ponder the storm in his eyes. Something unspoken moved in the space between us. I whispered out an answer.

"Yes."

"That wasn't a question." His brow arched with confusion.

Obediently, I lifted my wrist and placed it inside the cuff. Buttery smooth on the inside, X tightened the leather around my wrist. He lifted the other sturdy cuff, the unspoken command lingering between us.

"That is my answer."

"To?"

"I won't beg. I'll never beg, but I can give you that one word. When you ask, that is my answer."

"Raven..." He staggered back a step and gripped his jaw. "You will be my undoing."

"Promise that you won't make me beg. Do what you must and take what you need, but please don't ask that of me. It will destroy me and I'm barely hanging on as it is."

X wrapped his powerful arms around me.

"But don't you understand, my dear? That's exactly what I'm meant to do. I will destroy you."

It would be too easy to sag in his arms and lean against him for support, but for what would come next, there would be nothing but whatever strength resided within me to endure. I'd never felt so alone. I reached over my shoulder and tugged the wrist cuff out of his hands. He released me, a shocked expression on his face as I pressed the cuff to my belly, placed my wrist inside of it, and locked it in place. I held out my hands to him, wrists crossed and locked in leather.

"Then do it." A single tear tumbled down my cheek and I closed my eyes to take in a fortifying breath. I wish I'd kept my eyes open, but then I would've seen the hood. I would have screamed. Instead, the suffocating fabric surprised me as X plunged the world into darkness.

I gasped with shock, disoriented and confused, exactly what X wanted. Before I could catch my breath, I'd been bound in chains and my wrists lifted. I soon understood the sturdiness of the thick leather cuffs as he lifted my arms overhead. I balanced on tiptoe. He'd given me a choice, hang from my wrists or support my weight on my toes. With all that happened next, that had to have been the most diabolical torment inflicted on me.

With my vision forcibly taken away, my other senses came to the forefront. The tread of his feet walking away. The clanking of chains. The slapping of leather against his hand. All of it transmitted to me through the hood. The rich scent of leather flooded my senses. There was a touch against my hip, across my belly, under my breasts, and circling my nipples. My breathing hitched with the anticipation of pain I knew would follow. Except it didn't, at least not yet. My calves screamed in protest as I struggled to stand on tiptoe. I tried hanging from the cuffs but found my arms straining from holding the weight of my body. I shifted from one agony to the other, trying to relieve the pain, and failing utterly.

Whatever he dragged against my body lit every nerve on fire. My skin prickled with goosebumps. Anticipation wound me tight, filled me with fear, and had me aching with desire. For now, fear held me firmly in its grip. I refused to speak. Whatever X had planned, I wouldn't reward him with my voice. He would have to take, because I'd already given more than I could stand. I'd said yes.

And I wasn't standing anymore. My calves exploded in agony as a Charlie horse held me in its iron grip. My scream came from that pain, but turned to a shriek with the first strike of what could only be a whip.

"You're being punished, slave," X ground out, punctuating his words with another strike.

A wave of fire ripped through my back. I tried to count the strikes, but there was no breath in my body to make sound. Air squeezed out of my lungs and pain tightened my chest. The struggle to breathe became my universe as he struck again.

Eternity swallowed me as X worked my body to exhaustion. I screamed. I begged. I cried and howled. I danced away from the whip, only to trip and hang suspended above the ground. The whip would strike again and I'd regain my feet. X's fury bit at my flesh and crawled deep inside my bones. He became an extension of me, and I think, somehow, a part of me bled into him. Sweat poured from my body as I struggled to breathe. I lost count of the number of times the whip bit at my flesh. The power of X's strikes landed with surgical precision turning my world into a constant stream of torment. At some point, I gave in. The pain settled in. I hadn't escaped it, but somewhere along the way, I no longer seemed to care. I floated in a haze and rode the wave of sensation flooding my body.

A whimper escaped me when the strikes stopped falling. Bound by the hood, I'm not sure what happened next, except I floated on a cloud and the strain on my arms suddenly fell away. My wrists landed in my lap and I curled against the most delicious scent of coming home. Then I was moving. I clutched at X's neck and nuzzled, then stilled at a grating noise.

"Well done, boy. A few more sessions like that and she'll..."

"Get out of my way, Zane," X growled. "I don't need you to tell me how to handle my slave."

"Not telling you how to do shit. I could care less what you do with her."

"Then you won't mind getting out of my way."

X pivoted and stepped past my father, then everything faded as my lids closed and I shut out the world.

CHAPTER TWENTY-THREE_

BRIGHT LIGHT STREAMED THROUGH A WINDOW. SOFT FLUFFY sheets covered me and a muscled arm draped over my waist. My thoughts stilled as I wrapped my mind around what happened last night, the pain, the acceptance, and my father's presence.

Had Z been watching the entire time? X mentioned I would be a part of the evening's entertainment. Was that why X had whipped me?

No.

I'd earned that punishment on my own. That whipping hadn't been planned. In fact, it seemed to have done something to X, brought out a darkness which both terrified and soothed me at the same time. The explanation behind how that might be wasn't something I wanted to ponder. I chose instead to accept what happened. I'd triggered something in X; something that couldn't easily be put away.

His soft snores told me he had yet to wake and I froze, unwilling to stir the sleeping monster. A quick glance around the room had my eyes widening. This wasn't my room. It lacked the spartan lines and utilitarian furniture, and most importantly, the presence of one of my four guards. Why had X taken me back to his room, and why had he put me in his bed? More importantly, why had he crawled in with me to sleep? He stirred beside me and tugged me against his hard body.

"You awake, Raven?"

My entire body stilled and I dared not move.

He nuzzled my neck and whispered in my ear. "Relax. You're safe."

I felt anything but safe, then remembered my place.

"I'm awake, Master."

"You feel good in my arms."

X moved behind me, the long length of him jabbed against my backside. He could take me right now. I wouldn't stop him. To my surprise, he shifted away, placing distance between me and his morning erection.

"How do you feel?" He traced a line down my back. "Any pain?"

Was he tracing the marks from the whip? Surprisingly there was little pain.

"It doesn't hurt. How can that be?"

"I put cream on the welts last night." He massaged my neck. Knots of overworked muscles eased beneath his attention. I gave a soft sigh and allowed myself to enjoy the sensation. I didn't feel threatened by X's presence, and for the first time I found myself relaxing. He attacked the tension in my body, coaxing the tight cords in my back to relax.

"I don't remember that." There was little I remembered after X scooped me up in his arms and carried me off.

"You had your first experience with subspace. I brought you to my room, rubbed in the cream, and then crawled in next to you. I haven't slept so soundly in months."

Neither had I, come to think of it, and I wasn't in a hurry to leave either. I should want to escape X's bed, but I luxuriated beneath the power of his hands.

"The tightness will ease. Coming out of subspace brings back some of the pain. Your muscles will be sore for a couple of days."

"What's subspace?"

"It's when endorphins flood your body, helping you process pain."

"I remember feeling floaty."

"That, would be subspace. It's not unusual to feel a little detached."

"You didn't...um, do anything else to me?" It didn't feel like we'd had sex and I would hate not to remember it. He shifted beside me, coming up on his elbow and turned me to my back. Instead of hardness, he gazed down at me with tenderness and concern. I felt...cherished.

"When I fuck you, Raven, you'll be fully aware of it. I would never violate you, especially when you're in subspace."

And just like that, tension coiled back in my gut. There was no escaping that eventuality, although I didn't fear it as I had once before.

"I just assumed, especially after..."

"I've taken what you said into consideration. We'll get there, and when the time comes, I'll take you. There won't be any doubt in your mind, or regrets. This is happening between us, but I'm not like your father. I won't hurt you."

"But you trade in slaves."

"It's not what you think."

"I saw what happened in that room, what those women were forced to do. Ben said he was building a resort—"

"Ben is not building a resort."

"But, he said..."

"Come on Raven, you're smarter than this." He rolled out of bed and looked down at me. "Now put that brilliant mind of yours to work. I'm going to take a shower while you think about what might be happening here. We'll talk later, and you have some decisions to make. I need to play host to my guests, which leaves you free to explore the house." He pointed to my wrist and I noticed the dolphin pendant. "You can get breakfast in the kitchen. If you need anything, you can give Bay or Chad a call."

"How do I do that?" My guards weren't going to be with me? How had I earned the right to roam free?

"You'll see square panels next to practically every door. The RFID chip in your bracelet gives you access to most parts of the house. When you come to a doorway, sensors will read the chip and you'll see a red or green light. Green and you're free to pass. Red means that part of the estate is off-limits."

"And what if I keep going?"

"The discrepancy will be logged."

"And?"

"You know what comes next. Unless you enjoy counting to ten over and over, I suggest you adhere to the rules. As for me, I don't mind spanking your ass as many times as possible. If you enjoy the act of sitting, I suggest you don't push."

The thought of his punishment made me squirm and I pressed my thighs together, failing to soothe the sudden ache building between my legs. It wasn't the punishment which set me off, it was yielding to the authority X represented. What the hell was wrong with me?

"Just like that? You're going to let me wander free?"

"Free is a relative term. You're being given certain freedoms, respect your boundaries, Raven. Respect me. Also, no more going outside. Don't test me."

"And what will you be doing?"

"I must attend to our guests. We have a breakfast meeting to finalize the sale of the slaves, then I'll see them off the island."

"Will you tell me where we are?" I desperately wanted to know where in the world I might be.

"You need to be in the library by two pm. We'll talk about what happened last night."

He left me to ponder his words. What was it about last night that he wanted to talk about? The whipping? What led up to the whipping? My father's presence? Or something else? I hated the uncertainty brewing in my mind. A moment later, the shower turned on. I lay in the bed and pulled the covers around me. I had the day to roam and finally explore my surroundings. If I understood what X said, I was being allowed to do so alone. So why then did my attention keep popping to the bathroom, and my thoughts kept turning to joining X in that shower? The needy ache between my legs hadn't slackened with his departure. Instead it had grown, leaving me a needy mess.

I rose from the bed, torn between marching into that bathroom and leaving all pretenses behind, or running out the door. Without any clothes, leaving X's room didn't seem wise, but then I spied another sundress. It seemed X had a definite preference for what I wore, at least when allowed clothes.

The shower stopped, removing the option of joining him,

and I breathed out a sigh of relief. Too much temptation pulled at me, because I wanted to give myself to X. Something between us had shifted, and while I didn't understand, it felt right. No longer my adversary, X was becoming something else.

He exited the bathroom, towel wrapped around his waist. Water beaded down the smooth expanse of his chest. I didn't try hiding my open admiration and he said nothing as I blatantly checked him out. He ripped off the towel and tossed it on the bed, giving me full view of his naked ass. This was the first time I'd ever seen X in anything other than his pressed black suit and he wandered around his room as if it was nothing for him to be strutting his Greek glory in front of me.

"Shower is yours Raven. Be a good girl, behave, and I'll see you after lunch." He pulled on boxers and covered up with dark pants. A shirt came next and I shook my head as all his glorious skin was once again hidden from my sight. He gestured at the chair where the dress had been laid out. "I had Chad bring you something to wear."

"Thank you," I said, and at the hard stare X leveled at me, I remembered to add Master to what I said. He said I would be forced to say it until I couldn't separate him from the word. Today, it didn't grate on me to say the title. Like many things between us, it no longer felt burdensome.

X slung his tie around his neck and came to me. Palming

my cheeks, he tilted my face up. I lost myself to the heat burning in his eyes. "You're incredible, strong and resilient. I cherish this about you, but mind yourself out there. Don't let your willfulness get the better of you. You don't want to disappoint me."

"I won't."

CHAPTER TWENTY-FOUR_

AND I DIDN'T. I DID NOTHING TO DISAPPOINT X. I PLANNED ON being the perfect slave.

I showered, dressed, and ventured into the stark white halls of his home. I was on my own, without guards, and terrified of making the wrong decision on where to go. I removed the dolphin pendant from my wrist and clutched it in my hand. Holding it in front of me, I scanned the walls for the panels which would flash green or red.

When I came to red, I went left or right, or turned around. I would not violate the rules given to me, at least not until I could turn them to my advantage. But was that what I wanted anymore? Honestly, I didn't know. I couldn't deny my attraction for X, but there were a lot of things he had to answer for. My abduction aside, I'd seen him traffic in human flesh. That wasn't something I could live with.

It only took three turns until I became hopelessly lost. The tiny squares guided me, in a way. Most flashed red, blocking my passage, but enough turned green and allowed my exploration. I stumbled about for the better part of an hour, backtracking and getting hopelessly turned around until I started paying attention to the artwork. Where the halls looked indistinguishable from one another, the unique-ness of art started forming a pattern. Once I figured that out —and I don't know why I hadn't noticed it before—I was able to sketch out a rough map of the estate.

I stumbled across several inner courtyards like the one by my room. Each differed from the other. One had a waterfall cascading down from the second level. Another had a series of interconnected carp ponds with tiny waterways the bril-liant fish used to navigate from one pond to the next. The third courtyard was devoid of water structures. Instead of the serenity of flowing water, sand filled several basins and had been raked into calming designs. I stopped there to rest my feet and admired the simplicity of the Zen garden.

Not once did I see my guards, although I was under no illusion my walkabout wasn't being monitored. I kept to the green lit halls and stayed away from those blocked by the red lights. Temptation pulled at me to wander outside, but that would bring punishments I didn't want, and besides, I didn't want X to be disappointed. Abusing this privilege would send me ten steps back.

Eventually, I turned a corner and the most mouthwatering aroma hit my senses. The kitchen had to be close. I'd missed breakfast, too excited with exploring my new home to eat, and it had to be close to lunch, if not past time for the midday meal. I had to meet X back in the library at 2pm, and while I didn't have a watch, I felt certain I still had plenty of time.

Following the mouthwatering smells, I only backtracked once after making a wrong turn. The kitchen was exactly as it had been before, full of men I didn't know; kneading bread, butchering meat, and tending cook pots over a massive stove. One of the men came to greet me.

"Miss Raven, we were expecting you some time ago. I see you found your way."

"This is a big place! I got turned around at least twenty times."

He gave a deep, rumbly laugh and guided me over to one of the bistro tables sitting beside the glass wall looking into the wine cellar.

"It is at that. Now, what can I get you?"

"What do you have?"

He gave a sweeping gesture. "Anything you want."

"Anything?"

He winked at me. "Pretty much, but of course, some things might take more time."

"In that case, how about a tuna melt?"

"Now that's an easy request. Do you want fries with that or a salad?"

"My stomach is a bit unsettled, maybe just the sandwich."

A few of the men looked up, took me in, then went back to work. They were aware of me, yet made no effort to look me in the eye, smile, or otherwise acknowledge my existence. I had no doubts that all of the men in this room knew every tiny detail about me.

"Of course." The man wiped the table for me, although it looked spotless.

"Thank you." I settled back into my chair and prepared to wait.

"Would you like something to drink?" His eyes crinkled at the corners and made me feel at ease. Even though this wasn't my home, this kitchen felt warm and inviting. I didn't feel so alone, almost as if I shared something wonderful with all these men I didn't know. I knew what that was. We were all slaves to one mysterious man, but I got the feeling, that unlike me, they were here by choice. How did X instill that kind of loyalty and devotion in others?

"Water is fine." I didn't want to impose.

"Water it is, although if you want wine, we have plenty."

I glanced at the wine cellar and the thousands of bottles stacked inside.

"Um, I don't know if Master Xavier would allow that."

"We have received no instructions to the contrary. For such a big day, a little celebration is in order. No?"

If not being locked in my small room counted as a celebration I was all for that, but something told me adding alcohol into the mix might not be the best idea. I needed to remain sharp and keep my wits about me with X.

"Thank you. Perhaps another time? Maybe just the water?"

"Of course. Do you take lemon with your water?"

"Yes, please."

The man walked away and shouted orders to the others, leaving me to watch them work. Without a phone, I had nothing to occupy my time. What I wouldn't give for a magazine or newspaper, anything which might connect me to the outside world.

How long had I been locked up? A month? Longer? I felt disconnected from the outside world and oddly at peace with that too. The constant dichotomy swirling inside my head never ceased to amaze me. My mind drifted, watching the men knead dough and chop at the butcher's block. The sounds lulled me into a trancelike state and I jerked with surprise when an overwhelming presence approached.

Thinking X had found me, I opened my eyes, then my mouth gaped in surprise. If I thought X had been intimidating, the blond giant standing in front of me rendered me speechless. Like something out of a Norse legend, the towering man reminded me of a Viking king with white-blond hair, more white than blond, and piercing blue eyes. Those glacial eyes held a subdued warmth.

"You must be Raven." He extended his hand. "It's nice to

finally meet you. I see now how you've captivated Xavier's affections."

Affections? I wasn't sure I'd call what X and I shared as affection; locked in a battle of wills maybe, but affection? I lifted my hand in greeting before noticing X's laptop clutched in the man's massive hand. I drew back as if shocked.

Suddenly hyperaware and cautious, I treaded carefully, not eager to give anything away. "And you are?" Why did this man have X's laptop?

The stranger didn't ask permission to join me, he just dropped into the chair opposite me. None of the men in the kitchen reacted to the stranger's presence, making me wonder what was going on.

"I'm impressed," he said. "That's a rather large compliment from me by the way. It takes a lot to impress me."

"Excuse me?"

He placed the laptop on the table and pressed his hand over the lid.

"Xavier says you're an MIT graduate, Computer Science." He wasn't asking a question, but rather stating fact.

"I am." *Who the hell is this man?*

"They don't teach the kind of coding you wrote in Computer Science, especially in undergraduate classes. Your skill is impressive." He tapped the top of the laptop.

"Thank you?" I said it as a question and glanced around the room, wondering if Xavier was setting me up. The whipping from last night had been earned after telling X about the malicious programming in the source code I installed on Z's laptop. I used it as a threat against X, but I'd also left something else; a call for help.

"It took me almost an hour to crack," the man said.

"There's no way you cracked that in less than an hour."

"I did. It's no longer active." He flipped open the laptop and tapped on the keys. When he turned the computer around, I wanted to be sick to my stomach. Good thing the cook hadn't brought my lunch yet. "I also canceled the S-O-S you had set to send and informed Xavier."

My entire body shuddered. If X knew about the S-O-S there would be no end to his fury. Wait? If X knew, what the hell was I doing still wandering free? Shouldn't I be hanging from chains and at the mercy of X's whip?

"How did you do that?" I'd buried the S-O-S deep into the programming. No-one should have been able to have found it.

"Don't feel bad. I'm very good with computers." He smiled at me. "There aren't many people who give me a run for my money. I found your code intelligent and sophisticated. We could use someone like you working with us."

I sank back feeling defeated. All my hard work; erased by this man and worse. There would be no way to escape punishment for that S-O-S. The cook who'd taken my food order brought my tuna melt. He sat something resembling macaroni with meat in it down in front of my stranger.

"Thanks, Jasper," the man sitting across from me said, "it looks perfect." He took a scoop of the macaroni and swallowed it down. "Tastes even better."

"Thank you, Mr. Summers." The cook looked pleased and left with a smile.

"I'm sorry, but who are you?" I leaned back and scanned the kitchen. Where were my guards? Where was X? Why was I still free?

"A business associate of Xavier's, and you have me intrigued. I want to offer you a job."

"You're kidding, right?"

"I don't kid."

I rolled my eyes. "I'm sorry, but you obviously don't understand my position here."

"I understand it very well."

"If you're offering me a job, then you don't."

"You're Xavier's slave." He shoveled a massive bite into his mouth and wiped his chin. "Trust me, I know exactly what your position here is."

"Then you know it's ridiculous offering me any kind of job."

"Not really. I've had my eye on you for quite some time."

"Is that so?"

"I'm the one who intervened when your father put you up for sale to the highest bidder. You can thank me for Xavier stepping in to prevent an unscrupulous buyer from getting hold of you."

"Excuse me?" I blinked, hard, because the things coming from this man's mouth made no sense to me. "What do you mean you intervened and X stepped in?"

"Oh, it gets better." He said with a smirk. "You actually have a lot to be thankful for."

"What the hell are you talking about?"

"You said I have no idea who you are. I'm merely explaining that I know exactly who you are."

"I'm sorry, but I don't know you from Adam. And if you're with Xavier—"

"Your Master," the man corrected, bringing a huff from my lips. "I believe Xavier is a stickler for titles. He doesn't just believe in the lifestyle, he's embraced it to its fullest, but then you should know this."

"Okay...if you're with my Master, I have no reason to believe anything you say." I was to use the honorific in X's presence, but when he wasn't around? I shook my head.

"Why is that?" X's sudden arrival surprised me. He'd come from somewhere behind me. I jerked in my seat and spun around, only to find myself facing the indomitable presence of the man I called Master. X picked up a chair from the adjacent table and placed it between me and my stranger. "I see you've met Forest."

Technically, *Forest* and I hadn't officially met, but at least now I had a name. This was the man X had spoken to over the phone last night after I told X about the malicious programming I'd left behind for insurance. Forest wasn't a code word, it was this man's name. Forest Summers. His name sounded familiar, but I couldn't figure out why that might be.

Too many questions flooded my mind.

"Have your guests left?" Forest asked, turning his attention away from me and speaking to X. His face twisted with distaste.

"Yes, and good riddance." A look of relief passed over X's features. "I'm fumigating their rooms."

Forest burst out in laughter. "Good one." He sobered almost immediately, an odd shift in mood, then leaned toward X. "And the product?"

"They're being debriefed as we speak, and given their options."

The product? Forest meant men and women who'd been enslaved. My gut churned with the casual way these men spoke about stripping humans of their most basic rights.

I hooked my hands beneath my legs, my hunger forgotten in the presence of X. Forest said he'd found my S-O-S and had told X about it. Why didn't X have me over his knee? Or worse, strung up for another whipping?

"Good," Forest said, shoveling a bit of what looked like a concoction of macaroni and hamburger into his mouth. "I wonder how many will decide to stay?"

"One of the men at least. It's harder with the women, but I have a feeling one or two might choose to join the organization. Mel is handling their transition."

I tried to glean clues from their conversation about what was going on. X told me he was disappointed I hadn't figured certain things out, but what was I missing?

"Raven," X said, "aren't you going to eat?"

I stared at my food, but with the churning in my stomach that wasn't going to happen.

"I'm not as hungry as I thought, Master." I refused to forget the honorific and wind up over X's knee in front of this stranger. My core ignited with an achy flare of arousal and I pressed my knees together. Since when did I get excited about the prospect of X spanking me?

X lifted his finger and the cook came running. "I'll have what Raven is having."

"Yes, Master Xavier." The cook took the order and rushed off.

"You missed breakfast, Raven." X patted my knee. "You must be starving. Go ahead and eat." He propped his elbows on the bistro table and glanced at the plate sitting in front of Forest. "What the hell is that slop?"

Forest gave a grin. "Chili Mac! It's delicious. You should try it."

X pulled a face. "I think I'll pass."

I kept my gaze bouncing between the two men, unable to figure out how they might be connected. Finally, I couldn't stand it any longer. "I'm sorry, but how do you two know each other?" And what else did Forest know about me?

Forest jerked his thumb toward X. "I'm his boss."

CHAPTER TWENTY-FIVE_

"YOUR BOSS?" MY MOUTH GAPED AND I SHOOK MY HEAD. I thought X was the boss? When I realized I'd forgotten the honorific, I gave a tiny gasp, then rushed to correct myself. "I'm sorry, Master."

X gave a soft laugh and gripped my hand. "It's okay, I'll give you a pass, this one time." He turned to Forest. "I think it's time we come clean."

Jasper returned with X's sandwich. "Master Xavier, is there anything else I can get for you?"

"No, Jasper. This is good, thank you." X took a look at his plate, then glanced at me. "It's been years since I've had this. I think I was twelve."

Jasper gave a low bow, took two steps back, and retreated. I scanned the kitchen, watching the deference all these men gave, not to Forest—the man who claimed he was X's boss—but to X himself.

"Yes, please Master," I said, not at all concerned about begging for answers, "please, come clean."

X rolled his wrist and glanced at his watch. "We have less than an hour," he said to Forest.

With his mouth full of chili mac, Forest responded with a nod.

"Xavier!" I pushed my plate away. "What's going on?"

X arched a brow, reached out and pushed my plate back in front of me. "Are you that eager to bend over my knee, Raven? Do not forget your place, or what happens when you disobey."

I glared at him and curled my hands into fists. Instead of lashing out, a surreal feeling of calm came over me with the reprimand. Back and forth, back and forth, my emotions regarding X boomeranged inside of me, constantly flying about. Keeping hatred for him alive felt wrong, especially after the past few days. He'd exposed me, degraded me in front of my father, apologized for it, and sheltered me as he could. He'd been both tender and cruel. How did any of that make sense?

But, I felt a truth. My heart had already accepted it. At some point, I would have to trust my feelings about this man. What he'd done had been wrong. This couldn't be denied, but I felt an overwhelming protectiveness and affection coming from him. He kept telling me things weren't as they seemed. Instead of pushing back from the table and shouting something I would most definitely regret, I chose to trust. I took in a deep breath.

"I didn't mean to raise my voice, Master, and I didn't mean to disrespect you. I'm sorry, but I'm really confused. Please—" I stopped and changed the wording of what I was going to say. "Master, will you please tell me what's going on?"

He took my hand in his and raised my knuckles to his lips where he gave the lightest of kisses. "I will, Raven, but first, finish your food. We don't have much time."

Time? Time for what? My entire body buzzed with the anticipation of finally getting answers, but a glance at my master told me he wouldn't be explaining further. I had to trust him, and it killed me to sit in silence and take a bite of my sandwich. But I did. I cleared my plate, and then waited for my master and Forest to do the same. Hopefully, the answers I received were ones I could live with.

As if to torture me, X and Forest talked about inconsequential things.

"I hear you're an uncle now," X said. "Congratulations." He took a bite of his sandwich.

Who cared about Forest's personal life? I wanted to hurry up to this big revelation they had for me.

"Thanks." Forest gave a lopsided grin. "You know, I

thought Ash was going to have a cow when they rushed Skye to a c-section. He was practically pulling his hair out. Good thing Tia was there."

"Tia? Why do I know that name?"

"Tia's the certified nurse anesthetist leading Skye's surgical team. Her husband, Ryker, is the respiratory therapist."

"Ah, I thought that name sounded familiar."

"Yeah, Tia's a champ. She didn't even bat an eye when she had to put Skye under. That woman is scary as shit when she's working, super smart and gorgeous as hell."

"Everything went okay, though? Mom and baby?"

X appeared genuinely concerned, not that I cared. He took another small bite of his sandwich. This conversation was killing me. These were men! Why weren't they scarfing their food down?

Forest gave a nod. "Yeah, everything turned out perfect. The baby and my sis made it through just fine. Skye's an amazing mother. I couldn't be happier for her."

"That's wonderful news."

"Yes, but don't worry, the team will be ready."

"We can delay if needed." X put his sandwich down on his plate, and I groaned inwardly. "I don't want to rush," he said, taking a drink of his water, "but every day...it's another—"

"No rush. Skye knows her limits and she pushes herself

hard, besides we still don't know where Snowden is, and Skye wants this as much as me. She's smart enough to pace herself and not push."

There was that name again, my father's business partner, the one involved in the more heinous business practices. What interest did Forest have in Snowden? For that matter, what about X who did business with my father? But wait, if X worked for Forest, then Forest had his hands in the entire sex slave operation as well. Nothing made sense.

"Good," X said, "And the rest of the team?"

"With the men you've recruited, and the team Skye's put together, we're good. Not ready by any means, but give a few months of prep and everything will be set."

"That leaves only one thing." X looked at my empty plate and then to me sitting on my hands. He took another bite. Over half his sandwich remained.

I couldn't help it. I wanted to gouge both their eyes out and that was the only thing keeping me from acting on it.

"Can you find Snowden?" X turned the power of his gaze on Forest, who returned the intensity without flinching.

"With time and digging." Forest pointed to me. "Of course, it'll be a lot faster if we use her."

"Me?" I pointed to my chest. "Use me for what?"

X leaned back and crossed his arms over his chest. "Well, to take down your father's operation of course, but more importantly, to put down a real monster for good."

My focus shifted from X to Forest then back to my master. "I'm sorry?"

Forest huffed out a gruff laugh. "Honey, despite what you think, we're the good guys."

CHAPTER TWENTY-SIX_

FOREST CALLING ME HONEY DIDN'T SIT WELL WITH ME. HE WAS a stranger, and not someone I trusted. I turned to X, remembering all the times he told me he wasn't a monster. Could this be true? Was there good in my master?

"Good guys?" I looked at X with my stomach twisting in knots. "If you're one of the good guys, then explain what you did to me."

I pulled my hands out from under my legs and placed the dolphin bracelet, and all it represented, on the table. I no longer had the rights to it. X looked at it, then looked to me. Nothing else transpired between us, except an unspoken flow of power leaving me and filling him.

Forest leaned back while X returned his attention to the dolphin pendant. It granted me freedom, limited, but was no different from any other chain. The ties that bound us weren't pretty, but they tightened around my heart and held me fast.

I flicked my fingers in the direction of the laptop, highly conscious of the fact X knew about the message I tried to send. Nothing had been said about that, and it still hung in the air between us. He knew, and I knew he knew. We were in a standoff.

Unable to hold my own against the severity of X's gaze, I shifted my attention to Forest. He was no less fierce, but I felt more comfortable confronting Forest than my master.

"You don't need me. You said so yourself. You broke my code and have full access to Z's information. You can find this Snowden guy without me."

"I could, and on the surface, it would seem it should be that easy." Forest rubbed at his chin. "But it's not. You understand your father. Don't underestimate your value."

I didn't and turned to face X. "Is this true, Master?"

X gave a nod.

"Did it ever occur to you to ask? If you knew so much about me, then you would've known how much I despise my father. You could have come to me rather than abduct and enslave me."

"We considered it," X acknowledged, "but your father forced our hand."

"How so?"

"How much do you know about your inheritance?"

"I don't have an inheritance." I'd always assumed some of

my father's assets would transfer to me, but my father was healthy and not yet fifty. He had decades left to live.

X exchanged a look with Forest. "Let's take this conversation to the library."

I didn't want to take our conversation to the library. My questions finally had answers rushing to fill in the gaps. If we paused, and went to the library, I'd lose the momentum I'd gained. My mouth opened, I was ready to demand we stay put, but one look from X had me snapping my mouth shut. My master was back and fully in command. He'd released some of the restraints binding our roles, but his authority had returned.

I wanted to kick and scream. I wanted to shout at the top of my lungs about the injustice of it all. What I did instead was nothing. X stood. Forest followed suit. I numbly stared at my empty plate. X picked up the dolphin bracelet and tucked it into the breast pocket of his suit. My limited freedom had been rescinded. He came to stand behind me and put his hand on my chair to scoot it back. His attention to my needs made me want to scream, especially after he took something as precious as the bracelet from me.

"Forest, we'll meet you in a moment," X said.

I gulped at those words, because they didn't bode well for me.

Forest gave a nod and left me alone with my master. We weren't really alone, the entire kitchen was full of waitstaff and cooks, but I had no illusions they would ignore whatever came next.

"Follow me," X said, his tone stern.

I said nothing and followed meekly behind as he led me out of the kitchen. We didn't go far. Two turns through featureless white hallways and he stopped by a nondescript door. With a press of his palm to a keypad, the door swung inward. X ushered me inside with a wave of his hand. I stepped into darkness, confused, trembling, and strangely aroused when X shut the door behind us.

"On your knees," X said.

His clipped words had me dropping to my knees and bowing my head. A light flickered, revealing shadows around me. I faced the door, but sensed a vastness to the room.

"What we discuss in the library changes nothing between us. You are my slave. Given to me to pay off a debt, but enslaved to me by something much more profound."

My head snapped up.

"Eyes. Down!"

The force of his command had me bowing my head. My palms slicked with sweat and my entire body shuddered. Tension coiled within me and sparks danced down my nerves. X had an undeniable effect on me, irresistible and intoxicating. Like a sponge, I soaked in his dominance and rose to meet it with...something else. Was this my submission? I didn't know, because it felt like I needed to defy him, meet strength with strength, until he overpowered me. I hated the constant indecision warring within me. Why couldn't I simply give in?

"You want to fight what's inside you, rather than embrace it," he began.

I swear the man could read minds. Did I give off some vibe that betrayed my innermost thoughts?

"I've been sensitive to the stress this places on you, but that stops now."

How? How did I make it stop? How did I stop fighting not only him, but myself? Because, I wanted what he offered. I simply couldn't take it.

I meant to look up at him, a display of my defiance. And I did. I glared at him then gave a startled gasp. Shadows cloaked him from the dim lighting, making him fiercer, stronger, and more potent than I remembered. Power radiated off him, mingled with his overwhelming confidence, and fell upon me in a flood of conviction. Nothing about X was soft and gentle. I both respected and feared that about him. He held no confusion about his place and stood above me with absolute assurance, knowing that was where he belonged. How did someone fight the strength of his will? The short answer was they didn't. I didn't.

I couldn't.

"You gave me your consent," he continued. "You said the answer was *Yes*. You'll be tested. I don't expect you to say yes for what comes next and you asked me not to make you beg.

You have my word to honor that request, but the moment you say *Stop,* this ends."

I wrapped my arms around myself and shook, but I didn't cry. For the first time, in far too long, my eyes remained dry. Those words had been spoken to X under a different set of circumstances. My options had been limited, but I had meant them...at the time. A corner of my mind finally whispered to me and granted permission to embrace the firestorm between us. With what I knew now, did that change? Or was I finally ready to burn?

Once again, the boomerang took flight. Accepting X, acknowledging his power, and granting him authority over me, would change everything. I would no longer be able pretend I was a victim. I would no longer be able to feed my anger over my abduction and subsequent enslavement. Choosing to continue meant I became an active participant in my fate. I had no idea which way to jump.

"Turn around," he ordered.

I scooted on my knees and took in my surroundings. Similar to the room where that wretched business meeting had occurred, this one was kitted out with similar implements, a cross, a padded bench, and other pieces of furniture I couldn't quite figure out form or function. X stood behind me and dangled the dolphin pendant in front of me.

"This gives you access to many parts of the estate. This room is one of them. You have a series of punishments waiting for you. Using my name rather than calling me master, raising your voice to me, and let's not forget what Forest found. I'm going to give this back to you, then you and I are going to the library. I'll answer all your questions. After that, the choice is yours."

Choice? What choice?

"When you enter this room, a signal will be sent to me. The door will lock behind you, sealing you in. There will be no exit, no reprieve, except what is granted by me. When you enter this room, that is the choice you're making. There's no turning back. All or nothing. That's what I demand, and you know I'll take everything from you."

"Xavier..." The word came out a breathy whisper. I struggled to process his words, and I knew it was wrong not to call him master, but this moment demanded a more personal touch.

"We won't speak of this further. This is what I want, for you and for me. We're two halves of a whole. I've been looking for you my entire life. When I took you, I didn't understand the tremendous chance I'd been given. I've been nothing but honest about my desires or intentions. What you've seen is what you'll get with me, unwavering domination and uncompromising rule. Don't run from what terrifies you. It's my hope you'll run toward your fears rather than away. When you do, I'll be waiting for you. I'll give you everything you need. You'll want for nothing, but you will choose. I can't do it for you."

X turned and the door opened behind me, letting in

more light into the dimly lit room. A future of pain waited for me here, and maybe something much more profound. This would be the crucible in which I would break and be reformed. I took to my feet and followed X out of the room. We said nothing as he guided me to the library. My only question was whether I would ever return to this room.

CHAPTER TWENTY-SEVEN_

WHEN WE ARRIVED IN THE LIBRARY, FOREST WAS SEATED IN one of the leather chairs. He held a book open and had it propped on his knee. X walked over to the chair facing Forest, sat down, then pointed to the floor by his feet. His command required no interpretation.

Forest glanced up, gave me an indecipherable expression, and turned his attention back to his book. "I didn't think you would be here so soon," Forest said with a chuckle. "I settled in to wait."

"Raven hasn't made her choice, yet."

I moved to where X indicated and took to my knees. The position wasn't the most comfortable. Not interested in incurring additional punishments, I obeyed without complaint. My choice? How did my abduction become a choice?

"So, you're going to tell her, lover boy?" Forest snickered.

"Don't use that tone with me, unless you're feeling a need to howl. I can certainly use a workout with the whip."

Forest put his book down. "We've moved past that, Xavier."

"Have we?"

"Fine," Forest said with a huff. "I won't say that word again."

"Good." X snapped.

"Doesn't mean it ain't true," Forest mumbled.

"Forest!"

"Oh relax." Forest gave another chuckle, then turned his attention to me. "Raven, Xavier is a complex man, kinky as fuck, and uncompromising in his beliefs. Never forget it, because I have a feeling you'll be on the receiving end of much of his attention."

"Forest, you're crossing a line." X reached down and put his hand on my head. He ran his fingers through my hair, massaging my scalp. The tenderness behind his touch surprised me.

"We only have a few minutes before the conference call," Forest said, "if you're going to bring her in, we should probably do it sooner rather than later."

X glanced down at me, then stood. He bent down, crouching before me, and placed his forehead to mine. He placed his hands on my arms, rubbing them gently. "Listen first. Questions only after I'm done. Do you understand?"

"Yes Master."

He kissed my cheek with more tenderness than I was prepared to handle. With my head spinning, he lifted me up and put me in his chair. X raked his fingers through his hair and stared down at me. For the first time since I'd met him, he appeared uncertain, but he gave a sharp jerk of his head, as if coming to a decision, and his confidence returned.

"We'll begin with your inheritance," he said.

"I don't have an inheritance."

"Do not interrupt. That's the last time I'll say it."

I swallowed against the lump in my throat and glanced at Forest.

"You're going to want to hear this. That's only one of many things your father has kept from you." He set aside the book.

With my head on a swivel, I glanced between the two men. While hundreds of questions flooded my mind, I kept silent.

"Let's begin with your mother," X said.

I'd never known my mother. She'd died giving birth to me. Z never spoke of her. There were no pictures of her growing up. Everything I knew about her had been gleaned from what little the nannies told me. I'd only recently discovered she had been nothing but a slave.

"I know your father went to great lengths to hide who she was, and I also know he told you she was a slave."

I gave a nod. This was true.

"That is and isn't the entire truth. Your mother came from a prominent family, old money. She was not forced into slavery, but rather chose to enslave herself to your father. They met in college and married shortly thereafter. It's my belief your father introduced her to the M/s lifestyle. Unfortunately, she didn't know the monster she gave her submission to, or the depths of his depravity. Zane Carson is a businessman, well off, but not wealthy like your mother, and he has certain dark tastes. He took advantage of her, used her to climb social circles, and was in the process of gaining access to her trust to fund his side business, the one you've seen in action. Unfortunately for him, your mother became pregnant before he could withdraw anything from the family trust. This forced him to take out certain loans which he wasn't able to pay."

My eyes widened. "What?" Then I remembered my orders. "I'm sorry, Master. I won't interrupt."

X gave a slight nod, then continued. "According to the terms of the trust, individuals marrying into the family are specifically excluded from accessing it. Zane Carson attempted to pull out assets, and secure them for himself. With your mother as the sole heir, he could do so only with your mother's consent, at least until she became pregnant with you."

I stared at X, not understanding. The urge to interrupt overcame me, but with a sharp shake of his head, I pushed my questions to the background, trusting he would reveal everything if I only gave him time. Forest sat across from me, the weight of his gaze heavy upon me as he measured my every response. I ignored him, at least as much as a person could ignore the giant of a man.

"Your birth wouldn't have been a problem. Your mother, as your guardian, had the power to transfer assets out of the trust, which I believe was the plan. Unfortunately, she died giving birth to you, making you the sole heir to your family's fortune. This put a stop to Zane's plans. The trust took care of the family home and what was needed to raise you, but his debts piled up. He couldn't access the trust until you came of legal age. With no way to access your family's money, he concocted a new plan. That would come with your twenty-first birthday."

I rubbed my palms over the fabric of my dress, smoothing out wrinkles which didn't exist. I glanced to Forest and he nodded, supporting the revelations X bestowed upon me.

"Selling you into slavery gave your father two things. As you've already seen, enslavement effectively removed you from the world. You would disappear, and could be forced to comply with whatever your master demanded."

I knew this to be true. X had full control over my life. His wealth allowed him to control me, isolate me, and erase me from the world.

"Your father put a reserve price of five million and announced your auction to the highest bidder. Through his associate, John Snowden, they arranged several potential buyers. Trust me when I tell you, that fate would have been worse than death."

I didn't know whether to be horrified or impressed. Horror filled me knowing what my father planned, but five million? Who would pay such an extravagant price? I wasn't that pretty, or special.

"I sense your confusion, which is where the second benefit comes in. Your father's debts were well over five million. Proceeds from your auction wouldn't be enough to settle what he owed, but with your sale came a way to gain access to your trust. Once you turned twenty-one, you gain control over the trust. With that comes the ability to dissolve it. This is what your father intended, and he offered a kick-back to whomever bought you. Once they obtained your signature, they would receive two and a half million of your purchase price back. Your father, obviously, would get the rest."

"Why would he do that?" I couldn't keep silent any longer.

"Honey," Forest said, his voice deep and rumbly, "the amount of money we're talking about is not insignificant."

"Who would agree to such a thing?" I couldn't help the questions. They spilled out of me. "And I never would've signed—"

"Raven," X interrupted, "what you've experienced with me is nothing to what you would've been subjected to with another. You have no idea what you would've done to survive. Trust me in this. You don't understand what these men are capable of."

"But you..." I glanced to Forest, who continued to watch me. "You didn't buy me. A debt paid..."

"When Forest became aware of what your father intended, he approached me. Knowing who I am, the life I lead, and how I've positioned myself in certain aspects of the slave trade, I offered to settle your father's debts in exchange for you."

"You could have told me."

"We couldn't risk it," X said. "Not with what's at stake, besides it wouldn't have worked. There's no way you could've pretended to be my slave. Your father would've picked up on it. Your reactions needed to be real, because your father and I are involved in certain business trans-actions."

Yes, I couldn't forget X traded in slaves. He wasn't an innocent here, and despite everything was still involved in ruining lives.

"Why did you do this to me?"

"Because," Forest interjected, "we're after a true devil. As bad as your father is, and we will deal with him, Snowden is the true monster, but we couldn't get to him directly. We need your father to get to Snowden, and as it turns out you offer an exceptional opportunity."

My head spun with these revelations. I didn't know what

to process first. My mother? A secret family trust? My father's auction plans? X stepping in?

"If my father was going to auction me to the highest bidder, why not just grab me at auction?"

"Because, I couldn't risk being out bid, and I'd already decided I needed to have you."

With the amount of money invested in X's estate, I had a fair idea of the money he had access to. Maybe I wasn't worth five million? It's insane that thought went through my head. I shouldn't have a price attached to me at all.

"What do you mean you needed to have me? You didn't know me. How much did my father owe?"

"Twenty million, give or take a million," Forest answered. "As for the other half of your question, that is something you and X will need to discuss later." He glanced at his watch. "We only have five minutes. Xavier..." Forest stood. "I'm going to use the restroom, wrap this up." With that, Forest left us alone.

I stared at his retreating backside, unable to turn my attention to the man who I called master.

X took the seat Forest vacated and leaned forward, placing elbows to knees. He looked at me and I shrank back. I couldn't help it. When X turned the ferocity of his gaze on me, I reacted instinctually.

"I need to know if you're willing to work with us."

"How can I answer that?"

"Like Forest said, we don't have much time. Do you remember what I said to you earlier?"

"Yes."

"What did I say?"

He'd said many things, but I knew what he was after.

"You said what we discuss in the library changes nothing between us." My insides quivered with the understanding of what that meant. X intended for me to remain his slave, and everything which came with that.

"You gave me your consent," he reminded me, repeating some of what he'd said earlier. "I said you'd be tested. This is your test."

"But..."

"Let me finish."

I gave a nod.

"Forest is exceedingly wealthy, brilliant, and committed to taking Snowden down. And he's methodical. He's been planning this for a very long time, putting pieces into play. When I say he's brilliant, I need you to understand what that means. Forest operates on another plane than the rest of us."

I didn't understand.

"Ten years ago, Forest came to me with one and only one goal in mind, but it would take years of preparation. A piece of that was positioning me and establishing me in the slave trade. I've been buying slaves for years..."

"And selling them." I couldn't help my anger. This was the one piece I couldn't reconcile.

"Yes and no."

"What do you mean no?"

"Slaves move through my operation. It's necessary to maintain my cover. These are not people who have families or lives to get back to. They're those who have been discarded, orphans without families, forgotten people."

"But they're still people."

"Let me finish," X chided me. "They come through my operation and are offered a choice. Some choose to stay, to work with me to bring down slave rings across the globe. Others choose to work for Forest, in any number of different jobs, but all aimed at one thing. One common goal. Forest has been building an army, but there is one person who has escaped his grasp."

"John Snowden," I said, suddenly realizing something important. This was personal to Forest, but how? What connection did Forest have to this man?

"Yes," X said, confirming my guess. "We only recently tied your father to Snowden, but had no way to insert ourselves into his operation. Then Forest uncovered what your father planned to do to you. This provided an unprecedented opportunity. Because of you, your father owes me."

"I thought he paid off his debt?" With me. Wasn't that what they had said. I was payment of debts owed.

"I erased his debt in exchange for you, but he still owes me. Now that we're in business together it's eating him up.

You saw some of that earlier. I need to know, are you with us? Will you help Forest and I bring John Snowden down?"

Forest returned. "Well? What's the answer?"

I looked between Forest and X, knowing another issue remained to be resolved, but I didn't hesitate. I moved from the chair and came to my knees in front of X. He and I would have a conversation later, but for now I took his hands in mine and kissed the backs of his knuckles.

"If it means bringing my father down, I'm in."

CHAPTER TWENTY-EIGHT_

MY ANSWER SEEMED TO SATISFY X. HE GAVE ME ONE appraising look, then smirked. An easiness flowed between them, a sort of settling and acceptance. Bastard looked pleased with himself. As for me? My pulse roared past my ears because I knew exactly what I'd done. Or what I would do. Whether I was ready for it or not remained a question.

I didn't follow much of what happened next. Forest dialed in a video conference. As if given a silent signal, my bodyguards arrived.

"Raven is with us," X pronounced to the men.

Chad gave me a huge smile. Bay grinned. Mel gave a nod of respect.

Ben came over to me. "Are you okay?"

"It's a lot to take in," I admitted.

"It is. I hope you can look back on the past month

through a different lens. Perhaps someday, you'll find it in your heart to forgive us."

The funny thing was that I'd already forgiven my guards. I think I forgave them weeks ago. They were simply following orders. I understood that now.

Chad plopped down in the chair facing me. "I'm glad you decided to stay."

Stay? Was leaving an option? I glanced at X, knowing full well he would never let me go.

Forest waved Ben over, and then turned his attention to the laptop screen. "Detective Summers, I want you to meet Ben Chambers, our FBI lead."

My attention snapped to Ben. FBI?

"It's nice to meet you Detective Summers, is your asset in place?" Ben asked.

"Davenport is moving into position under protest." The woman's voice was sultry and low, almost hypnotic. "He's not happy."

"Will he be a problem?" Ben shifted to better see the laptop.

"I have it under control," the woman said, "and it's not Detective. I lost that title a long time ago. Please, call me Kate."

"I'm sorry, Kate," Ben said. "My apologies."

I watched the exchange between Ben and the woman on the screen. Xavier hadn't officially introduced me, keeping me off screen, but he'd announced to those gathered that

Zane's daughter had agreed to join the operation. It felt odd hearing him refer to me as anything other than Raven, or slave. While Xavier, Forest, and Ben huddled around the screen, I leaned forward and whispered to Chad.

"Is that Forest's sister?"

Chad shook his head. "No. Despite the name, they're not related."

The conversation between Xavier, Forest, Ben, the woman, and two others continued for some time. Chad settled into the chair and grabbed a book off the nearest shelf. Mel and Bay went to join the others, remaining at the periphery and listening in while my curiosity continued to grow.

"Ben's FBI?"

"Yup," Chad said.

"So, he's not a slave?"

"Oh, Ben is very much Master Xavier's slave."

I cocked my head, not understanding.

Chad gave a low laugh. "Don't think too hard about it. Xavier has been building his team for over a decade. He picks men he knows can do the job required, and who are unwavering in their loyalty to him."

"I just don't understand the slave thing?"

"Really? Coming from you, I find that interesting. You feel the pull he has." Chad sounded as if he worshiped X, and I realized he probably did. "And when you finally realize his vision, you can't help but want to serve him."

"I suppose so."

"Kitten," Chad said, "stop overthinking it. Ask yourself what feels right, and do that."

Was that all I had to do? He made it sound simple. I felt myself heading into an all-out panic attack. The air seemed to grow thick and the walls hemmed me in.

"Um, Chad..." I pulled at the bodice of my dress, feeling it tighten around me.

"What's up kitten?"

"I can't breathe." I opened my mouth, tried to gulp air, and felt the room spin around me.

"Let me get Master Xavier."

I reached out to Chad. "No, I don't want to disrupt his meeting. I just need some air."

While I didn't know all the details, this conference call clearly was a meeting of the minds. From the way tension bunched in Forest's shoulders, to the stiff way Ben held himself, they were planning something big. It felt as if that decade of positioning X in this world was coming to a head. There was more, but it was too much for me to process.

"Please," I begged, "I just need some air."

Chad gave a nod and straightened his bulk from the chair. He went to X and whispered in his ear with great deference. X said something back and Chad gave a nod. He returned to me and held out his hand.

"Come, kitten."

I took his hand without hesitation. A quick glance at X

and my heart stopped beneath his penetrating stare. The room felt claustrophobic to me. I couldn't breathe. With the weight of X's gaze upon me, my heart struggled to beat. Chad led me out of the library. My expectation was to be led back to my room, or perhaps one of the many atriums. Instead, Chad surprised me when he turned to the front door. Surprise pulled me back.

"It's okay." Chad tugged me forward. "Master Xavier's instructions."

Warm, humid air greeted us and soft, floral aromas hit my senses. Xavier had picked paradise within which to build his empire.

"Chad, where are we?"

He cocked his head. "What do you mean?"

"Where is this place?" I'd flown into it hooded and bound. Curiosity was getting the better of me. If this was to be my home, I needed to know.

"It's nice, isn't it?"

"It is." It was more than nice. A peaceful tranquility fell upon me breathing in the rich scents, and feeling the heat of the sun bake my skin. The faintest scent of the ocean whispered to me of an endless ocean of possibility. I could breathe. The overwhelming suffocation of a few moments ago faded into nothing but a bad memory. I stopped at the top of the steps, knowing the limits of my freedom, but Chad continued down the steps.

"Are you coming?"

My attention snapped to him and my stomach tumbled about. "I thought..."

"If you don't mind a short walk, I can take you to the beach."

"He's going to let me?"

"I think you're going to find you'll be allowed to do a great many things now, Raven."

It was the first-time Chad said my name. I'd always been his little kitten, the one he was charged with caring for. Nothing about the past month made sense and reconciling what I was learning about X and my guards was going to take some time.

A quick turn had me facing the imposing doors of X's mansion. It had been my prison for weeks and I turned new eyes to it now. The overwhelming theme of white and gray continued on the outside of the house. Plantation shutters covered the windows and ornate woodwork framed the window. Tall columns supported the front of the house, integrating a massive porch into their design. Touches of blue, here and there, provided relief from the stark whitewash of the exterior. It was a grand home. Would it become mine?

"Come on, Kitten. My instructions are to show you around the grounds."

Knowing the price of failure to comply with X's commands, I pulled my attention from the structure which had been my prison and faced the jailor who had become something approaching a friend.

"Chad, can you tell me how you met Master Xavier?"

He reached out and gestured for me to join him down on the gravel of the drive. "It's a long story, but we have time. Master Xavier will be tied up for some time with the others. Now, how about we take a walk?"

"I'd like that very much."

We walked beside each other, two people tied to one indescribable man. Chad did not take me immediately to the beach, choosing to show me the expansive gardens surrounding X's estate. I learned about his induction into X's world. Recruited like the rest of my guards, he first met X in a gay BDSM club.

"Master Xavier needs a cadre of men, loyal to him, who are beyond reproach."

"How so?"

"It's an ugly world out there, kitten, but Master Xavier does what he must, and saves those precious few he can. All of the men embedded in his operation are gay. It's his one rule."

"Why is that?"

He gives me a look. "We handle the slaves, move them from place to place. These are women who've been battered and broken, trained to please men. Master Xavier ensures there's no temptation within his operation. He doesn't have to trust we won't avail ourselves of the merchandise. He knows we won't."

A shudder ripped through me with all that word implied. These weren't people, but goods in trade.

"I'm still wrapping my head around this. I don't understand."

"What's there to understand?"

"If he's against slavery, then why is he involved in the business of it? Why did he enslave me?"

"Those are complicated questions. I'll answer the first, but I think you already know the answer to the second."

It wasn't clear to me that I did.

"Master Xavier, Mr. Summers, and Ben have spent nearly a decade building this operation. Master Xavier is embedded deep in the business. He wishes he could free all the slaves, but that's the unfortunate price which must be paid. Mr. Summers finances most of it, and Ben uses his position within the FBI to track leads and position assets where they're needed most."

"How can he live with himself?"

"Master Xavier?"

"Yes."

"Because he saves a great many along the way. Think of it as an underground railroad. The slaves which funnel through his operation are *sold* to buyers who work for him. It's all a shell game. These are forgotten people, street kids, orphans, people who have no family and nobody who will miss them. They disappear from the world. Those who come through Master Xavier's operation are recruited back into the cause. There are scores of former slaves who work for Master Xavier, working from the inside to funnel information."

"Wait." I pull up short. "From the inside?"

He cocks his head. "Yes."

"But that means..."

"They are given into a highly-curated list of buyers who are known for taking care of their slaves. Master Xavier doesn't place people into positions that jeopardize the integrity of the operation or place them in harm's way."

"How does he do that?"

"Most of the areas of this estate, which have been closed to you, are the induction facilities. Remember, kitten, these are people without homes, without families. Master Xavier gives them a cause to fight for and a family which welcomes them. They choose to stay."

"And what if they don't want to stay?"

"Well, Mr. Summers offers a rehabilitation and relocation service. They are debriefed, what information that can be taken is taken, and then they're placed into witness protection with the FBI and Mr. Summers rehabilitates and retrains them to begin new lives."

A sense of profound awe overcame me with the realization of all that was going on around me. "I had no idea."

"You weren't meant to know all the details."

"I suppose not."

I wasn't a rescued slave, funneled through X's organization and given an option to fight for a cause, or retire to a quiet life. My life had been taken by the very man who made it his life's mission to free slaves. What was it about me that made X need to keep me?

A rhetorical question, I knew the answer. X took me because he had no choice. It was the only way to save me, and then something else happened: *the other half of a whole.* Those were the words he'd used, or something close. I brought something out in him as surely as he brought something out in me. Destiny brought us together and I had a choice to make.

"You still haven't told me how you met Master Xavier."

"I told you I was recruited."

"But as his slave? Why not just a hired gun?"

"Well, that's not what I needed."

"I don't understand."

"I'm ex-military and came from a world steeped in discipline with life and death stakes a part of the job. When I left the military, I spun out of control without the discipline military life provided. I was in a self-destructive spiral; one which Master Xavier took me out of."

"How?"

"He gave me the structure I craved, the discipline I need, and rules to bind my life. My life is his because he saved me from a very dark place. He mastered me and I bound myself to him and chose to submit to his authority. You know a little of what I speak, the power he wields is a potent thing. The stories are similar for the others, differing only a little."

"Does he..." It felt weird to ask, but I didn't need to complete my thought.

"Are you asking if he whips us?"

My cheeks heat and I glance up at the massive man walking beside me. "Yeah."

"Yes, among other things, but it's not a sexual relationship. It's deeper. For me, I needed the release of pain when I was fighting my demons. It's been years since I've needed to feel his whip. The same isn't true of others, but they fight battles different from mine. Master Xavier provides me structure and consequence. Discipline can be any number of things as can rewards."

"It's hard to wrap my head around that."

"Fortunately, you don't need to worry about me, or the others. Master Xavier has made his intentions clear about you, and to be honest, I was a little concerned when he went down that path with you, but I'm glad for it now."

That got my attention. What did that mean?

"Why is that?"

"You're the first woman in years to have captured his heart."

"Years?"

"Yes, didn't you know?"

"No."

"Well, suppose there was no way to know, but Master Xavier hasn't—"

"Hasn't what, Chad?" X's deep voice had Chad stopping in his tracks.

"Master Xavier." Chad gave a deep bow. It should seem odd to see a man with a linebacker build bow before X, but the motion came easily to Chad.

I didn't have years to perfect my reaction to X. He took me by surprise each and every time. Butterflies fluttered in my belly. My heart slammed into high gear. Blood roared past my ears. And a feeling of anticipation skated across my skin as my nerves awakened and my body prepared for battle.

"I believe my instructions were to show Raven the island," X said, "not divulge my past."

"Forgive me."

"We'll speak of it later. Now, return to the house. Mr. Summers needs your assistance settling in our new acquisitions."

"Yes, Master Xavier."

Between one breath and the next, Chad spun and ran toward the house, leaving X and I terribly alone. A breath caught in my throat as the full intensity of X's gaze turned on me.

"Are you feeling better?" he asked.

I shook my head. I had been; up until a moment ago. Chad's words worked magic on me, relaxing me, but all that was now gone beneath the powerful presence that was X.

X passed beside me and headed down the trail Chad and

I had been traveling. "I want to show you the beach. If I recall, you're a scuba diver?"

"Yes, Master." Among other adventurous activities, I held advanced certifications in scuba.

"You're going to enjoy our reefs. I'd love to dive with you."

X ducked beneath an arch of thick vegetation. I followed, then gasped at the expanse of white sand extending along a private beach. Turquoise waters filled my view, dotted by darker colors of the coral reef hidden below. Several hundred yards offshore, waves broke upon a break wall. The inner water of the protected bay barely rippled and mirrored the picturesque blue sky above.

"This is incredible." I couldn't contain my excitement and bounced on my toes. The urge to remove my shoes and feel the sand on my barefeet was nearly overwhelming.

"Wait until your first dive."

"I can dive?" My mouth gaped with surprise. I was going to be allowed outside the house? To dive? I missed the calming sensation of diving beneath the surface. It was an escape from the world, and I sorely needed a little of that now.

"You can do anything you want." While his gaze was sincere, his actions spoke volumes to the contrary. There was one thing I could not do.

"Except leave."

X pulled me to his chest and tugged me tight. The

ferocity of his hug surprised me, but not nearly as much as the tremors in his body.

"You're free to leave, Raven, although it's my hope that's not what you choose."

My heart slammed in my chest, coming to a thundering halt.

"What?" Had I heard him right?

"Come."

His command couldn't be ignored. My body reacted on instinct, following where he led. X brought me to a chaise protected by an umbrella overhead. The shade eased the heat of the day and the wind sweeping off the ocean dried the preparation beading my brow. He gestured for me to sit and I obeyed without question.

X dropped to his knees and focused his smoldering gaze upon me. He gripped my calf and lifted my foot, propping it on his bent knee. Deft fingers worked at the clasp of the anklet which had been my constant companion since my abduction. It fell away from my skin and I felt lighter without it. I stared at the bare expanse of my ankle, not sure what to think by these series of events.

"A wise man told me that if I truly loved someone, I needed to set them free."

He took my wrist and removed the bracelet, then did the same to my other wrist. His powerful frame straightened and he moved behind me, while my mind stuttered with what was happening. A tugging at my neck preceded the removal of the collar around my neck.

X moved back in front of me, standing over me, and tucked the bracelets and collar into his pocket. "Forest's plane will depart after lunch. You may go with him if you choose." His head cocked to the side. "Unfortunately, it won't be possible for you to return to your previous life, at least not until our operation concludes. I can't risk your father knowing I've set you free. That would endanger countless lives and destroy everything we've been working toward. Ben is prepared to move you into witness protection. You have unique skills and I'm not sure what your plans are for graduate education, but Forest's organization should be able to provide you any of the training you require as well as the certificates and diplomas you may need down the road."

"Why are you setting me free?"

"Weren't you listening?"

He said if he truly loved someone...But there was more to that saying. In letting go that which a person loved, they hoped it would return to them. X didn't want me to leave, but he was willing to lose me...in the hopes I came back to him.

I was being set free! This was everything I wanted. Why then wasn't I running to that plane?

I gazed over the bay and imagined swimming beneath the pristine waters with Xavier by my side. The idea of not being around him turned my stomach and a hollowness lodged in my chest. I would miss Xavier. Despite everything, or maybe because of everything, he wouldn't be a man I could forget.

"Is this Forest's doing?" I turned my attention back to Xavier and felt my heart race. My head swam. It was a good thing I was already sitting, or I might have fainted from shock.

Xavier shook his head. "You know my desires. And my needs. What I said before has not changed. I won't keep you against your will, but you need to know that if you choose to stay nothing between us changes. I'm sorry to have caused you harm. It was necessary, as I suspected your father would send men to check in. That he arrived instead, and forced me to...well, I'll never forgive what he made me do."

I rubbed at my wrists, feeling naked without the bracelets in place. This was too much. Too fast. Too overwhelming.

Xavier turned to the ocean. "It's beautiful here, but will be desolate without you. I'll miss you terribly. Despite every-thing, know that is the truth." He turned away from me. "If you decide to stay, the collar and bracelets will be yours again, as well as everything that comes with them." He hung his head and jabbed his hands deep into his pockets. "Choose well, my sweet Raven, but it must be your choice."

Xavier turned and left me on the beach. In my head, I chased after him. My body shuddered as I wrapped my arms around him. My entire body came alive beneath the fury of his kisses. The ache to be possessed by him burned inside of me and I yearned to surrender. Instead of chasing after him, I tugged my knees to my chest and cried.

How long I stayed on that beach wasn't something I would remember. At some point, I stripped out of my dress and cooled off in the water. Long sure strokes took me almost to the breakwater and the ground dropped beneath until I swam in water over forty-feet deep.

With deep breaths, I submerged myself beneath the waters and dove until the world disappeared. Saltwater stung my eyes and I gazed at blurry shapes in the water, blinking until they came into better focus. I dove again. And again.

Each time, I extended the duration of my dives, counting the beats of my heart until the pain in my chest became intolerable and I could no longer resist the urge to breathe. I sought the surface of the water and sucked in air. Then, I did it again.

And again.

The ache I felt was only from the need to breathe. Xavier had freed me. I should be celebrating, but I never felt so lost.

CHAPTER TWENTY-NINE_

THE SUN DIPPED TOWARD THE HORIZON AS I LAY ON THE BEACH confused and dazed by the sudden change in my status. A plane took off and disappeared into the setting sun. Forest had left the island and I wasn't with him. Yet, this didn't mean I made any decisions.

A war waged inside of me, desire and want battling it out with reason and need. I'd never felt this conflicted and that terrified me more than anything else.

Eventually, I'd have to get up. I couldn't stay out here all night. But when I returned to the estate, where would my feet take me? To my stark and barren room? Would it wait for me, empty of guards? Or would I take a different path? Make a different choice?

Xavier's words spun in my head; a never-ending repeat. *When you enter this room, a signal will be sent...The door will lock...There will be no exit, no reprieve, except what is granted by me...That is the choice you're making...*

But could I give him what he craved? Was I brave enough to make *that* choice? Could I bow beneath his dominance and not lose who I was in the process?

The sun sank further, painting the sky in a vibrant canvas of reds, yellows, and golds. Time forced me to move from the beach and return to the estate. I felt at my wrist, at the emptiness there, then touched my bare neck. The feelings sweeping through me with those simple gestures couldn't be ignored. I took to my feet and left the beach behind as the horizon swallowed the sun.

Dusk swept over the island, bringing a curtain of dark purples sweeping over the sky to usher in the darkness of night. I had no problem finding my way back to the house. Lights along the path illuminated my way, bringing me closer to an inevitability. Salt and sand covered my skin and dried saltwater turned my hair crusty. I needed a shower. I needed more time. I needed to make a choice.

I turned down one of the many halls, moving on autopilot as I retraced my steps. I didn't have the dolphin pendant to guide me based upon a flash of red or green. I stopped by a door and wondered if the keypad would work for me, or not. A press of my palm answered that question. The door swung inward and I stared inside as adrenaline spiked in my veins.

Unlike my last time here, there was no fear. I took a step

inside, then another. I walked all the way in, and behind me, the door closed and a lock turned. A deep shuddering breath rattled into my lungs and my palms slickened with sweat. Was I making the wrong choice?

Lights turned on, giving me ample opportunity to explore this room. I didn't know the function of many of the pieces of furniture, but had no doubt I would soon. My gaze went to the wall and the precise, ordered rows of all manner of devices. These too, I would soon know intimately. An ache settled between my thighs, a delicious throb I would soon ease.

Xavier said I would wait for as long as he pleased, so I was surprised when the door creaked open a few moments later. Had he been waiting? His large frame filled the doorway and I could see nothing but his silhouette.

His coarse voice vibrated the air, heavy with his need. "Raven?"

I crossed my arms over my chest, then looked down at my dress. With my eyes glued to his face, all hesitation faded. This was what I wanted, and everything which came with it. I lifted the fabric over my head and let it fall to the floor. I released the clasp of my bra and dropped it on the dress. Then I hooked my fingers beneath the waistband of my panties and took those off as well.

A hiss escaped him. I expected him to rush me. To take. To claim. But he stood solid and unmoving as my panties joined the waiting pile of clothing at my feet. The need to cover my nakedness had me folding my arms across my chest, but I bit at my lower lip and forced myself to place my hands to my sides. It made no sense to hide from this man.

"You gave your consent before," he said, voice vibrating with barely contained restraint. "You said the answer was *Yes*."

"Yes, I did." My admission came easily. Now that I had made my choice, I felt at peace.

"The consent you gave before was given under duress. I need to know if this is what you want? Do you want to be mine?"

"It is, and I most definitely do. My answer is still *Yes*." The truth of those words sent the butterflies in my belly off on a stampede. My world shifted, tumbling about, with the reality of this choice I freely made. I felt nauseous and excited all at the same time. "May I make a request?"

He took a step inside. "You may."

"One day a week..." My voice hitched and I stumbled over my words, but I needed a concession from him.

"Yes?"

"One day a week..." My voice steadied and my nerves quieted. "Can it just be you and me? Raven and Xavier? No master. No slave. Just us?"

"You entered this room knowing there was only one way out. You made that choice."

"I did."

"Are you withdrawing your consent?"

I shook my head. This was what I wanted. "No."

It hurt that he didn't give me the concession, but he was right. I knew what stepping inside this room meant, and what I was giving up—correction—what I'd already given up. I belonged to him, freely this time, and he would determine everything that came next.

He took in a deep breath and blew it into the silence stretching between us.

"I need this Raven. It's not a thing I can ignore. It's a deep-seated need within me. One day a week is too much time away from what we'll become."

"Yes, Master."

I should've kept the disappointment out of my voice, but I couldn't manage it. I needed something too. Submission wasn't something I knew existed within me. I was still learning what it meant and how to handle the things Xavier made me want. It had taken Xavier to show me the darkness I craved and the great strength within me to give in and surrender. *His missing piece*, that's what he called me. Well, he was mine, too; the other half which made me whole. Never would I have believed such a thing possible, but I'd fought a war within me until only one truth remained. I needed him and everything he represented.

"One weekend a month," he said, almost as if he were testing the words.

My head snapped up.

He repeated himself. "One weekend a month, we drop our roles, be just you and me. That's all I can give you."

Truthfully, I didn't care whether he gave me a day, a weekend, a week or more. That he cared enough to not only consider my request, but concede to it, filled my heart with joy. I wanted to run to him and hold him tight, never letting go. Instead, I locked our gazes together with the inevitability of our future.

"Xavier..."

"Yes, Raven?"

"I'm terrified." I breathed out my fear.

"You don't need to be."

CHAPTER THIRTY_

"THIS IS OUR BEGINNING, RAVEN." HE KNELT DOWN MEETING me at eye level. "Surrender is the most difficult step, but it's a part of who you are. You crave what I can give."

I gave a tight nod, but couldn't find my voice.

"I've seen the way you respond to my touch and how you bend to my authority. I promise to give you everything you need, take only what you can give, and devote myself to being the master you need. I wish we had met under different circumstances. I would have liked to have taken you slowly and introduced you to this life differently, but your father made that impossible. I ask that you forgive me for the pain I've caused you."

"Master...it's not."

He placed a finger to my lips. "It's necessary. I need your forgiveness."

My lashes grew wet from unshed tears, but I gave a nod. "I forgive you."

He tugged me to his chest and held me tight. It was just the two of us, two souls bound by an indescribable force, needs and wants which tied our lives together. The beat of his heart, deep, solid, strong and true, set a rhythm which mine met. Even our breathing came together as time stood still.

Xavier took to his feet and undid his buckle. "It's time to please your master, slave."

He would take and I would give. The ebb and flow of our roles formed the structure of my new life. The rasping of his zipper sounded as he unzipped his pants. I gazed up at him while he pulled out his long length, grasping it in his powerful hands. He stood before me, staring down, hand gripping the root of his shaft as his eyes blazed with lust.

"I've thought of nothing but this moment for far too many weeks. Are you ready to serve your master?"

Heat bloomed at the apex of my thighs and I held back a needy groan. I wanted to feel his touch upon me, but understood why this came first. This was about me pleasing him, serving him. The rest would come later.

X put his hand on top of my head and rocked his hips toward me, pressing his cock toward my mouth. Deep uneven breaths surged out of his lungs. He moved back, leaving the salty taste of him on my mouth. "Last chance, my sweet Raven. Say the word and all of this stops."

I glanced up, meeting the heat in his gaze, and shook my head. "I never want this to stop." And I believed the truth of those words. The future terrified me. I didn't know what things would look like in a week, a month, or even a year, but I embraced this moment. The rest, I'd figure out along the way.

He held his very prominent erection in his hand, stroking it from root to tip. "Now, open that pretty mouth." He stepped toward me, his hand moving up and down his shaft in long sure strokes. He placed a hand on my shoulder. My heart leapt at the darkness in his eyes.

He moved his hand to cup the back of my head, then rocked his hips forward, brushing the tip against my teeth. The saltiness of his precum had me opening for him. A single thrust forward and the hot length of him invaded my mouth. He slammed into me, seating himself to the hilt. I gagged as the tip bumped against the back of my throat. He filled me and I couldn't breathe. I tried to pull back, but he gripped the back of my head, holding me in place.

A groan of satisfaction filled the room as he seated himself deep. He held still, his cock pressing against the back of my throat as I struggled to accommodate him.

"You need me to force you, Raven. You and I both know this. It's okay to resist, if it becomes too much, tap my thigh three times and I'll stop."

I could barely breathe with him filling my mouth, and fought against the urge to gag and hurl the contents of my stomach. But he was right. I needed him to take control and force what I couldn't give. Now that he had pried his way inside my mouth, the responsibility for what came next was no longer mine. I needed to fight him, but more than that, I needed him to overcome my resistance. Only then could I respect his strength and grant him the authority to master me.

His eyes widened as I took him and licked the underside of his cock. I reached up and gripped his balls, stroking him with my fingers, knowing if not from personal experience but from what I'd read, that he would like it, and was rewarded by a jerk of his hips and an indrawn breath.

"More," he said. "Harder...squeeze my balls."

His hand gripped the hair at the crown of my head, fingers twisting in the strands. "God, I want to fuck you. Tell me you want me too."

I opened my jaw and let him plunge into me.

"Suck," he hissed. "Wrap your lips around me and suck."

I breathed around him, not daring to move, as he rocked his hips. His hands held my head in place, even as I tried to rear back. I accepted the intrusion knowing accountability for whatever happened was his and not mine. He took over, thrusting in and out, rocking up and down. When he went too deep, making me gag, he backed off, adjusting his thrusts to the last depth I was able to manage.

He started slow, but the tempo increased, until the end

when his thrusts came hard and fast. Panic overcame me and I tapped his thigh.

One. Two.

He slowed down and allowed me to recover. I never tapped a third time. Xavier chased the limits of what I could endure, pushing me to the edge, pulling back, then pushing even harder as he tested my resolve.

He gripped my hair and tugged. I nearly tapped out, but then his breathing changed. He pulled my head to his belly and curled around me as his climax overtook him. As his body shuddered and shook, a deep masculine groan vibrated through his body. I choked on the salty mix as his release slid down my throat. He held me there, breathing deeply, as his erection softened inside my mouth.

"Swallow, slave," he commanded.

I obeyed and a fire burned in my belly, stoking the unbearable ache between my thighs.

Tears dried on my cheeks. Pressure released from my chest. I had done it. I sent him over the edge. An upwelling of satisfaction filled me and flooded me with pride? Pleasure? Happiness? Satisfaction?

I stared up at him, a feeling of blissful contentment plastered on my tear streaked face. I was a hot needy mess and seconds from begging him to take me. He stepped back, met my gaze with a hooded expression with the flames of lust heating his eyes.

"Never forget you're my slave, Raven."

I wiped my chin and regarded him with a mix of emotions.

He pulled out and took a step back. "Raven..."

No response was required, because I felt it; this thing between us. No longer taken, I'd given myself to him. He owned me not as payment of a debt owed, but because I gave myself to him freely. A moment passed between us, but then his fierceness returned.

"Come." He led me deeper into the room, moving with purpose, as he grabbed a set of leather restraints. "Lay down."

He pointed to a padded table and I followed without question. He didn't specify how I should place myself, but I lay on my back, eyes glued to his every move. He went to a drawer and removed a black hood. Fear coiled in my gut. I hated that hood and my entire body shivered.

"I want you to trust me," he said. "Can you do that?"

My heart jumped in my chest. My breaths quickened. What rights did I have as a willing slave? Were they the same as when I'd been unwilling? Could I refuse? I didn't know and that paralyzed me.

He came to me, stroking my shoulder, brushing my hair away from my face, trying to ease the panic building within me.

"You can always make this stop. Say the word, call out

Red, and I stop, but know this is something I believe you need. Removing your sight heightens your senses."

"But I'm afraid."

"I want you to trust me. Believe me when I say I will not harm you. Put your faith in me."

"But..." I couldn't tear my eyes from the hood. It terrified me and reminded me of all the times before when I'd been forced to wear it. "Please, not the hood."

One word would stop everything, but I didn't want any of this to stop. I needed this. Xavier was right about that. I was here of my own free will. But could I give Xavier what he wanted?

I didn't know if I could get over the hood.

He bent over me, brushing his lips over mine. The gentleness of the kiss surprised me. I was used to hard and rough; gentle confused me. But, it eased the beating of my heart. Slowed my ragged breaths. I relaxed beneath the gentleness of that kiss.

"Trust." He slipped the hood over my head.

I could pull it off. He hadn't restrained my hands, but I decided to trust and prayed my faith wasn't misplaced. I don't know if I'll fully understand everything which came next. The expectations in my head didn't prepare me for what followed. Xavier wrapped the leather restraints around my wrists and ankles. Those he attached to rings bolted to the table. I was bound and unable to move. Hooded and blind.

He began by running his fingers over my shoulder, across my collar bone, and to my other shoulder. His light touch moved down first one arm and then another, bringing goosebumps to my skin. I shivered beneath his touch. His lips followed, taking the same leisurely path as I ached for more beneath his touch. I heard him move around me, check my circulation in hands and feet, then walk away. Drawers opened and closed, bringing all kinds of images to my head.

A sadist, Xavier loved pain. Pain turned him on. Forcing me to endure excited him. I expected the worst and therefore wasn't prepared for what came next. He took what I decided must be a feather, and traced every curve of my body. I writhed on the table, squirming away from the delicate touch. Something soft came next, not silk, but some other fabric which felt buttery smooth. Something cold touched my skin, but warmed immediately. It was hard, curved, and I had no idea what it might be. Then he tickled me, running something sharp across my skin. With more pressure, I had no doubt it would hurt, but he used the lightest of touches. I felt pinpricks, nothing more, and moaned beneath his touch. Not once did he touch my most private places, leaving my breasts and pussy achingly untouched during the delicious torment he subjected me to.

In between implements, he surprised me with the heat of his mouth. I screamed when he sucked my nipple into his mouth, not expecting the touch, or my body's reaction. I arched into him, pressing against his mouth, needy and aching for more. He deepened the suction on my nipple, drawing out a deep soulful moan from my lips. I jerked in my restraints as his hand moved over my belly and settled over my mound.

Without warning, he pressed his finger to my clit and I let out an agonized scream. He circled the sensitive bundle of nerves then dipped between my thighs, finding the wetness of my slit. A single thrust and he was inside.

My heart beat too fast. My breaths came too fast. I couldn't help but breathe him in. His rich scent of spice and musk intoxicated my senses as his body enveloped me with an explosion of erotic need. Coiling inside of me, tension demanded release. I panted against my bonds and gasped as his fingers crooked forward. Unintelligible sounds spilled from my throat.

"My sweet Raven." He stroked in and out, firing up all the nerves, until I writhed beneath him, moaning and begging for more. "I take what I want, and give you what you need. You're powerless to stop me. Your submission is my drug, just as the power I hold over you is yours."

My climax swelled and I felt like I was going to explode.

His thumb swirled around my clit, and I prayed he wouldn't stop. My release was only a few strokes away. It was an inevitability. His fingers crooked up and continued to stimulate my g-spot. I cried out as he brought me to the brink and held me on the edge.

"Pleasure is your drug, but pain is mine. We're two sides

of the same coin: Yin and Yang, hard and soft, strong and weak. We're the knife's edge when pain becomes pleasure." Another stroke kept me hovering on the edge of bliss. He branded me with desire. His voice trickled power down my spine and turned me to ash with a whisper of truth. He gripped my throat, establishing his dominance, and squeezed, stealing my ability to breathe. My mind went wild, trapped between two disparate sensations; pleasure mixed with pain.

My mind swam in vicious circles, my thoughts stumbling and drowning, no longer eager for release. He stroked me, enflamed me, and I caved beneath his power. He controlled my body, choking off my air, as he stroked me to climax.

"Come for me slave," he said with a whisper.

I gave in to his power and surrendered to his control. I couldn't stop myself. With a flick of his thumb against my clit, he sent me tumbling over the edge. Wave after wave of pleasure washed over me and my world splintered into a million pieces. My pussy clenched around his fingers, my heat pulsing against him as I cried out. He ripped off the hood and captured my screams with his mouth. His lips embraced mine, taking my cries into his lungs. He devoured me and released his grip on my throat.

"Imagine what it will feel like with my cock inside you." He brushed my lips with his. "I can't wait to bury myself deep into your wet heat."

I gasped as he forced me to look him in the eyes, because I wanted that too. I wanted everything this man promised.

He ran his fingers up and down my slit, plunging in deep. Another orgasm began to build. The inevitability of it flared to life under the command of his hand. His finger stroked and I crested, a barreling flurry of sensations crashing toward me. I gasped as his finger breached my barriers, slipping between my folds. He stroked my sensitive nub with his thumb, stimulating my clit, while his fingers curled within me and brought a moan to my lips.

But then he pulled his fingers out and lifted his body from mine. I gasped with the loss of him.

He gave me a smirk as he undid the restraints holding me in place. He took three things out of his pocket and placed them on the table as I quivered beside him.

"Do you know what day it is, my sweet Raven?"

"No, Master." I'd lost track of what day it was weeks ago.

He huffed a low laugh. "It's Friday. Our first weekend together. I think Xavier and Raven need some time to get to know one another. Master and slave will wait.

"Xavier," I looked deep into his eyes and met the fierceness of his love. I had given myself to a master and found the heart of a man.

"My sweet Raven, it's time I take you to bed."

I understood nothing about this new life, but then again, I understood it all. He had no choice in taking me and saved me from a much worse fate. After everything we'd been through, he needed to know this was what I truly wanted. What he needed, and what he would take from me, made me shiver with the most delicious anticipation. In setting me free, I had found a new home.

EPILOGUE_

———

THE LAST RAYS OF SUNDAY'S SUN SPREAD ACROSS THE HORIZON.
We were out on the water, beyond the breakwater getting
ready to dive the reef wall. Tomorrow, Xavier and Raven
would once again become Master and slave, but for now, he
was simply the man I'd grown to love.

Xavier held my tank while I put on my scuba gear. The
dive boat rocked beneath my feet and I moved with the
swells using my legs to keep my balance. This would be our
last dive of the day and I couldn't help but be excited.

Anticipation thrummed in my veins as the sun sank
beneath the horizon. We would be doing a night dive and I
couldn't wait to show Xavier where I'd found the colony of
basket stars. They only came out at night and were stunning

to watch as they unfurled their multitude of arms and formed a basket of living lace.

While I finished adjusting my gear, Xavier slipped into his scuba gear. Bay sat at the helm with Chad beside him. They would mind the boat while we dove below. My previous guards spent much less time guarding me than in the past. I adhered to the stringent rules set forth by my master—mostly. They still watched over me, four overly protective men who'd become obnoxious older brothers to me.

While Bay and Chad weren't joining us on this dive, Ben and Mel would be diving with us. They readied themselves on the other side of the boat, completing their buddy checks as I strapped the canister of my high-intensity dive light to my waist. A cord snaked from the black metal tube to the back of my wrist where halogen lights would turn night into day below the waves. I secured the support for the lamp around my wrist. We had a few minutes before our dive. The basket stars only came out after the sun went down.

Xavier turned to me and we did our buddy check. The last rays of the sun lit his face, turning hard lines into a canvas of warmth and love. He smiled, an easy expression reserved solely for me. These weekends were special to us both and I was beginning to think he looked forward to them as much as I did. He always planned special surprises, although I'd told him this weekend would be mine to plan.

Tomorrow, my master would stand before me, hard and

unyielding, terrifying and utterly devastating. I yearned to bend beneath his mastery, but cherished what remained of this day. For a few more hours, it was just me and Xavier, the man who'd stolen my heart. Tomorrow would bring back the roles which defined us.

With our buddy check complete we took our seats while I gave the pre-dive briefing and described our depth, time, and general route for the sixty-minute dive. We wore doubles and bailout tanks and planned for a decompression dive.

"Your excitement is infectious, my sweet Raven." Xavier gripped my hand and gave it a squeeze.

If we weren't wearing nearly two-thirds our body weight in gear, he would've leaned over and kissed me. As it was, the rocking of the boat made that an unwise endeavor. I still had yet to strap in my side mount tank. Chad would hand that to me once I was in the water. We did one last safety check of our gear, then settled in while Bay drove us over our insertion point.

"I can't believe you didn't know they were here." My leg bounced with restless energy.

Bay, Chad and I had found the colony weeks ago. Now that they were no longer charged with guarding me, the three of us had bonded over a mutual love of diving. I spent much less time with Ben and Mel. Their roles in Xavier's operation kept them busy most of the day, but they too enjoyed diving. They suppressed their eagerness for what we'd found. Neither of them had seen basket stars. They checked their dive computers, watching the time. If we went in too early, our dive would end before the basket stars emerged for a night of feeding on plankton.

"Unlike my adventurous Raven, I don't have as much time to explore these waters." Xavier squeezed my hand. The solid connection bound us together. Even through the thickness of my neoprene gloves, his touch excited me and set my heart pounding.

He was right. The boredom I'd experienced in that tiny room hadn't been as much by design as necessity. Running a slave operation took up most of Xavier's time. It no longer turned my stomach, thinking about what he did. Not all the slaves who moved through his channels could be saved, but he freed dozens each month, funneling them through an operation he'd built over a decade.

My stomach churned because the pace of things had stepped up with the intelligence we pulled from my father's computer. Xavier involved me where he could, and I worked with Mr. Summers to track down a ghost. I'd found proof of John Snowden's existence, finding Snowden's base of operations had been another matter. But, I'd done it. We had the final piece to the puzzle and Mr. Summers was in the process of activating his team. Xavier planned on moving his pieces of the puzzle into play beginning tomorrow and I wanted to be by his side.

"Xavier..." I leaned toward him, hoping to plead my case one last time. "It doesn't make sense that I not go."

"We're not discussing this, sl—Raven."

He'd nearly slipped and called me slave. I walked a dangerous line pushing him, but I was right in this. The meeting scheduled for later this week would have both my father and Snowden in attendance. It would look *off* if Xavier didn't have his newest slave by his side. Xavier refused because he didn't want to subject me to the degradation which would be necessary. I disagreed. With Xavier by my side, I had nothing to fear. That, he said, was the problem. I should fear him. My father would expect to see me broken.

"But—" I had only a few hours left to plead my case. Once the sun rose in the morning, I would again be his slave, yielding to his authority and unable to defy his command to remain silent on this matter.

"Raven," he said, "don't push. You've said your piece and I've said mine. You're not going."

For now, I wouldn't force the issue. Our weekends without titles, rules, and consequence meant too much to me to jeopardize by pushing limits I should otherwise respect, but I wasn't done. I would hold my tongue for now. If he was going to walk into the lion's den, there would be no way I wouldn't be by his side.

"Time," Mel pronounced. "You two ready?"

Xavier took to his feet and braced against the rocking of the boat. He gave me a hand up and a penetrating stare. "I sense a tough week ahead of you, if you don't put this issue to rest."

He meant every word. Xavier's love for me didn't mean he stayed his hand, quite the opposite occurred instead. My defiance enflamed his desires. He was a sadist after all, and I was finding how much I truly completed his other half. My wetsuit covered the bruises and marks, but I felt the burn left behind.

I gave him a wink. "I would expect nothing less, but you know I'm right. And, I'm coming with you."

Shock rippled across his face, but I didn't give him time to yell at my defiance. With a giant step off the back platform of the boat, I plunged beneath the dark waters. While we dove, Xavier was effectively silenced. Our conversation would continue, no doubt in the morning, but I was prepared to fight and win. I was learning a thing or two about the man I loved. He loved me fiercely, but I loved him more.

Xavier joined me a moment later, and from the look in his eyes, this would be a conversation we continued tomorrow. Draped over his knee, or tied to the cross, I would endure whatever punishment he devised, but there was no way my master would walk into danger without me by his side.

———

I HOPE YOU ENJOYED THIS BOOK AS MUCH AS I ENJOYED WRITING it. If you enjoyed reading this story, please consider leaving a review on Amazon and Goodreads, and please let other people know. A sentence is all it takes, but a book lives or dies based upon its reviews. Thank you in advance!

CLICK ON THE LINK BELOW TO LEAVE YOUR REVIEW

Goodreads

Amazon

BookBub

ALSO BY ELLIE MASTERS_

Sign up to Ellie's Newsletter and get a free gift.
https://elliemasters.com/FreeBook

The Angel Fire Rock Romance Series

EACH BOOK IN THIS SERIES CAN BE READ AS A STANDALONE AND IS ABOUT A DIFFERENT COUPLE WITH AN HEA.

Ashes to New (prequel)

Heart's Insanity (book 1)

Heart's Desire (book 2)

Heart's Collide (book 3)

Hearts Divided (book 4)

Romantic Suspense

She's MINE: a Captive Romance

Twist of Fate

The Starling

Redemption

HOT READS

Changing Roles Series:

Book 1: Command

Book 2: Control

Book 3: Collar

Off Duty

Nondisclosure

Down the Rabbit Hole

Becoming His Series

Book 1: The Ballet

Book 2: Learning to Breathe

Book 3: Becoming His

Sweet Contemporary Romance

Finding Peace

~AND~

Science Fiction

Ellie Masters writing as L.A. Warren

Vendel Rising: a Science Fiction Serialized Novel

ELLIE MASTERS is a multi-genre and best-selling author, writing the stories she loves to read. These are dark erotic tales. Or maybe, sweet contemporary stories. How about a romantic thriller to whet your appetite? Ellie writes it all. Want to read passionate poems and sensual secrets? She does that, too. Dip into the eclectic mind of Ellie Masters, spend time exploring the sensual realm where she breathes life into her characters and brings them from her mind to the page and into the heart of her readers every day.

Ellie Masters has been exploring the worlds of romance, dark erotica, science fiction, and fantasy by writing the stories she wants to read. When not writing, Ellie can be found outside, where her passion for all things outdoor reigns supreme: off-roading, riding ATVs, scuba diving, hiking, and breathing fresh air are top on her list.

She has lived all over the United States—east, west, north, south and central—but grew up under the Hawaiian sun. She's also been privileged to have lived overseas, experiencing other cultures and making lifelong friends. Now, Ellie is proud to call herself a Southern transplant, learning to say y'all and "bless her heart" with the best of them. She lives with her beloved husband, two children who refuse to flee the nest, and four fur-babies; three cats who rule the household, and a dog who wants nothing other than for the cats to be his best friends. The cats have a different opinion regarding this matter.

Ellie's favorite way to spend an evening is curled up on a couch, laptop in place, watching a fire, drinking a good wine, and bringing forth all the characters from her mind to the page and hopefully into the hearts of her readers.

FOR MORE INFORMATION
WWW.ELLIEMASTERS.COM

g goodreads.com/Ellie_Masters

CONNECT WITH ELLIE MASTERS_

Website:

www.elliemasters.com

Amazon Author Page:

amazon.com/author/elliemasters

Facebook:

https://www.facebook.com/elliemastersromance

Twitter:

https://twitter.com/Ellie__Masters

Goodreads:

https://www.goodreads.com/author/show/

14502459.Ellie_Masters

Instagram:

https://www.instagram.com/ellie_masters/

Google+:

https://plus.google.com/110364901628776604366

FINAL THOUGHTS_

I hope you enjoyed this book as much as I enjoyed writing it. If you enjoyed reading this story, please consider leaving a review on Amazon and Goodreads, and please let other people know. A sentence is all it takes, but a book lives or dies based upon its reviews. Friend recommendations are the strongest catalyst for readers' purchase decisions! And I'd love to be able to continue bringing the characters and stories from My-Mind-to-the-Page.

Second, call or e-mail a friend and tell them about this book. If you really want them to read it, gift it to them. If you prefer digital friends, please use the "Recommend" feature of Goodreads to spread the word.

Or visit my blog https://elliemasters.com/, where you can find out more about my writing process and personal life.

Come visit The EDGE: Dark Discussions where we'll

have a chance to talk about my works, their creation, and maybe what the future has in store for my writing.

Facebook Reader Group: The EDGE

Thank you so much for your support!

Love,

Ellie

THE END_

———